W9-ABW-743

NO ONE KNOWS MY NAME

FELLOW MYSTERY WRITERS PRAISE THE NAME OF JOYCE HARRINGTON:

"A MARVELOUS READ. . .
FINE, SCARY SUSPENSE."
Thomas Chastain, *HIGH VOLTAGE*

"SUSPENSE THAT GRIPS THE READER
from the opening sentence to the
astonishing conclusion."
Franklin Bandy, *DECEIT AND DEADLY LIES*

"THE PERFECT MIX OF MURDER AND SEX."
Lucy Freeman, *WHO IS SYLVIA?*

"THE DRAMA IS UNBEATABLE."
Dorothy Salisbury Davis, *SCARLET NIGHT*

"CHILLING. . .WELL-PLOTTED,
STYLISHLY WRITTEN."
Bill Pronzini, *BLOWBACK*

"ABSORBING AND EXCELLENT FROM
START TO FINISH."
Stanley Ellin, *THE LUXEMBOURG RUN*

"WHAT A MYSTERY OUGHT TO BE."
Hillary Waugh, *MADMAN AT MY DOOR*

NO
ONE
KNOWS
MY
NAME

JOYCE HARRINGTON

AVON
PUBLISHERS OF BARD, CAMELOT, DISCUS AND FLARE BOOKS

AVON BOOKS
A division of
The Hearst Corporation
959 Eighth Avenue
New York, New York 10019

The St. Martin's Press, Inc. edition contains the following
Library of Congress Cataloging in Publication Data:

Harrington, Joyce.
   No one knows my name.

   I. Title.
PZ4.H31113No   [PS3558.A6284]   813'.54   80-14644

First Avon Printing, December, 1981

AVON TRADEMARK REG. U. S. PAT. OFF. AND IN
OTHER COUNTRIES, MARCA REGISTRADA, HECHO EN U. S. A.

Printed in the U. S. A.

WFH 10 9 8 7 6 5 4 3 2 1

This book is for Phillip
and Chris and Evan.

CHAPTER I

It's time to make an exit.

No applause, no curtain calls for the little drama just ended. The final tableau is perfectly staged, the setting impeccably correct. A small shabby room with cheerful posters on the walls to hide the peeling paint, a daybed covered with a bright cotton throw, a cheap pine table and two straight-backed chairs amateurishly enameled an acid green, on the floor an ancient brown shag rug suffering a terminal case of mange. And on the rug, sprawled but still graceful, long legs poised as if in flight, wheat-blond hair seductively tumbled, the girl lies still and beautiful.

Her face shows astonishment, but no pain. That's good. It's hateful to think of causing pain. She looks as if she can scarcely wait for the curtain to ring down so that she can leap to her feet and gracefully acknowledge the contribution of the rest of the cast. But, for her, the curtain will not rise again, and the single remaining member of the cast is about to tiptoe quietly offstage. The spreading stain on her blouse is not from a broken capsule of red dye; the knife whose handle protrudes from her breast is not a breakaway stage prop. For her, make-believe has ended and reality has proved fatal. Good-night, sweet princess.

Let us not wax poetical. She's dead and it's time to think of practical matters. She probably won't be found for some days. She was new in town and had few friends. In this business and at this time of year, an unanswered phone could mean a touring company or summer stock. No one would raise the alarm or report her missing for at least a week or possibly longer. She had been chosen for just that reason.

It had been simplicity itself to win her confidence. A few kind words at a casting call, commiseration and coffee afterward, a tip on a show looking for a replacement, sage advice from an old trouper. Well, not precisely old, but wise certainly in the ways of that most treacherous of all the arts, the theater.

And from the neophyte, bubbling boundless hope, an almost religious dedication, and a catalog of small-town triumphs. She had come to New York on her own savings and in the face of her mother's opposition. Silly mother, to be so worried. She would be pleased to know that her daughter had found such a good friend.

And so, good friends, meeting by chance on a midtown street, she struggling along with a heavy package wrapped in brown paper and tied with thick twine, it was only natural to offer help.

"My mother," she laughed. "She sends me Care packages. She's afraid I'll starve. They're getting to know me at the post office."

Help was accepted and the burden shared as far as the odorous vestibule of the ratty West Side building that offered rooms at a price the budding actress could afford.

"Why don't you come up?" she invited. "We'll see what Momma sent this time. We'll have a feast. You've treated me often enough."

The package was postmarked somewhere in Nebraska. Momma was far away, a vague round figure in a printed housedress rooted in a flat, dull landscape. But sharp enough to be worried about her beautiful, trusting daughter. The girl, unwary and unwise, couldn't yet know what it was like to be turned down time after time, to be passed over for roles that would have been perfect, roles that meant the difference between fame and nonentity. She didn't yet know the awful indignity of laying bare your soul for the inspection of every callous keeper of the right to cross the stage. She hadn't yet had to face the calculated insults dished out regularly at the unemployment office.

"You again? Why don't you get a *real* job?" Implied if not actually stated by the iron faced guardian of the state's kitty for the artful unemployed.

She hadn't felt the poisonous rage that must hide behind a smile and a gallant shrug when even the second-rate summer stock companies up and down the East Coast judge your talents to be insufficient, and you force yourself to accept the only offer you're likely to get—a semiprofessional repertory group in a dinky resort town somewhere on the shores of Gitchee Gummee, salary barely scale, room and board thrown in.

She didn't know any of that. Yet. Just as she didn't know that she could be hated for the very youth and beauty that she

8

took for granted. And she didn't know that it was singularly unwise to boast.

"Guess what?" she bubbled, using a kitchen knife on the string that was wound several times around the package and tied with tight, sensible knots. "I got a job! A real job! It's a new play, very Off Broadway. I'm not sure I understand it, but the playwright says it's a totally new concept of theater. Oh, look what Momma sent!"

She had finished with the knife and torn open the brown paper. She lifted the flaps of corrugated cardboard and plunged her hands into a mound of fluffy white popcorn.

"Momma packs everything in popcorn. She grows it herself and pops it herself and says it's the best packing material in the world, better than Styrofoam, and besides you can eat it."

She munched a handful while excavating half a dozen jelly jars, some glowing a deep dark red, thick with chunks of fruit, others a clear golden amber. Next came a huge plastic bag of raisin-studded cookies, and finally a shoe box full of brownies bulging with walnuts.

"Look at that, will you. My Momma's really something else. I'll make some tea," she said. "And then I'll tell you all about this play. I just got the callback this morning and I haven't seen a soul yet to tell the good news to. Except the man at the post office. He must have thought I was crazy to be so excited about two lines in a play. But it's a start, isn't it? Maybe I'll call Momma tonight after the rates go down."

A start. A finish. And all that lay between. Once it had been possible to have high hopes, to read fame and fortune into a two-line walk-on in an experimental play that's sure to fold after three performances. But spend a few years on the fringes, in the land of almost but never quite making it, live long enough on a steady diet of hope without even the feathers to pick your teeth with, and you get very hungry. And very, very angry.

Once it had been possible to watch others succeed and be glad for them. That was when faith in the future and in the magical power of sheer determination were as much a part of your theatrical baggage as the interminable singing and dancing lessons, the acting coach, the agent taking his cut of next to nothing, and, of course, your talent. Your God-given, immutable, nontransferable, everlasting talent.

Let determination shrivel to a grim reflex and watch the

future turn into a season in the boonies, but never, ever, doubt your agent or your talent.

So much for faith and hope. What about charity? Wouldn't it be charitable to put this golden girl out of her misery before it starts? Wouldn't it be an act of mercy? Save her from the good old fate worse than death? But if the fate is really worse than death, and if charity begins at home, why not do yourself a favor? Slit your own throat, pick up the bare bodkin and eliminate all those creeping tomorrows and tomorrows and tomorrows.

Better yet, split. Get out of here before the pressure gets unbearable. You know what happened before. Make your apologies, tell her you have an appointment, an important audition, a lunch date at Sardi's, the usual lies. She'll eat it up. Get out of here before she starts spouting back at you all the delusions you used to feed yourself. The fantastic break that's just around the corner, the chance of a lifetime, the show must go on, the play's the thing, there's no busines like show business. And the saddest part of all is that you still believe it. Otherwise, you would have given it all up long ago and gone off to sell shoes in East Dubuque. Otherwise, you wouldn't have this crazy confused mess of rage and pity and envy boiling away in the blood that feeds the muscles that inch by wicked inch force the hand closer to the knife lying on the table twinkling through the popcorn spill.

"I said, I hope you don't take milk, because I don't have any."

The dime-store kettle rocked slightly on the hot plate as it began to steam. She set two cheap Japanese mugs on the stained drainboard of the chipped, ungainly sink and dropped a teabag into each.

"I'll make some toast, so you can try the strawberry jam. Oh, I still can't believe it! I've only been here a couple of months, and already I've got a speaking part. Rudy, he's the playwright, says it's a fine showcase for me, and he says it's practically a sure thing that we'll move it uptown after the first six months or so. It's a very spiritual play, a quest. A man's search for his soul in the miasma of today's commercialized, technologized society. That's what Rudy says. I'll never understand it all, but Rudy says I'm perfect for the part and he's asked me to have dinner with him sometime. Rehearsals start as soon as they can find a hall. Aren't you happy for me? The toast is ready."

So she prattled, and so it wasn't possible to leave. Rudy, the playwright, would undoubtedly be selling shoes in East Dubuque before too very much time had passed. But not before he pinned her and half a dozen like her to cotton-covered daybeds all over town. And she? She would say her two lines and console Rudy when the play closed. And then there would be two more lines and other consolations. She might get lucky and land a featured role. She·might even get smart and go home to Momma after she had her fling. Or she might hang in there and get tough and make it to the big marquee in the sky. But the odds were against that happening. Just ask me sometime. I've been playing the odds for years.

In the meantime, here she comes gaily treading the five paces between the tea kettle and me, a steaming mug in either hand. My own hand brushes aside the spilled popcorn to make room for our feast, and the knife winks up at me, inviting. I wait until she sets the mugs on the table. No sense in making a greater mess than necessary. Then as she straightens and turns to fetch the toast, the hand moves, the knife flashes, the blood wells, the look of astonishment settles forever onto her pretty, unguarded features. The entire scene is marvelously underplayed. No warning, no overwrought speeches, no screams of fear or agony. Only the swift movement, the startled intake of breath, and the graceful collapse to the scurfy brown rug. A beautifully acted scene. An act of charity.

Who am I kidding? Was it charity that strangled the sweet kid from Sheepshead Bay? The one with the Streisand nose and nothing else but enthusiasm. That was almost a year ago. That's when it all began. But the feeling is still fresh. First the slow certainty that some kind of turning point had been reached. The dear old "many are called but few are chosen" syndrome. Then some wasteful hours of railing, in private, of course, at the injustice of it all. And then, ah, then, the rising tide of hatred, the sleepless nights, the loss of appetite, a blessing to a skimpy wallet but bad for the morale, the restless wandering through the midnight streets seeking answers but finding only death's head scavengers, each intent in his own petty way on "making it." They'd all be better off dead. My own sick imagination or the real world revealed? A little of both, perhaps. Afterward, when Sheepshead Bay lay with her mouth stretched wide, belting a soundless tune, there was peace, calm, renewal.

It is a mighty and comforting precept to the readers of sensational newspapers that your average everyday homicidal maniac does not know what he is doing. The familiar "red haze" descends, the force beyond control takes over, commanding voices are heard. He's a killer, certainly, an animal, and should be castrated, mutilated, and exterminated. But it's an article of faith that the creep is merely an instrument of evil, godforsaken, outside the pale of common humanity. Otherwise, any man could kill his wife in a murderous rage knowing that he hated her for being a constant daily reminder that tomorrow would be just like yesterday, instead of just bashing her about for a bit of Saturday night sport. Otherwise, anyone could be a victim, not randomly selected, but singled out for his sins. A comforting fantasy.

In other words, I was well aware of what I was doing. Maybe this makes me unique among legendary crazed killers, but I doubt it. It's true that I have long experience of character analysis, delving for motivations on which to build a dramatic portrayal, and maybe this makes it easier for me to avoid deluding myself on the subject of why it becomes necessary to kill. The Stanislavski method of murder, utterly believable, utterly true, completely conscious of means, opportunity and motive.

Don't get me wrong. If I am ever caught, there will be no talk of motivations. I will plead insanity with the worst of them. I will act the greatest role of my career. I will *be* insane. But there's no need to rehearse that role. I have no intention of being caught.

What I hadn't anticipated that first time was the tremendous sense of well-being, the almost superhuman urge of power that swept me into a state of euphoria. If I could do this, I could do anything. It carried me through more than six months of minor defeats and insignificant successes, just enough work to pay the rent and get me back on the unemployment rolls.

When the buildup began again, it was the tail end of winter, one of the coldest on record. But that didn't stop the boy from West Virginia from practicing his routines on the deserted midnight decks of the Staten Island ferry. A dancer he was, and gay, but I'm not prejudiced. He wanted a friend, an audience, an adviser, and I was only too happy to oblige. His room was too small for leaps and springs, and the ferry was romantic. I only hope the icy waters of the bay made his death painless and swift. He went in just past the Statue of Liberty. He didn't make much of a splash.

That was just over three months ago. It's interesting to note that the beneficial effects of this therapy I've discovered for myself wear off after a time and have to be renewed. It's too soon to know how long the present state of exaltation will last. But it's early summer in Manhattan. Outside the air is balmy and the sky a bright clear blue. The city sparkles in the sunshine like a jewel of great price, a sapphire city well worth fighting for and winning. Never mind that it's only a stage jewel, a tarnished backdrop to an endless drama of tedium and frustration. Today, take it at its face value. Walk out of this mean little room and onto the great stage where anything can happen and probably will, where tomorrow can mean the leading role you've been waiting for all your life, a Tony award, a movie contract—the sky's the limit. Even a couple of months in the north woods can lead to something wonderful. At least it's a job and a pleasant way to spend the summer, away from the heat and the madness of the city in July and August. Tomorrow, I'll be on my way.

But first, make certain there's nothing in this room that says I've been here. I've touched nothing but the knife. No one saw me come up. The two mugs of tea will cool and grow cloudy, but that's nothing to do with me. And so, I kneel beside her, both to bid her farewell and to polish the handle of the knife with my ancient handkerchief, once a fine translucent lawn and now riddled with holes where many launderings have eaten away the fabric. Tomorrow, before I leave, I'll buy some new handkerchiefs.

"Farewell, farewell, a long farewell to all thy . . . hopes of greatness."

Five paces to the door, a final glance around the room. Soon it will grow warm in this cramped space. She will not be pretty when they find her. I wish I could spare her that, but she won't know and I'll remember her as I do the others. Bright, young, and hopeful. There is no one in the hall as I open the door and peer through, careful to hold the knob with my handkerchief shielding it from my hand. Once in the hall, I do not look back. I pull the door closed behind me and listen for the click that tells me the lock has engaged. Then away down the stairs and out into the brilliance of the streets where no one knows my name.

CHAPTER II

I hate airports! I hate planes, I hate stewardesses, and I hate you! I'm not walking another step. I want to go home.''

"Don't make a scene, Glory. There's no one here to take your picture. Besides, you look like Maria Ouspenskaya when you're angry.''

"Who's Maria Whatever?''

"Never mind. You wouldn't know.''

Behind his dark glasses, Barney Gross's tired old eyes drooped with fatigue. I'm insulting Ouspenskaya, he thought, by comparing her with this featherbrain. No, I take that back. Glory's not dumb. She's tough, shrewd, and single-minded. She's also beautiful, stacked, and blond. From her, an agent could make a fortune. If only she could act. The whining voice grated into his thoughts.

"I could have spent the summer at Malibu, lying in the sun.''

"And getting laid by moonlight. Be a good girl, Glory.''

Glory giggled. "What's wrong with getting laid? Don't tell me you wouldn't like a piece, Barney.''

"Never screw the clients. That's my motto.''

In-fucking-credible! All you ever had to do to put her in a good mood was talk dirty. She loved it. And she could always go you one better. If she'd done only one-tenth of the things she talked about, she had to be some kind of sex champion. In the old days, she would have been whispered about, ostracized, no work. Could you imagine Irene Dunn talking like that? In the old days, everybody toed the line, at least in public. What they did and said in private was their own affair, but the least little hint in the columns of extracurricular hanky-pank could mean the end of a career. Nowadays, everybody played musical beds and compared notes afterward. At least, that's the impression you could get from ten minutes of conversation with Glory Hayes.

"Barney, why can't we just get on the next plane back to

L.A.? I don't like this place. Everybody looks fat and ugly and stupid."

Barney Gross surveyed the airport concourse. She was right, of course. Not everybody, but most of the people plodding by looked solid, substantial, and dull. He saw them from a slightly different viewpoint. To him, they were the marks, the suckers, the good citizens who would lay out four or five dollars to sit in darkness for a couple of hours watching the worst crap that Hollywood could grind out, and loving it. Barney Gross wanted a share of that escape money, and Glory Hayes was going to get it for him. She was his escape ticket. There weren't too many years left, and she was his last chance to enjoy them with some small degree of dignity.

"Look, honey," he pleaded, "all you have to do is walk down this corridor and get on the next plane to Traverse City. There's a rental car waiting for you at the airport. They'll tell you how to get to Duck Creek."

"I don't want to go to Duck Creek. What am I going to do in Duck Creek for three months?"

"Everybody you can, baby. And maybe learn something about acting. Just remember who's gonna be the greatest thing since Monroe."

"She died. And she never had to go to fuckass Duck Creek."

She was pouting now, the temper tantrum stage forgotten. God, but she was a knockout! That mouth, fleshy and sensuous; those eyes, an unbelievable green, awash with promises and just a hint of tears. Vulnerability, that's what she projected and that's what she had to sell. It was great, terrific, but by itself it wasn't enough. She tested out like a great big beautiful wooden dummy. She had to learn about timing, how to get the most out of a line, a look, a comic situation. She could sing, in a tremulous baby whimper, and she could dance, flinging that incredible body about in a frenzy. She had energy and youth going for her. What she needed was control, discipline, and experience. Barney Gross's own private natural resource was about to be harnessed and exploited, for her own good, of course. That's what the Duck Creek Playhouse was going to do; a summer in the boonies working with a semipro repertory company and a director who had brought along more raw talent than anybody in the business. And if she hadn't learned anything after that, she could just drift back into the third-rate porno films where he'd found her.

But she'd learn. She had to. She was just as hungry as he

was. Hungrier. And she knew that good old Barney was right. She'd seen the tests and had the intelligence to be embarrassed. Naturally she'd taken her embarrassment out on him in an hour-long poison-mouth tirade and then disappeared for two weeks. When she returned, looking subdued, sleek, and satisfied, she was ready to go to work on herself. She knew, too, that good old Barney had invested a sizable amount of cash in her future, and she wasn't ungrateful. She bitched constantly about the lessons he made her take: acting, singing, dancing. But she went and he paid. She didn't know that he'd had to pay off the playhouse director to get her taken on. Larry Devine was an old friend who had once been top of the heap and was now on a downer, struggling to keep his playhouse afloat. Even old friendships can get strained when you're asking a favor and the guy you're asking can't pay his bills. To Larry Devine, Glory Hayes meant the difference between mimeographed programs and a slick professionally printed playbill. Larry had been on the point of hiring some scrawny New York actress, girl friend of his leading man, but when Barney got out his checkbook and backed it up with an eight-by-ten glossy of Glory in a string bikini, well, everybody's human.

"Come on, baby."

He took her arm and began steering her toward the departure lounge. "You got three minutes to get on that plane. Your luggage is checked through, and if you don't turn up to claim it, they'll give it all to the Indians."

Glory allowed herself to be propelled along the corridor.

"Barney, come with me."

"Sweetheart, I can't. You know I have to be in New York tomorrow morning."

Two perfect fat tears rolled out from between Max-Factored lashes. "Barney, I'm scared."

"Oh, baby! If you could only do that in front of the cameras."

He dragged her into the departure lounge just as the tail end of the line of passengers was disappearing through the gate.

"There's nothing to be frightened of. You're gonna get out on that stage and knock 'em dead. You don't need me along to do that."

"That's not what's bugging me," she wailed. More tears. Barney got out his handkerchief.

"Don't cry, sweetheart. You'll spoil your makeup." He

dabbed at the wet on her cheeks. The stewardess at the gate was making impatient clock-watching motions. "Now, what are you scared of? Tell Uncle Barney."

"Just cut the 'Uncle Barney' shit!" She backed away from him. "You got me into this and now it's giving me nightmares. You wanna hear this? I never dream, right? I mean, I flunked out with my shrink because I never could tell him any dreams. Well, night before last I had this dream. I was on this enormous stage, all the lights and everything. I was standing there all alone and I couldn't remember what I was supposed to do. I tried to say something, but I didn't have any voice. And then, my clothes started melting. I mean, they just turned into liquid and ran off my body and made a little puddle on the floor, just as though I'd pissed myself. So there I was, stark naked."

"You should have got a round of applause for that."

"Shut up, you old pervert, and listen. So there I am without a stitch. I can't move and I can't speak. And all these New York actors come out on the stage and they're laughing like maniacs. At me!"

"How could you tell they were New York actors?"

"They were all sick and creepy looking, that's how. Now, Barney, listen. This is the worst part. They all got out knives and started throwing them at me. And I couldn't *move!* That's when I woke up. Oh, Barney! They're gonna kill me up there. They're gonna cut me to pieces!"

"Excuse me, Miss. Are you boarding this plane? We can't hold much longer." The stewardess, exuding plastic concern, hovered antsy in the doorway.

"Just a minute, Stew. She'll be right along. We have a little panic situation here."

Barney gripped the drooping, tearful girl by the shoulders and forced her to stand straight. "Look, kid," he said. "Is this the first time in your life that you've been scared, really scared shitless?"

She nodded, woebegone.

"Well, you better get used to it. It doesn't get any easier. If anything, it gets worse. The higher you go, the greater the panic. It's the price you have to pay. In a way, you're right to be nervous about working with the pros. They know a lot more than you do, and they've had light years more experience. But you're going up there to learn from them. Watch them, listen to them, use them. And if anybody starts cutting you down, just blister them the way you do me. There's nobody on God's green earth can out-bad-mouth Miss Glory Hayes, America's future superstar. That's all the pep talk you're gonna get from me. Just remember what you're supposed to be doing up there and don't screw any wooden Indians. Okay?''

She grinned. "Okay, Uncle Barney. I'll save it all for you. Maybe by September you'll be able to get it up.''

"Atta girl. Get on the plane now before the Stew has Siamese twins. I'll be in touch. Anything you need, let me know.''

"So long, Barney." She ran to the departure gate, haunches swaying, breasts straining against the thin green jersey shift which was obviously all she was wearing. At the gate, she turned.

"What kind of car did you get me, Barn?''

"I asked for a red T-Bird.''

"Fantastic!" She disappeared.

CHAPTER III

The Gristede's shopping bag was heavy, but it would be a lot lighter by the end of the trip. It was balanced on the other arm by an overnight case and a large black leather handbag. The trunk had been sent on ahead and would be waiting for her at the other end. Tina Elliott waddled through the bus terminal looking for the ramp that would lead her to the bus to Detroit.

On all sides she was assaulted. People rushed this way and that; transistor radios squawked and shrilled at her; the harsh lighting hurt her eyes and made them water; two open-mouthed, large-eyed children stared at her as she passed. "What are you gawking at?" she wanted to scream. "I wasn't always fat. Once I was thin—pretty, too. You don't believe me? Look at my feet. How many size-two feet do you ever see in a lifetime? And not just small. Fine, the bones are fine. Finest bones you could ever wish for. You think you're staring at a funny-looking fat lady, but a million years from now when they excavate the remains of this civilization, they'll think my skeleton belonged to a particularly tiny and delicate princess. It's all in the bones, my dears, that's where true beauty lies. So stare your miserable little eyes out."

Breathless, she leaned against the plate glass window of one of the countless shops that lined the terminal. All this walking was difficult, especially with the bags dragging at her arms. It wouldn't hurt to rest for a few minutes. She had plenty of time to find the bus and get a nice window seat. Tina liked traveling by bus. In the first place, it was cheap. But even when she could afford to fly, she hated the narrow airplane seats with the hard little armrests that dug into her sides. And airplane food wasn't enough to feed a circus midget. Trains were all right, but nothing like what they were years ago when she used to travel with Pa and dining cars served beautiful, magical food. She had a vague memory of oysters and champagne on a long-ago train, but couldn't remember whether it was something that had happened to her or that she had seen in an old movie. Anyway, dining cars had suffered a sad decline and so had Pa, spending his last years in a home for aged actors, completely lost in a world of his own.

So, Tina preferred to travel by bus. She brought along her own food, a shopping bag full of the sweet things she loved so well: datenut bread and cream cheese sandwiches, chocolate-covered Mallomars, ripe yellow pears and cantaloupe quarters neatly sliced and wrapped in plastic film. At the bottom of the bag, cushioned by play scripts and paperback romances, were two Thermos bottles of lemonade. At the last moment, she had thrown in bags of potato chips and pretzels and a box of Turkish Delight. It was a long trip, and while she might sleep for part of the night if no one occupied the adjacent seat so she could spread out and be comfortable, still it was a good idea to be prepared for some wakeful hours of reading and studying lines. Fortified, of course, by a good stock of munchies. Tina felt a little like a pioneer woman setting out for the great unknown.

She pulled her weary body away from the plate glass, ready to resume looking for the Detroit bus. Change at Detroit for a bus going north, a bus that would deliver her practically on the doorstep of the Duck Creek Playhouse. Now there's a name for you. Who could ever admit to having worked in a place called Duck Creek? It sounded ridiculous. But it was a job, wasn't it? And you can't knock that. Four good plays, and four good parts for Tina Elliott. If she could just hold up and not let herself get too worn out to handle the stiff pace of rehearsing by day and performing by night.

Come to think of it, maybe she was just hungry. Maybe that's what was making her feel so tired. She'd been rushing around all week getting ready to go and hadn't been eating regular meals. She hadn't had anything since breakfast and that was hours ago. Her stomach rumbled at the thought, and at the same moment, a rich, sweet, doughy aroma reeled its way out of the shop whose window she had been leaning against and past her quivering nostrils.

"Just what the doctor ordered," she murmured softly as she waddled into the shop, and then remembered that the doctor had, in fact, ordered her to lose weight.

"Or you won't live to regret it," were his exact words. Well, that was two years ago, and she hadn't lost any weight. Had put on a few more pounds, if the truth be known, but was still alive and kicking. And eating.

"I'll have six of those, and three of those and three of those over there," she told the girl behind the doughnut counter as she pointed first to the sugar-sprinkled jelly doughnuts and then to the ones iced with shiny thick chocolate and the ones prickly with white coconut shreds.

Before she tucked the bulging sack into her shopping bag, she plucked out one of the jelly-filled cakes and devoured it with quick, gulping bites. Her small, even teeth chomped up and down like soldiers marching quick time. Powdered sugar sprinkled down the front of her purple tent-like dress and glistening red jelly squirted onto her pudgy fingers. When she had finished the doughnut, she licked her fingers, avidly collecting each sticky smear of jelly.

"Ah, better," she sighed. "Much, much better."

Her spirits restored, she moved quickly through the terminal, her feet in their red patent-leather pumps practically dancing along the echoing tile floor. The red shoes were among her favorites. She wore them for good luck, because they made her feel like Dorothy in the Land of Oz, and it was all she could do as she skipped along to keep from breaking out into her impression of Judy doing "Over the Rainbow." She'd done it once on the Ed Sullivan Show and everybody had loved it. But it hadn't really led to anything, not even a return engagement, and now she only did it once in a while privately at parties where a faithful Judy fan might get drunk enough to want to close his eyes and pretend.

She had other favorite shoes. Lots of shoes. Over a hundred pairs. All styles and colors. Well, when all your dresses have to be cut from practically the same pattern, large and loose, you have to do something to feel pretty. Twenty pairs of her best shoes were in the trunk on their way to Michigan.

Tina spotted the ramp, numbered and marked with her destination. Oh, it was good to be working again, to be on the road just like she used to be with Pa. Of course, this was different. She was on her own. Pa had made it all seem like fun, a different hick town every few days and never having to go to school. Pa had taught her everything she needed to know—how to read by declaiming Shakespeare to each other; enough arithmetic to know when she was being cheated on a contract. The first shoes that she could remember were darling silver tap shoes with great big bows. The act was "Tom and Tiny," song and dance and a line of patter that always made tall, elegant Tom come off second best to the tiny moppet who

23

danced circles around him. At the end, after they'd taken their bows, he would always sweep her up onto his shoulder where she would smile and blow kisses at the audience.

Things were certainly different now, but they said that tap dancing was making a big comeback. Tina had her tap shoes ready and she could still shuffle-ball-change with the best of them. Well, maybe she had slowed down a trifle, but only a trifle. In the meantime, there was Duck Creek and a busy summer season. Nothing could be finer.

She boarded the bus, clambering up the high steps with difficulty.

"Don't know why they make these steps so tall," she complained to the driver as she handed him her ticket. "Not everybody's a giant, you know."

The driver nodded noncommittally as he punched her stub and handed it back to her.

The interior of the bus was airless and stuffy and smelled of hot vinyl and old cigarette butts. She scanned the rows of seats, only a few of which were occupied, to choose the one that suited her best. Not too far back where the ride was likely to be bumpy, and not right at the front where the evening sun would shine in her eyes. Somewhere in the middle. As she began edging down the narrow aisle, she glanced into the seat immediately behind the driver. In it, an old man lay back with his eyes closed, his seat already in the reclining position. He wore an ancient cream linen suit and a pale brown silk shirt of equal vintage with a carefully folded ascot at his corded and wrinkled throat. In the rack above his head rested a Panama hat, just like the one that Pa used to have, its brim drooping through the steel bars.

With a shock of recognition, Tina tiptoed past the sleeping man. Peverill Martin! Who would have thought he was still alive? She hadn't seen or heard about him in years. Well, no reason why he shouldn't be alive. He was younger than Pa, but not by much. And he was one of the few who could remember the days when she was "Tiny" in fact as well as in name. She sank into a window seat halfway down the aisle and directly behind the old man. That way, even if he turned around, he'd have a hard time seeing her over the tops of the intervening seats. She deployed her shopping bag, handbag, and overnight case on the empty seat beside her to discourage company, and settled down to wait for the trip to begin.

24

Pev Martin. What do you suppose he's doing on this bus? Well, she'd have to talk to him soon enough. There'd be rest stops along the way and she couldn't very well avoid him for the entire trip. Memories were fine, as long as you kept them to yourself and remembered only the good parts. Pev would ask about Pa and that would hurt. He would talk about the old days and graciously pretend not to notice that dear little "Tiny" had changed a bit. Good God! Could it be possible that he was going to Duck Creek, too? She'd never bothered to find out who the rest of the company was. It just hadn't seemed important. Surely he was too old to be working. But Pa had worked until he couldn't remember lines anymore and missed performances because he forgot where he was supposed to be.

The bus was filling up. Tina rummaged in her shopping bag and pulled out a play script and a pear. Might as well get started. Juice trickled down her chin while her lips mumbled over the lines she would speak on opening night, just two short weeks from today. No one asked her to clear her belongings from the unoccupied seat. The doors closed with a hydraulic hiss and the air-conditioning system groaned into life, blowing first warm then cooler air around her neck and shoulders. The bus rolled and Tina Elliott ate another pear.

CHAPTER IV

Did you get through this time?"

"No. First the line was busy. Then nobody answered. I must have let it ring twenty times. I'll try again in a while. If we're lucky, we won't be more than a day late. Damned car!" He kicked the offending vehicle's right front tire.

Anita stared at the oil-streaked pavement through the open door of the stranded Volkswagen. "Maybe I ought to go home, Tony," she whispered. "I can probably get a plane back to New York from here."

"Dammit, Anita! Let's get the car fixed first and then talk about who's going where. Without the car, nobody's going anywhere. Where the hell is that mechanic?"

Tony Brand strode across the blackened macadam toward the service station's glass-enclosed office. Anita watched him through the rain-streaked windshield of the old VW. It wasn't fair, she thought, swallowing hard against the tears that threatened to spill down her cheeks in a storm more torrential than the steady downpour through which they had been driving for the past two hours. If he didn't want the job, why did he take it and then complain bitterly for almost the entire trip about the injustice that condemned him for the whole summer to working in a backwoods theater where no one would recognize his talents? Sure, he was entitled to something better. So were we all. Everybody had talent and everybody ought to be a star. But not everybody got the breaks. He didn't once consider how she might feel, tagging along with no real reason for taking up space. She didn't even have a job to complain about. Oh, it had sounded wonderful when they'd talked about it back in New York.

"Make it a vacation," he'd said. "You deserve it. You know what New York is like in the summer. And besides," he'd added, nuzzling her neck with tender kisses, "now that I've gotten used to you, I can't live without you. You wouldn't want me to waste away out in the wilderness, would you?"

Larry Devine had been encouraging, too. "Sure," he'd

27

said, "come on along. It's really beautiful up there. Miles of beach, and the air is as fresh and clean as on the first day of creation."

Or maybe he was only being polite after half-promising her the job and then at the last minute giving it to some Hollywood sexpot nobody'd ever heard of. Glory Hayes. What a phony name. Anita wondered what her real name was. Probably something like Ethel Frump.

She shrugged and rested her head against the door frame, letting the stray raindrops cool her cheeks. The car had been stuffy with the windows closed against the rain and overheated with Tony's angry words as he inveighed against the other drivers on the road and an unappreciative theatrical establishment that steadfastly refused to recognize that he was Pacino, Stallone, and a young Robards all rolled into one glorious package. To hear him tell it, there was no role beyond his scope, no medium in which he could not reign supreme, if only the idiot directors would give him his rightful chance.

She'd heard it all before, of course, but never in such a concentrated dose. At home, she could quietly agree with him and then go into the kitchen or take a shower or leave the apartment. Often she was too busy herself, making the rounds or working when she had work, to pay too much attention to his moods. But in the car, on this long drive from New York to Duck Creek, Michigan, she was a captive audience and she began to wonder if she shouldn't have paid closer heed to the signals he'd been giving off in the six months they'd been living together. He was enormously self-centered, that much was obvious. But actors need to be in touch with their emotions. Especially an actor like Tony who relied almost exclusively on instinct and a deep well of private feelings to come to an interpretation of a role. It didn't always work, but when it did, he was very, very good. When she compared herself to him, Anita often felt that she had nothing more than a moderately pretty face and a bag of clever, meaningless tricks that brought her the occasional week's work in a soap opera and the odd television commercial.

"Oh, God!" she muttered. "There you go making excuses for him again."

But he could be kind, she reminded herself, adding, yes, when it suits him. He could be boyishly charming, maddeningly thoughtless, surprisingly repentant. He was alternately a passionate lover and an indifferent stranger. His moods swung up and down like a crazed barometer responding to some internal weather which she had no way of forecasting. There were times when he would become so violently angry over some inconsequential issue that she thought he might strike her, only to switch gears suddenly and sweep her into gales of relieved laughter with his ridiculous clowning. It was like living with a dozen different men and never knowing which one was going to turn up for dinner. Perhaps it was the uncertainty that kept her tied to him, the feeling that, even after six months of sharing meals and bed, triumphs and disappointments, there was still much that she didn't know about this intense, mercurial man who was now trudging downcast through the rain back to the car.

"How much money have you got?" His voice was dispirited as he leaned against the car door, gazing sadly at the highway where trucks, buses, and cars hissed by in the watery gray afternoon. Raindrops glistened in his hair and ran down his cheeks like tears.

"Two hundred, more or less. What's up?"

"Well, we can either junk the car and hitchhike the rest of the way or wait till dawn's early light and hope that Buddy, who comes on duty at eight in the morning, can diagnose the trouble and fix it. Wayne over there," he nodded at the stocky plastic-coated figure stolidly pumping gas into a battered farm truck, "says he 'don't know nuthin' 'bout no engines.' But he can get his brother to come and drive us to the nearest motel. What do you think?"

Anita thought, there goes my plane ticket. But would I really have gone? Deserted him in the outskirts of dreadful Toledo? Who knows? The question has passed the point of receiving an honorable answer. She said, "Will two hundred be enough?"

"Won't know till Buddy looks it over in the morning." He reached down and took her hand in both of his. "Look, love, I'm sorry I was such a grouch in the car. I don't know what's bugging me, but I shouldn't have taken it out on you. What do you think we should do?"

Anita, after her first impulse to pull her hand away, got out of the car and pressed her lips to his wet cheek. The rain tasted clean and cool.

"Get it fixed, of course," she said. "It's a good old car. I wouldn't think of junking it. Everything will look better in the morning. It's probably some minor thing that won't cost an arm and a leg. And I could use a good night's sleep. Tell Wayne to call his brother.''

Anita followed him back to the service station office. That goes for people as well as cars, she thought. You don't junk them when they're tired and hurting. Sometimes he was such a child. Now that his anger was past, he was chastened and looking to her for help. Were those the moments she lived for, the moments that gave her the illusion of being in control of their relationship? Because it was an illusion. They always ended up doing exactly what he wanted to do, even though it was she who finally made the decision. Clever, clever Tony.

''I'll try to call them from the motel,'' he said. ''I wouldn't want Devine to think I don't cherish this golden opportunity to wow the yokels.''

CHAPTER V

I realize this isn't the Ritz, darling, but you could lay on something better than these dank little cubbyholes."

The only affectation the young man lacked was a monocle, but even without it his sneer was villainous.

Leo smoothed his already perfectly groomed dark hair and slapped his riding crop impatiently against the calf of his burnished leather boot. He'd been riding on the dunes earlier in the morning and cherished the occasion to appear in his horsey finery. His tweed jacket had suede elbow patches.

"Elena, dear chatelaine, keeper of the keys to my fickle heart, you simply cannot relegate these people to the attics like a covey of simpering scullery maids. They're actors, my dear, temperamental beasts. At the very least, they're accustomed to privacy when bathing. There are only two cantankerous bathrooms on this entire floor. It's not as though I were asking for a dozen bridal suites."

"If I put them downstairs, some of them will have to double up."

Elena St. Cloud thought the young man ridiculous, but she was glad to have the business. A sizable chunk of her regular summer clientele had defected last year to the brand new Rushing River Lodge, centrally air-conditioned, color television in every room, king-sized beds, an artificial waterfall, and a spectacular view of the old fish smokehouses across the road. But it was convenient to the new marina just on the other side of the wharf and, of course, to the playhouse, which had once been a cannery where the cherries from the orchards dotting the peninsula had been processed and shipped out by lake freighter.

"Double up!" Leo shrieked. "Are you mad? Actors are the most incompatible people in the world. It's sheerest insanity to ask them to work together all day, and then sleep in each other's pockets at night. You'll have murder, foul and most natural murder on your hands. No, my beloved, you'll have to do better than that. Otherwise, I'll ship them all over to Flushing Fountains and damn the expense."

Elena smiled. He was awful, a phony, shrill and demanding, but he *was* funny. And he was probably right. Although she was reasonably sure the playhouse couldn't afford to board the entire company at Rushing River, still she had agreed to accommodate them and she didn't want to take the chance of losing them along with the half of her remaining regulars who still hadn't sent in their reservations. Here it was mid-June, and if she didn't have a full house by the Fourth of July, she might as well close up and sell the old hotel to the first waterfront developer who came down the pike.

"All right, Leo. I'll let you have some singles on the second and third floors." She stared down the narrow uncarpeted corridor.

"We have a pair of lovebirds. We pay for him; they pay for her. Not my idea."

"A double, second floor front."

"Lovely, I hope they appreciate it. We also have a rather lardy lady and an antediluvian gent. Your elevator, I notice, is inoperable." Leo followed her down the creaking stairs.

"My elevator is nonexistent. I do have two adjoining singles on the ground floor, but I was saving them for ... oh, never mind. You can have them."

"Oh, mistress of the inn, you have soothed my careworn brow. Let me bestow upon you the kiss of gratitude."

They had reached the ground floor lobby, and Elena moved swiftly to maneuver herself safely behind the registration desk.

"For shame, ducky," Leo wagged a playfully admonishing finger at her. "I really didn't have rape and ruin on my mind. I seldom do. Only a brotherly sort of peckish thing. And speaking of brotherly, where's yours?"

"In the kitchen, I think. The sink was backed up and he said he would fix it."

"Oh, how unspeakably domestic. I think I'll just drift through and wish him Godspeed and a swift plunge. Oh, and Elena, before I disentangle myself from your affairs for the rest of the day, a word of caution. Dispose of the rest of this motley crew however you wish, but take notice that among them you will receive under your roof a certain Hollywood-type person. Nothing much is known about her except that she measures 38-24-36 and it would be as well to install a revolving door in her room. To save wear and tear, you understand. The

32

rest will be the usual assortment of nuts, mad Hungarians, moody method actors, and egregious egoists. It won't be a dull season. Cheeri-bye.''

Leo patted the bronze hand resting protectively on the hotel register and strutted off toward the double doors leading to the dining room and thence to the kitchen quarters, his riding crop tucked, military-fashion, under his arm. But before he had pranced halfway across the lobby, the front doors crashed open and a piercing voice cried:

"WHAT A DIVE!"

He whirled around and stared. Elena stood transfixed behind her desk. The vision in the doorway spoke again.

"WHAT A DIVE! Who said that?"

"You did," said Leo.

"No, stupid. I mean *who* said that? In the movies?"

"Beats me," said Leo. "Esther Williams?"

"No! Listen. WHAT! A! DIVE! Give up?"

"Up you may consider me given." Leo smiled. Elena stared.

"Elizabeth Taylor!" The vision spoke triumphantly. "In 'Who's Afraid of Whoevershewas.'"

"Oh, really?" said Leo. "Do you see many movies?"

"See them! I'm in them." The vision gave a self-congratulatory wiggle.

"Well, try this on for size." Leo flounced to the center of the lobby facing the entrance. With one hand on his jodhpured hip and the other miming a limp-wristed grip on a cigarette holder, he uttered in a throaty, disgusted contralto.

"What a dump! My name is Bette Davis, and you must be dear little Glory Hayes. We've all heard so much about you. Welcome to the dump!"

Glory narrowed her eyes, tossed her head, and undulated across to the desk. She spoke to Elena.

"A bellboy, please. I have tons of luggage in the car."

"Allow me," said Leo.

"Are you the bellboy?"

"No, but I've carried lots of bags in my day."

"Fuck off, faggot," said Glory, smiling sweetly.

Elena hurriedly tapped the bell and called, "Joe! Joe!"

"Oh, do I need a bath," said Glory to no one in particular. "I've been traveling since last night." She plucked at the green jersey, calling attention to the way it clung damply to her body, and leaned against the registration desk, throwing her rump into high relief. "Want me to sign in now, dear? I want

33

your best suite, a king-sized bed, a refrigerator that makes lots of ice cubes, and send up room-service with a bottle of chilled champagne."

"I don't think you want to stay here," said Elena, closing the registration book and sliding it onto a shelf under the desk. "If you'll excuse me, I have work to do." She stalked out from behind the desk and headed for the stairs.

"Wait a minute, ladies," said Leo, catching Elena's arm and halting her angry exit. "I think we can straighten this out." He turned to Glory Hayes and bowed deeply, almost making a leg in approved Restoration fashion. "Allow me to introduce myself. Leo Lemming, at your service. Duck Creek's general factotum, gopher, stage manager, makeup artiste, and sometime mummer. If you don't behave, I can screw up your entrances, put snakes in your dressing room and sand in your cold cream, and make you look like Grandma Moses. This lady is Miss Elena St. Cloud, your hostess for the season. She will give you decent accommodations and all the plain nourishment you can tuck away. If that isn't good enough, I suggest you leave instantly and wiggle your enticing tail back to wherever you came from. End of speech."

While Leo was speaking, Joe St. Cloud appeared in the dining room doorway behind them and stood listening. A lazy grin revealed his startling white teeth and his gray eyes moved insolently and slowly from Glory's absurd platform shoes to her tousled mane of brass-colored hair. Glory returned the appraisal with obvious relish.

"I'll stay," she murmured with a throaty catch in her much modulated voice. She crossed the lobby with long-legged strides that produced interesting configurations in the green jersey dress. "Are you the bellboy?" she asked.

"He ain't Jay Silverheels," said Leo, smirking.

"Are you for real?" pursued Glory, ignoring Leo and concentrating instead on Joe St. Cloud's bare bronze chest, his long black hair caught in two hanks and bound with strips of red cloth, his handsome arrogant face grinning down at her.

He stood well over six feet in his faded Levi's and, as he brushed past her, lightly grazed her unavoidable breasts. He moved silently, on bare feet, to his sister's side.

"You need some help, Elena?" he asked.

"Miss Hayes has luggage in her car, Joe. Will you please bring it in and put it in her room? She'll be in 304."

Joe ambled out the front door with Glory's green eyes glued

34

to his back. Elena returned to her station behind the registration desk. "Will you sign in now, Miss Hayes?"

"White woman brings dubious blessing of civilization to noble but deprived red man. Be careful, Glory. I hear he collects scalps." Leo waved his riding crop like a magic wand. "I hereby protect you with this potent spell. May your legs stay crossed and your luscious person remain safe from the incantations of the powerful witch woman at this moment giving you the evil eye." He tapped Glory lightly on the head and turned to Elena. "Cheeri-bye once again, my dear. If this popsie gives you any more trouble, just let me know and we'll give her a ducking in Duck Creek."

Leo pranced out, favoring Joe with a lascivious leer as he struggled in, burdened with five pieces of Glory's matching luggage. Elena opened the registration book and handed Glory a ballpoint pen.

"Is it true what he said? Are you a witch?"

Elena replied stiffly, "I am a member of the Wolf Clan of the Chippewa tribe. I am a healer. A medicine woman. I am not a witch. Leo is full of nonsense. But he can be troublesome."

"Well, okay," said Glory. "Sorry I asked." She tossed the ballpoint aside and rummaged in her handbag for a red marking pen with which she scrawled her name in the book. "I always use this for autographs," she remarked. Her eyes left the book and tracked Joe as he carried her luggage up the stairs. "Is he your . . ."?

"I'll show you to your room," said Elena, taking a large old-fashioned key from a board behind the desk. "Joe is my brother. He has made promises to the daughter of the chief of our tribe."

"Are you sure you're a real Indian? You talk just like the ones in John Wayne movies."

"Are you sure you're a real actress? You talk just like the whores on the streets of Detroit. Let's go upstairs."

Glory stared for a moment, with new respect in her appraisal of the woman who stood waiting for her to follow. Elena St. Cloud was tall and slender and moved with the straight-backed grace of a dancer. Her oval face and wide-spaced slanting dark eyes were framed by short-cropped shining black hair. She regarded Glory steadily and impersonally, daring her to continue the exchange of insults.

Instead, Glory smiled and tossed her head as if she were

35

tossing away the implication of hostility, received or offered. "You're okay, Elena," she said. "Sorry if I came on too strong. It gets to be a habit."

Elena merely nodded and started up the stairs. Glory followed, subdued. "Have any of the others arrived yet?" she asked.

"No. You're the first. Outside of Leo and Mr. Devine. Leo is staying in the hotel. Mr. Devine has a houseboat moored at the marina. Your room is at the rear where it's quiet. You share a bath with 306. I hope you'll be comfortable." Elena stalked the rest of the way in silence, with Glory Hayes trailing sulkily behind her.

Joe had deposited the luggage in the middle of the braided rug that covered the pine floor of Room 304. He was nowhere in sight. Elena opened the room's single window and indicated the bathroom and closet doors.

"Isn't it quaint!" said Glory, dubiously eyeing the single brass bed. "I'll be all right as long as that deliciously savage-looking brother of yours keeps within groping distance."

"Do you always ignore advice, Miss Hayes? Dinner is at 6:30. There is a television set in the lounge."

Elena left, closing the door behind her.

CHAPTER VI

Pev Martin woke from a dream of glory. Like most dreams it didn't make much sense, but while it lasted he was the star of the drama dearest to his heart. In it, he seemed to stand outside the action, a spectator in the farthest reaches of the balcony, watching a much younger version of himself perform scene after scene from all the hit plays of his youth. There was a constantly changing parade of leading ladies, all the great ones of the day, but the deafening applause was for him, Peverill Martin, with his wavy black hair, his magnificent profile, and his overwhelming stage presence.

When the applause died away, Pev awoke, cramped and slightly nauseous. The bus had stopped, its thrumming engines now silent, and the passengers were filing off to stretch their legs, visit the facilities, and feed. Still rapt in the glory of his dream, he watched them with dispassionate interest wondering vaguely what dreams they could have one-tenth so fine as his. Of course, he had never really shared a stage with Kit Cornell or Eva Le Gallienne, never even come close to it. His career had begun at a bad time. The Great Depression had meant that jobs were scarcer than usual on Broadway, and he'd drifted into the tail end of vaudeville, doing comic sketches based on Shakespeare's tragedies. His Hamlet was a bumbling German farm boy pondering the question, "To pee or not to pee." Two a day in the shiny movie palaces that had begun to spring up across the country, between the jugglers and the tap dancers and the new talking pictures. He made up for this sacrilege by giving readings from the classics to women's clubs along the way, letting the ladies feed him and fawn over him in exchange for a smattering of culture and the titillation of vying for his presence at their dinner tables. Some of them said he looked like Barrymore.

But that was long ago and the resemblance, if there was any, had been of little use in those disappointing years in Hollywood. The war years had been better. Older than most of the first wave of enlisted men, he'd been assigned to a Special Services Unit in England where his job had been to book entertainment for the troops. He'd seen all the plays he could, visited Shakespeare's birthplace, and actually met Noel Coward.

When he returned to New York after the war, he was dismayed to find a new generation of young actors gobbling up all the best parts, while he was left with a choice of character roles or nothing. It was criminal—he wasn't that old; more often than not, he had to make himself up to look older. But that was show business, and he resigned himself to playing bumbling old gentlemen, heavy fathers, eccentric lovable grandfathers, always hoping that the right play would come along and establish him at the top of the heap. There were plenty of actors who played leading roles long past their prime. But for Peverill Martin, the years drifted by until he no longer had to whiten his hair and paint creases on his face.

Finally, even the character roles came few and far between. He'd done some television in its early days, and even had a few small movie roles to his credit. But the theater was his first love and he remained faithful, despite the incontrovertible evidence that she was a fickle and deceitful mistress, promising the earth and delivering a lump of coal.

Pev sighed and shifted in his seat, trying to ease the cramped feeling in his legs. He debated whether he should join the hungry mob in the roadside restaurant. A cup of tea might settle his jumpy stomach. But the bus fare had taken almost all his ready cash. There would be plenty to eat once he got to Duck Creek; room and board were part of the arrangement, and he had planned to hold out until he got there. As soon as the bus got under way again, he would try to go back to sleep. But right now he was feeling faint and was afraid that he might not even be strong enough to walk the few yards from the bus to the restaurant.

The last few passengers were trickling off the bus, and Pev watched them go with a feeling of detachment. Let them stuff their faces, he told himself. They're made of common clay, while I am touched with magic. They will never know the enormous thrill of being loved by a whole theater full of people.

38

Let them have their small pleasures, their commonplace gratifications. The world for them is plentiful beer and overcooked hamburgers.

His eyes traveled pityingly over the woman passing by his seat. She filled the aisle with her bulk and breathed stertorously with the effort required to propel herself along. How terrible, he thought, to allow the divine human form to swell to such monstrosity. How much food she must consume in a day! There was something vaguely familiar about the shape of her head, the configuration of the ear that was visible beneath her piled up orange hair. But lately Pev had found himself seeing old familiar features occupying the faces of strangers. It was a trick of his failing vision, or maybe just wishful thinking on his part, trying to bring back old companions.

The woman, in passing, cast a surreptitious glance over her chubby shoulder, and Pev sat up in amazement.

"Tiny!" he cried. "Tiny Elliott!"

"Pev, dear. What are you doing on this dreary bus?"

"Keeping in touch with the *hoi polloi*. One never knows when one will be called upon to enact a sordid little life. And you, dear child?"

"Oh, I'm traveling for my health. Bad nerves, y'know. Doctor's orders. Get out of the city before the city gets you. But, darling, aren't you coming in for a spot of nosh? The next rest stop is four hours away."

"I can wait. Never could stand to be part of a mob scene. What news of your noble father?"

"Tell you when I come back. I'm starving. Sure you won't come in with me?"

"Quite sure. I had an absolutely monumental breakfast before starting out. Ham, waffles, eggs. I couldn't eat a thing right now." The lie activated the old man's salivary glands, and a wave of nausea shivered his slender frame.

"If you say so," said Tina. "Be back in a few minutes."

He watched as she maneuvered her bulk down the steps and off the bus. How grotesque! It must be all of fifteen years since he'd seen her, and then she'd looked so much like her mother it was heartbreaking. Her sweet, petite, gay sprite of a mother, dead well over forty years but still dancing merrily in his memory. Tiny, herself, must be close to fifty years old, and Mitzi Elliott had been run down by a streetcar in Cincinnati when Tiny was just a tot. He would never forget that terrible day. They were playing the Albee Theater; the movie was

39

Tugboat Annie. The stage show featured a magician, a team of tumblers, himself, and Tom and Mitzi Elliott singing love songs and dancing like a pair of angels. Mitzi had rushed out to buy some cough syrup for Tiny who had a cold, and when she hadn't returned by the last reel of the movie, he and Tom, already in stage makeup and costume, had gone out to look for her. They found her, or what was left of her, in front of the theater being loaded into an ambulance, limp, bloody, and already beyond hope. A river fog had come up, and the street-car conductor, pale and shaken, kept repeating, "I didn't see her. Poor little lady, I didn't see her."

Peverill Martin sighed and closed his eyes. Some memories were better left undisturbed. But for a twist of fate, Tina Elliott might have been *his* daughter. It was a tribute to Mitzi's sweet honest nature that she could have chosen between the two of them, himself and Tom, and still inspire devoted friendship in the loser. Pev had never married and still kept an old snapshot of Mitzi in his wallet.

"Sleeping again?"

"Not sleeping. Just resting." Pev opened his eyes. The grotesque parody of his beloved Mitzi was standing over him, holding out a white paper bag.

"You can't fool me, Pev Martin. I know dumb pride when I see it. And an empty stomach. Now eat this." She laid the bag in his lap. "I'll be right back. I've got some other goodies back at my seat."

"Tiny, wait! It isn't right. I can't take this from you." He tried to hand the bag back to her.

"Why not? You can't travel all the way to Michigan on thin air. Eat! Before it gets cold."

"Michigan! Tiny, are you . . .?"

But she was toddling back up the aisle. The shock of it was worse, far worse, than seeing her again after all these years. He'd been able to avoid her even in the small world of the New York theater, but if she were going to Duck Creek, too, if he had to see her day after day, work with her, perform in the same plays, always with the shadow of her mother's beauty imprisoned in that obese body, how would he manage to make it through the summer? The emotional strain alone would wear him out.

All the eagerness with which he'd started out the morning was dispelled. The purposefulness of at last having a job, even at such a remote place as Duck Creek, had turned to ashes and his mood of elation was crushed. It had never occurred to him that she, of all people, would turn up as a member of the company. His long thin fingers closed round the bag and an overpowering aroma of hot food rose from its mouth. His stomach lurched in anticipation. She was kind. He must overlook her appearance and think of her only as a fellow performer and a generous soul. He must hide his chagrin and be appropriately grateful. He opened the bag and drew out a single french fry.

"What? Haven't you finished that yet?" She plumped herself down beside him, distributing her parcels around her on the floor. "Well, take it easy. If you've been . . . ah . . . dieting for any length of time, you should eat slowly until you get back in the habit. When you finish that, I've got dessert here in the bag." She rummaged around and pulled out a box of Mallomars. "Now, if you tell me where you're going, I'll tell you where I'm going." She slit the paper wrapping with her fingernail, and popped a whole chocolate marshmallow cookie into her mouth.

"You're right. It's Michigan," he mumbled around a mouthful of hamburger.

"I thought so." Her voice was thick with chocolate. "And I suppose Duck Creek means nothing to you."

"Playhouse. Just a summer job." He couldn't bear to look at her. He knew what was coming next.

"Well, if that isn't a laugh and a half. Here we are old troupers, trouping again. I remember when we all used to travel together, you and Pa and me. Too bad he can't be with us now. He would have loved it. Ah, well, it's a funny old world."

"You have no idea," said Pev, already feeling better as a result of the food. "How is Tom?"

"Keeping alive. He doesn't know me anymore. Keeps getting me mixed up with my mother."

Pev shuddered.

"What's wrong? Are you ill?"

"No. It's nothing. Someone walked over my grave."

"Well, you can't die until the season is finished. Oh, Pev! It's going to be great fun! Remember those funny skits you used to do? Pa was so handsome, and so were you. You still are."

"It was a long time ago, Tiny. It all ended long ago."

CHAPTER VII

Duck Creek flowed deep behind the old cannery on its way to merge with the deeper waters of the lake. It was a clear, slow-moving stream where lazy pike could lurk and swoop without too much effort on smaller unsuspecting fish. Years before, its waters had run red in the summer months with the refuse of the tons of cherries that had passed through the cannery's hoppers and sorters and vats. Now, most of the peninsula's cherries were frozen into pies down in Traverse, and apart from an occasional beer can drifting downstream, the creek had returned to a glistening, almost primordial, purity. Local residents claimed that you could drink from it without fear of contagion, although none but stray dogs had ever been seen doing so.

On its southern bank, behind the sand dunes rimming the lake, the old cannery, an ugly rectangular, two-storied, weathered brick building, had undergone a face-lift. The long side of it, facing Cherry Lane, had been painted bright yellow and a tent-shaped green canvas marquee stretched across its front. Larry Devine had been tempted to name his playhouse after the meandering dirt road on which it was located and coincidentally after the venerable Off-Broadway theater in which he'd achieved his first success. But the town fathers had wistfully suggested that the tourist trade might benefit if the theater were closely identified with the town, and Larry had acquiesced. At night, floodlights shone on glass-fronted frames on either side of the entrance where photographs of last season's plays gave promise of entertainments yet to come. Wooden flower boxes bursting with pink geraniums lined the path from the parking lot. On the roof, colorful pennants snapped and fluttered in the lake breeze, while just below the ornate rooftop molding, an emerald green banner announced in foot-high yellow letters that this was the Duck Creek Playhouse.

That was the front. At the rear, where the paying customers seldom wandered, the building and grounds remained in a state of disrepair. Weeds grew tall between the ties of a rusty

43

abandoned spur line track. The splintered planks of the loading platform threatened to collapse at any moment, and the unpainted bricks set in crumbling mortar had mellowed to an ashy rose. A concrete retaining wall kept the creek flowing within bounds, but the level of the lake had been rising over the past few years and the wall had developed some new cracks as a result of last winter's subarctic temperatures. There were some ominous soggy spots in the sandy ground behind the theater.

"Ah, Leo. Sometimes I think I should just let the place fall into the creek and forget about it. It's going to do that anyway one of these days. Why fight it?" Larry Devine stood on the retaining wall staring morosely at the latest evidence of its decay. Two rifts in the wall had managed to come together splitting off a sizable chunk of concrete which now rested on the creek bottom. The water lapped innocently at the gap in the wall.

"*Nil desperandum,* Uncle. *Nil desperandum.* We'll get the old thing shored up and keep our little hoofies dry." Leo jotted a note on his clipboard and consulted the long list of items still to be covered. "Let's see. Fire inspection tomorrow morning. Must be sure that all the exit lights get brand new light bulbs. Rehearsal schedules distributed and posted on the backstage bulletin board. First read-through tomorrow at two. Assuming everyone gets here by then. Let's go take a look at the costume designs. Emmy's lurking in the office, awaiting your pleasure."

Devine slouched away from the water's edge and climbed the rickety stairs of the loading platform, with Leo bounding along beside him brandishing his clipboard like a shield. The stairs creaked and swayed ominously.

"Dangerous," muttered Devine. "I can't afford any accidents. One thing goes wrong, and we're out of business. See if you can get somebody to brace them up."

Leo made a note. "Joe said he'd send someone around. One of his clients is said to be a fair carpenter."

Devine sighed. "If we don't show a profit this year, Leo, I'm going to have to close it down."

"But you always say that, dear relative. Is it time for me to give my perennial lecture on the joys of operating a summer theater? Fresh air, sunshine, doing the plays you want to do. The pleasure of spending the summer in my company. What more could you want? We'll make money this year. Don't you fret. Emmy says the advance sales are spectacular."

"Emmy always says that." Devine kicked a a loose board at the edge of the loading dock.

"And Emmy's always right. If business gets much better, we'll have to hang seats from the rafters. Don't go broody on me, Uncle. I've got enough to do keeping the troops in line."

"Who's arrived so far?"

Leo snickered. "I personally witnessed the grand entrance of your protégée of the year. Honestly, Nunk, whatever possessed you to take on that one? Glorious Glory spells nothing but trouble as far as I can see."

Devine gazed up at the clouds massing solidly out over the lake. "Barney Gross says she's got something. Only needs a little experience."

"Her something is obvious, but I didn't think we were running that kind of an establishment. And as far as experience goes, she's probably had more of that than all the rest of us put together. You should have seen her move in on Joe St. Cloud."

A few huge raindrops splattered the gray boards of the loading dock, and Devine swung open one-half of the tall double door that served as an emergency exit.

"Joe can take care of himself. Don't worry, Leo. Barney Gross is an old friend and I owed him one. But if Hayes doesn't work out, we can always get someone else. Isn't Tony Brand bringing along that nice little girl friend of his?"

Leo shook his head as he slipped into the dim interior of the theater. Outside, the rain began to fall with a steadily increasing drumroll that echoed in the empty auditorium. "You're a crafty old maneuverer, Uncle mine. Here I thought you were losing your highly polished marbles inviting Stratton along for a *soi-disant* vacation while giving the job she coveted to a Hollywood popsie with an admittedly magnificent exterior but no other discernible reason for treading your cherished boards. But you obviously set the whole thing up. Give Hayes a chance, thereby fulfilling your obligation to old friend Barney, and when she muffs it, as you equally obviously expect her to do, slip in Stratton who has been discreetly waiting in the wings. Oh, Unk, you're a masterpiece. I couldn't have plotted it better myself."

"Hold on, Leo. I didn't plot it. It just worked out that way. But you can't blame me for taking advantage of the situation. Who knows? Maybe Barney's baby star will turn out to be the greatest thing since sliced bread. In that case, Stratton has herself a fine old time lolling on the beach. On the other hand, if Hayes bombs I can ship her back to Barney and let Stratton take over. That's all there is to it. No plot. And I hope no hard feelings. But I would like to talk to Stratton before rehearsals start. Have they got here yet?"

"Not yet. Tony wrote that they'd be driving, so they could arrive anytime."

The two men had reached the back of the darkened auditorium. From somewhere backstage came the muffled sound of voices and staccato bursts of hammering. Larry Devine paused at the top of the center aisle. "Who else is here?" he asked.

"Sounds like the stage crew is working."

"No. I mean members of the cast. Who else?"

"Well, two of them are supposed to be on the morning bus. Tina Elliott and Pev Martin. And you've already talked to the local talent."

"You know what I mean, Leo. Is *she* here yet?"

"She?"

"Don't play dumb, Leo. You know perfectly well who I mean. Has Hilda arrived yet?"

"Oh, Hilda. Well, I could check at the hotel. Want me to give them a call? If she's there, I'll tell her to pop on over."

"No. Don't do that. It's raining." He glanced down at the old gray slacks he was wearing, and brushed at the spots that decorated his ancient sweatshirt. "I guess I'll go down to the boat and get cleaned up. Wouldn't want the cast to see me looking like this the first time."

"What about Emmy? She wants to check those costume sketches with you."

"That can wait. It's almost dinner time, and I need a shave." He rubbed the gray bristles on his chin. "Tell me the truth, Leo. Do you think I made a mistake in bringing her here?"

"The Hollywood popsie? That could be the biggest mistake of your life. On the other hand, people may come from miles around just to gawk at her dimensions. Truly monumental."

"No," said Devine. "I mean Hilda. Do you think she'll think I have something else in mind?"

Leo displayed intense interest in his clipboard. "Do you?" he murmured.

Devine frowned. "I'm glad she's decided to make a comeback. I hope she succeeds. If I can help her, I will and I'll be glad to do it. It's the least I can do after all the misery I caused her. But five years is a long time to be hibernating in this business. People have short memories. It won't be easy for her once she gets back to New York. They'll all make a big fuss over her at first, but they'll be waiting and watching like vultures. If she has a hit, well and good. Everyone will rally round. But if she flops, well, you know what it'll be like. They'll all be too ready to pick over the corpse. I wish I could spare her that.''

"Your sentiments do you credit, Unk," said Leo, "but you haven't answered my question."

"Which was?"

"Do you? Have something else in mind? Like a reconciliation scene? Wipe out the divorce and the past five years in one brief summer of happiness?"

"Oh." Devine pushed open one leaf of the doors leading to the foyer. A dim watery light penetrated the first few rows of seats, revealing dusty chair backs and swags of cobwebs swaying gently in the disturbed air. "Got to get this place cleaned up, Leo. Make a note. And tell Emmy to go home. I'll see her in the morning. I'll be down on the boat if you need me for anything."

"When in disgrace with fortune and men's eyes
I all alone beweep my outcast state,
And trouble deaf heaven with my bootless cries . . ."

She got no further than that. With one joyous shout of "Hilda!" Larry Devine bolted down the aisle, leaped up the side steps onto the stage in two strides, and swept her into his arms.

At the back of the auditorium, Leo Lemming murmured, "Bravo, old girl. That was a fine entrance. And the answer to the question is obviously, 'Yes, he does have something else in mind.'"

He slipped through the door and let it close quietly behind him, leaving Larry Devine and Hilda Kramer to ask and answer their own questions.

CHAPTER VIII

Rain obscured the stars and the moon was only a dim efflorescence hanging low over the lake. There had been thunder and lightning earlier, and gusts of wind that had howled around the old hotel during dinner, rattling the windows alarmingly and seeping through them to chill the ankles. But the storm had since quieted to a dull steady downpour. On the deck of the houseboat, sheltered by a canvas awning, Hilda Kramer and Larry Devine sat in deck chairs.

"Can I get you a drink?"

"Relax, Larry. You've been fussing over me for hours. I'm not used to it."

"Well, I'd like one. You used to like Glenlivet. I just happen to have some around."

"I've lost my taste for a lot of things. Do you have any coffee?"

"Just instant."

"That'll be fine."

Devine heaved himself to his feet, a bulky silhouette in the light that streamed from the open door of the houseboat's main cabin.

"It'll take a few minutes. Don't go away."

"I won't," Hilda promised. "I'll stay right here."

Left alone with her thoughts, Hilda smiled at the recollection of her first evening's dinner at the Dune Haven Hotel. Her next door neighbor, Glory Hayes, after monopolizing their shared bathroom for well over an hour, had appeared in a shimmering crimson jumpsuit that looked as though it had been glued to her body by Frederick of Hollywood himself. The four of them, Glory, Leo, Larry, and herself, had sat at a large round table in the center of the dining room. The remainder of the tables, those that were not empty, were occupied by family groups with small children and dowdy middle-aged couples. The young fathers and the jowly, balding grandfathers alike had difficulty paying attention to their wives. Their eyes invariably drifted to the center table where Glory Hayes

49

basked in the warmth of their regard and poked scornfully at her food. The wives, after brave attempts at conversation, resorted to scolding the children or lapsed into injured silence. So that Glory, when she judged the time was right, had an undivided audience for her scene.

"Oh, waitress," she cried to the young girl who was edging past with a tray full of dirty dishes. "Take this disgusting mess away and bring me a poached egg on toast and a cup of tea."

"Just a minute, Miss. I'll be right back," said the girl, nervously maneuvering the tray with its heavy load toward the kitchen.

"Take it away right now," Glory insisted. "I can't bear to look at it another minute. Just pick it up and put it on your little old tray and throw it to the dogs. That's all it's good for."

"Yes, Ma'am. I don't think I can. I'll come back directly." The girl continued her teetering progress out of the dining room.

Leo intervened. "Pipe down, Glory. There's nothing wrong with the food. It's not your ordinary Southern California haute cuisine, but it's not kennel fodder either."

Glory ignored him and rose to her feet, a sinuous chest-heaving picture of indignation. Larry grabbed at her arm, but she shook him off. "Waitress!" she shrieked. "Take this plate away! Now!"

The girl stopped in her tracks, cups and glasses sliding dangerously close to the edge of the tray. "I can't," she mumbled, her round young face flushing almost as red as Glory's costume.

"Oh, yes, you can," said Glory, snatching up her untasted plate of food. Before anyone could stop her, she carried the plate over to the young waitress and dumped it upside-down on top of the stack of dishes on the tray. The girl clutched the tray with both hands and was forced to do a ludicrous kind of bent-kneed shuffle to keep her balance and prevent the dishes from sliding off the tray. She straightened up with tears in her eyes, only to watch helplessly as two water glasses tilted and toppled, shattering on the hardwood floor.

"Now, look," the girl moaned. "I'll lose my job."

"Serve you right," said Glory.

The girl fled, stumbling and sobbing, through the archway that led to the kitchen. Glory returned to the table beaming in triumph.

"You have to keep the help in line," she remarked as she resumed her seat.

"That was cruel, young lady," said Larry, "cruel and unnecessary."

"Maybe so," said Glory, "but I've had worse than that done to me."

"Deservedly, I'm sure," said Leo. "It was a bad scene, Glory. You've lost your audience."

It was true. An embarrassed silence blanketed the dining room. The family groups were deeply engrossed in their cherry pie, and the middle-aged couples were gulping their coffee and preparing to depart.

"Oh, who cares about them." Glory tossed her brassy mane and moved her chair closer to Larry's. "Let's find a place where there's some action. There has to be something in this town. A disco, or at least a bar with a jukebox where we can dance. I love to dance." She wriggled her shoulders and set the front of her jumpsuit quivering.

"Not tonight," said Larry. "We have a busy day tomorrow."

Hilda had kept silent during Glory's tormenting of the waitress. Now her hand moved slightly on the tablecloth, edging infinitesimally closer to Larry's, and she was gratified when he covered it with his own. Glory blinked and smiled.

"You really ought to care about those people, Glory," said Leo. "They're the ones who'll be buying tickets to come and see you perform."

"Well, they've just had a preview of coming attractions. Leo, won't you come dancing with me?"

Before Leo could answer, Elena St. Cloud entered the dining room, followed by the young waitress armed with broom and dustpan. While the girl swept up the shards of glass, Elena came straight to their table.

"Is something wrong?" she asked. Her face was expressionless but her dark eyes fastened on Glory Hayes.

"Yes. I ordered a poached egg. How long does it take to poach an egg?"

"I'm sorry," said Elena, "but the kitchen is closed."

Glory took a deep breath and her hands curled into fists on the table. Leo hurriedly interposed.

"Oh, too bad!" he exclaimed. "Are we too late for some of that marvelous cherry pie? You ought to try some of that, Glory, my pet. There's nothing like it in the world."

51

Glory subsided into a pout. "All right," she said ungraciously. I've got to eat *something.*"

Elena smiled at Leo. "Yes, we still have cherry pie. Would you all like coffee?"

They all agreed on coffee and cherry pie, and for the rest of the meal Glory maintained a sullen silence while Larry and Leo embarked on a short history of the Duck Creek Playhouse, its ups and downs, the plays and actors that had figured in the past summers. Then Larry spoke of his hopes for the coming season.

"I always like to do an original play. There are lots of people writing plays in this country, and only a tiny fraction of them ever have a hope of getting produced on Broadway. Or even Off Broadway. The regional theater keeps the art of playwriting alive. And there's always a chance that a play can move from the hinterland to Broadway. It's happened before and it can happen again. This year, we've got a historical drama with a feminist slant. It's got everything—costumes, romance gone awry, humor and compassion, a woman masquerading as a man. Although how we're ever going to convince an audience that Glory is anything but all woman is beyond me. She'll have to be a very good actress."

The mention of her name drew Glory out of her sulks and she turned to Hilda across the table.

"Barney said I could learn a lot from you."

"Barney?"

"Barney Gross, my agent."

"Oh. Barney's an old friend. That was very kind of him."

"Yeah. He told me all about you."

"Did he?"

"Yeah. He thinks you're some kind of terrific actress. Funny. The way he talked, I thought you'd be a lot older than you look."

"Sorry to disappoint."

"Oh, that's okay. Listen, some of us manage to stay looking young a long time. You wouldn't think I was twenty-ah-two, would you?"

"Don't tell me *you're* worried about getting old!"

"Well, I've got to make it in the next year or so. Otherwise I might as well forget about it and marry some rich old guy and just lie back and enjoy life. I might just do that anyway."

"A noble ambition."

"Yeah. Well, if nobody wants to go dancing, I guess I'll finish unpacking. I don't know how I'm going to get all my stuff in that crummy little closet. This place is really the pits.''

Glory pushed back her chair and undulated to her feet. She stood for a moment as if posing for a photograph, one hand resting on the chair back, the other modestly pressed to her bosom but at the same time indicating the point at which the cleavage of the jumpsuit cleaved the deepest.

"Well, good-night, all," she said. "I hope I can get my poached egg for breakfast. At this rate, I'm liable to waste away to nothing. That wouldn't do my image any good. I can't afford to get scrawny and wrinkled." She looked innocently at Hilda as she said this, then turned and strolled indolently away.

The three sat as if hypnotized watching Glory Hayes leave the dining room, cross the lobby, and start up the stairs. When she was out of sight, Leo broke the silence

"Ah, popsies," he groaned in mock dismay. "They never change. Makes you wonder about Neanderthal woman." He bent to retrieve his clipboard from beneath his chair. "I think I'll toddle on over to the playhouse for a bit. Larry may work from sun to sun, but poor Leo's work is never done. The program proofs came in just before dinner and I want to check them over and get them back to the printer tomorrow. Ta-ta, kiddies, don't stay up too late renewing old acquaintance.''

He rose from the table, dropped a kiss on Hilda's cheek, and drifted away. "Pay no attention to the popsie, Hilda," he called over his shoulder. "I don't believe she's house-trained yet. Maybe I should try boffing her on the nose with a folded newspaper every time she acts up."

'Good-night, Leo," they chorused after him. Then Larry turned to Hilda and smiled.

"Don't say good-night yet, Hilda. I want to show you something."

"Yes?"

"I want to show you the *Hilda Kay*. Well, she's not much, really, just an old tub of a houseboat. No disrespect to you. Just that I couldn't think of anything else to name her. I bought her the first summer I spent here, when I was fixing up the playhouse. She belonged to an old lady who bought it for her kids to party on. But the kids grew up and went away, so she was stuck with it. It was a terrible mess, so I got it cheap. The decks were rotten and the interior was a wreck. But I've been working on it and it's in pretty good shape now. Leo

53

stayed on it that first summer, but he says sleeping on a boat makes him seasick, so I've had it all to myself ever since. Would you like to take the tour?"

"Yes, I would."

"Great. I'll just borrow an umbrella from Elena."

The tour had revealed much to Hilda of the change in Larry Devine's character. The walls of his sleeping quarters were covered with framed photographs. A few were of Larry himself on memorable occasions in his life—the night he received the Obie, a crowded table at Sardi's after the opening of one of his hit shows—but most of the pictures were of Hilda. They were photographs that she had left behind five years ago when she had renounced Larry and all his works, and her own work, as fruitless and unrewarding. There was Hilda as Mother Courage, Hilda as Hedda Gabler, Hilda as Queen Gertrude. All the roles of her career were displayed on the walls of the *Hilda Kay*, from the very first walk-on as a Cockney maid in a revival of a turgid Galsworthy social drama, to her last appearance as a troubled middle-aged woman trying to come to terms with her grown daughter's lesbianism. The play had not been well received by the critics, but her own performance had been praised as sensitive and finely drawn. This was the role she had walked out on when life with Larry had grown intolerable and the nightly immersion in fictional miseries had added a sickening weight to her own despair.

Over Larry's bunk, the photographs were of a more personal nature. Summers in Amagansett, their trip to Greece years before to pay homage to the birthplace of the drama, a costume party they'd given once for no reason at all except to have fun. Larry had dressed as Oberon and she as Titania, while a very young Leo had had a fine time cavorting as Puck, wreathed in greenery and not much else. In the far corner, next to the wall, was a wedding photograph. Hilda almost wept when she looked at it. How young they all were, and how happy to be together. And there was Leo again, a member of the wedding party, knobby-kneed in short trousers and mugging for the camera for all he was worth. So much had happened since then.

"I never expected you to turn sentimental," Hilda remarked as she finished inspecting the photographs.

"It was a surprise to me, too," said Larry. "But it seemed like an idea whose time had come. Let me show you the rest of the tub."

And so he had shown her the trim galley where he prepared his own breakfast and sometimes cooked dinner when he wanted to get away from his actors for a breathing spell. The main cabin was small, but everything in it was carefully planned to lend a feeling of space. And everything was scrupulously clean, not a single used cup in the tiny sink, not a single pair of trousers thrown on the floor for someone else to pick up.

"Who does your housekeeping?" Hilda asked, remembering the disorder of their former life together.

"I'm on my own," said Larry. "All it takes is a little discipline. There are a couple of cabins I haven't put right yet, but maybe I can find some time to work on them this summer. How do you like it?"

"I'm very impressed," said Hilda.

Now, as she sat in the deck chair listening to the whisper of the rain forming a background to the sounds of her ex-husband clattering around in his shipshape galley, she mulled over her impressions. Larry had achieved a great deal, both in creating his playhouse out of nothing and in restoring his houseboat to livable conditions. But beyond that, he seemed to have returned to a dedication they had both shared in their early days together, and he had grown in generosity of spirit and in an open receptivity to the feelings of others. While she. . . ; she shivered slightly at the memory of how she had spent the last five years. Better to forget that. It was all over now. Larry had changed, and she was on the road to change. If he could do it, so could she. It was too soon to tell, but maybe, just maybe, there was some kind of future for both of them.

She wondered if it would have happened for Larry if she hadn't left him and if he hadn't suffered a series of defeats. Would he have changed at all if he were still one of the most successful directors on Broadway? Or would he still be the overbearing, inaccessible, arrogant monster she had run from? Not a question that could ever be answered. He was who he was now. That ought to be enough. And he'd aged, as she supposed she had, too. But she found his gray hair and his gaunt cheeks, his bearish shambling walk, even his incipient paunch considerably more attractive than the tense dark-haired martinet of her memory. She wondered if he had noticed any change in her appearance. As if in answer to her thoughts, he

55

emerged from the cabin with a glass for himself, a mug of coffee for her.

"Black, as I remember," he said. "You know," he added, "you've hardly changed at all. A little thinner, maybe, but we can take care of that. And a different hairdo. I like it. It suits you, all those little curls. You could almost stand in for Little Orphan Annie."

"Oh, sure. If I dyed it orange and blunked out my eyes. Not to mention a few years."

"Tell me," he said, settling down in his deck chair and sipping at his drink. "Tell me everything you've been up to since the last time I saw you."

Hilda was about to protest that the last five years of her life could not possibly interest anyone, when rapid footsteps pounding along the dock to which the *Hilda Kay* was moored drew their attention. A voice cried, "Larry! Larry! Where are you?"

"Over here," he answered, rising from his chair and setting his drink down on the up-ended barrel that served as a table. To Hilda, he muttered, "Now what in creation does *she* want?"

Hilda followed him as he skirted the cabin and approached the short gangplank that gave access to the *Hilda Kay*. The Duck Creek Marina was lit at intervals by electric lights made to resemble ships' lanterns placed on stanchions. Their glow was dimmed by the rain, but was sufficient to reveal the bedraggled figure of Glory Hayes running down the dock toward the houseboat.

"Here we are," Larry called again and waved.

The girl reached the gangplank and stumbled as she started to cross it. Larry caught her arm and helped her make the crossing, lifting her down the short jump to the low-slung deck of the *Hilda Kay*. When her feet touched the deck, she sagged against Larry, forcing him to support her with both arms wrapped tightly around her limp body. Hilda watched from the shelter of the awning, ready to help but not sure what form her help should take. Glory's long hair hung like a wet curtain flapping around her face and hiding whatever expression was there. Hilda wondered if she were sick, hurt, frightened, or merely creating yet another scene.

"Hey, now." Larry guided the drenched and trembling girl across the deck. "Come on in out of the rain and tell me what's the matter. Somebody put a frog in your bed?"

He nodded to Hilda to help him, and between them they hustled Glory, gasping and stumbling, through the door and into the shelter of the houseboat's main cabin. Along one wall, a low bank of storage lockers did double duty as a settee by virtue of the canvas-covered padding that lined its top. Here they deposited Glory, dripping and moaning. While Hilda arranged a pillow beneath her head, Larry rummaged in the lockers for a blanket to cover her. The red jumpsuit, thoroughly soaked, clung even more definitively to developments beneath, but Glory, for once, seemed oblivious to this display of her native talents. She glanced wildly around, then sank back onto the pillow and closed her eyes, sighing with relief.

"What's wrong with her?" Hilda whispered.

"Damned if I know," said Larry, shaking out a loudly striped afghan and spreading it gently over the girl. "See if you can find a couple of towels in that closet next to the head."

Hilda set off in the direction he indicated, down the narrow passage between the sleeping quarters. As soon as she was out of hearing, Glory opened her eyes and clutched Larry's hand.

"Larry," she whispered. "You've got to help me. You're the only one who can."

"Sure, kid," he answered with what he hoped was a confidence-inspiring smile. "If I can, I will. But first you have to tell me what the problem is."

Glory propped herself up on one elbow, still clinging to Larry's hand. "Promise you won't laugh at me," she begged, her green eyes gleaming moistly as she searched his face for signs of ridicule.

"I promise." He sat beside her and with his free hand brushed aside a wet strand of hair that was plastered to her cheek.

"I don't want *her* to hear this. I didn't know she'd be here. Otherwise, I wouldn't have come."

"Hilda? Oh, listen, kid. Hilda wouldn't laugh at you. She probably could help you more than I could. Why don't you tell us both what's wrong, and then we'll see what we can do."

Glory shook her head vehemently. "No!" she cried. "You don't understand. She may be part of it. You're the only one I can trust. The Emperor came up and that's usually Barney but he's not here, so it has to be you."

"What?"

"I found a couple of beach towels." Hilda came through

57

the narrow doorway from the passage. "And here's a robe she can put on. She really ought to take those wet clothes off."

At the sound of Hilda's voice, Glory lay back on the pillow, closed her eyes, and turned her face to the wall.

"That's great," said Larry. "I still don't know what's bothering here. Maybe a cup of tea. . . ."

"Good idea," said Hilda, gazing down at the recumbent girl with a bemused expression on her face. She handed Larry the towels with the terry-cloth robe. "Why don't I make it, while you get her dried off a little. At least, wrap a towel around her head."

Hilda retreated once again to the passage, this time turning in the direction of the galley.

"Make it good and strong," Larry called after her. "And put a shot of brandy in it."

"Right," came Hilda's voice from the galley, followed by the faint sound of water rushing into a kettle.

Glory's eyelids flickered. "Thanks," she murmured, and turned to face him.

Larry eyed her sternly. "Okay. Now let's have it. What is all this about Emperors and Barney and Hilda being part of it? Part of what?"

"Well, first of all the Moon came up. That's always bad luck." She took a towel from Larry's lap and sat up and began toweling her hair. "So I knew the rest of it was going to be pretty awful. But I didn't think it was going to be so fucking scary."

Larry stared at her, perplexed. "Glory, the moon comes up all the time. What's so scary about that?"

"No. You don't understand."

She draped the towel around her head with the ends hanging down behind her back so that she looked like a figure in a Passion Play—Mary Magdalene in purple terry cloth.

"Most of the time I get something good to offset the bad. But this time, except for the Emperor, it was all bad. Nothing went right. I feel better now, just talking to you about it. But when the Tower came up in my Future Influence, I knew I was in for trouble. So whatever it is, you'll help me?"

"The tower? What tower?"

"The Tower Struck by Lightning. That means disaster. It didn't help that it was raining like a bitch outside and the thunder and lightning and all. Maybe I'm going to break a leg or something. And then when the Death card came up at the end,

58

well, I guess I just panicked and came running to you because the Emperor was sitting right there in the number five spot. So you've got to help me."

Larry shook his head. "Glory, Glory." He almost laughed, but remembered his promise and stopped himself just in time. "You've been telling fortunes, haven't you? You don't really believe that stuff, do you?"

"It's not fortunes. It's the Tarot. And you better believe I believe it. I never do anything without asking the cards. But I don't usually read them myself, so maybe I did something wrong. Miss Angelique never gave me such a bad reading, even though she wasn't too happy about my coming here."

"Who's Miss Angelique?"

"She's my reader back in L.A. I go to her once a week. I don't know how I'm going to get along without her. That's why I brought the cards. I thought I could do the readings myself, and tonight when nobody wanted to go dancing and I didn't have anything else to do, I just laid them out and what do I come up with? Death and disaster."

"Where does Hilda come into it?"

"Maybe it's not Hilda. Maybe it's that Indian bitch at the hotel. The Queen of Swords. A dark-haired, dark-eyed woman. That's a bad lady to mess with. You have to be careful with that card. Last time I had the Queen of Swords in a reading, I got in a fight with a snotty salesgirl who didn't want to let me return a dress that didn't look right. She claimed I already wore it and there were stains on it."

"Had you worn it?"

"Well, of course. How else would I know it didn't look right? I wore it to a party and somebody said I looked like the Mummy's Revenge. It was white and it had these fringes all over it. Could I help it if somebody spilled Kahlua on me? I tried to get if off. But I knew I'd win that one because I had the Ace of Swords in that reading, too, and that means conquest. So I just kept after her until she took it back."

Glory seemed calmer and in possession of her normal combative disposition. The fear that had turned her into a whimpering infant had apparently dissipated. Larry wondered if these were the only two faces that Glory Hayes presented to the world—dependent child and aggressive virago—and he shrank from being elected father confessor to the child. It could create enormous problems with the rest of the cast if it seemed that Glory was getting special attention. Somehow, he would have to nip that little notion in the bud. She prattled on, pressing herself against him so that he became uncomfortably aware of the heat of her body radiating through her damp clothing.

"I just remembered," she said, "that the Death card doesn't necessarily mean that somebody's going to die. Miss Angelique always says it could mean a spiritual change. What do you think, Larry? Do you think my spirit could use a little change? I guess I just read the cards all wrong. But, you know, there I was up in that dingy little room, all by myself, nobody to talk to, and that damn' skeleton jumped out of the pack. Well, I just got scared." She shook off the afghan and stretched invitingly. "But I feel a whole lot better now. I just remembered something else about the Emperor. He's very sexy." Her hand went to the zipper of her jumpsuit. "I'd better get out of these wet clothes before I catch a cold."

"Hey! Wait a minute!" Larry leaped to his feet and held the bathrobe out before him like a bullfighter's cape. "Here. Put this on. Better yet, go down to one of the cabins and change."

She grinned at him, green eyes lewd and mocking, and slowly rose from the settee. "What's the matter, Larry? Haven't you ever seen bare naked skin before?" The zipper plunged.

Hilda walked in from the galley, carrying a laden tray. She glanced at Glory and, without breaking her stride, crossed the room and placed the tray on a pedestal table set into an alcove. "The tea's ready," she said, "and I freshened up your drink for you, Larry. The rain seems to be letting up a little." She turned and scrutinized the half-naked girl. "Glory, dear," she said, "I think your zipper's broken."

"Heavens!" said Glory, glancing down at her navel. "How in the world did that happen!" She wafted the bathrobe out of Larry's hands and scampered away down the passage. "Be back in a momentito. Don't start the party without me."

Larry shrugged helplessly. Hilda tried to maintain a frown, but her eyes twinkled.

"The girl's a menace," Larry whispered.

"And you're a dirty old man." Hilda collapsed into his arms, choking with stifled laughter. "You should have seen yourself," she gasped. "The reluctant lecher. Pop-eyed and drooling in spite of your best intentions. If I'd come in a moment later, she'd have had you snorting and pawing the deck."

"Believe me, Hilda, I didn't encourage her. I was only trying to find out what was bothering her."

"I believe you. Come and sit down." She took his hand and led the way to the captain's chairs surrounding the pedestal table. "Did you find out?"

"Oh, just some fortune-telling nonsense." Larry sipped his drink and sighed. "Barney didn't tell me that she runs her life according to the cards. I've worked with crazies before, but this one really takes the seven-layer cake with frosting on it."

"Did the cards tell her to play flasher for your benefit?"

"No. That was an afterthought. Poor kid. She really worked herself into a tizzy over what she thought the cards were telling her. Death and disaster. And I guess she really believes in it."

"Well, don't feel sorry to her. I have an idea that little lady knows exactly what she's doing." Hilda yawned. "God, but I'm tired. Would you feel safe if I deserted this little party? It's been a long day and I feel like I could sleep for a century."

Devine thoughtfully rattled the ice in his glass and fixed his gaze somewhere past Hilda's left ear. "Why don't you stay here?" he murmured diffidently. "You could have the spare cabin. It would only take me a minute to make up the bunk."

Hilda got up from her chair and walked around behind Larry. She put her hands on his shoulders. "Let's take it slowly, Larry," she said. "I'm glad to see you again, and God knows, I'm glad to be back among the living. But I'm not ready to think about what tomorrow's going to be like. All I want to do is live each day as it comes along. That's about all I can handle. In my own way, I suppose I'm just as superstitious as Glory. She tries to psych out the future through the cards, while I try to ignore the fact that there is a future just in case it might be bad. If I don't plan anything, then I can't be disappointed. Let me say good-night and go back to the hotel. If I'm lucky, I'll see you in the morning."

Larry remained silent, pondering his empty glass. Hilda had left her coffee mug untouched on the table. Glory's tea was steaming and he breathed in the aroma of brandy that rose from it. He felt Hilda's hands lift from his shoulders and heard her move softly to the door. There was so much he wanted to say to her, so much lost time to make up for. He wanted to tell her that he was sorry for the past, for driving her away, for wrecking their marriage. He wanted to tell her that he'd never blamed her for any of it. Most of all, he wanted to tell her that he loved her, and that he'd never stopped loving her and longing for her through all the years since she had left him. Maybe

61

she was right and there'd be time for that later. No sense in rushing things. Take it slowly and make it last this time. Larry turned in his chair to say good-night, and the door burst open. Leo stood on the threshold beaming. Hilda stepped back to let him enter. Behind him, there was a clatter of footsteps on the deck.

"Looky who's here, Uncle! The midnight travelers!" Leo pranced into the cabin followed by a weary-looking couple, both wearing wrinkled faded blue jeans. "They just arrived and, of course, the hotel bar is closed, so when I saw that the *Hilda Kay* was still lit up, I brought them down for a nightcap. They need it. They've been driving through that rain for hours."

Larry rose and moved to the door to welcome the arrivals. "Glad to see you," he said, extending his hand.

Tony Brand stepped forward and exchanged a handshake with him. "Sorry to barge in on you like this, but Leo said it would be all right. I was afraid we weren't going to get here at all. The car broke down just outside Toledo and we were all set to spend the night and a couple of hundred dollars to get it fixed. You know how it is at these backwoods service stations. They can't possibly do anything until a week from tomorrow and when they do, they charge you five times the going rate. But we got lucky. The mechanic was off-duty, but he decided to come back and tinker on his hot rod. He fixed up the old bug in nothing flat. It was only a blocked fuel line. So we decided to drive on through. Rained all the way, and we got lost a couple of times. But here we are, and wouldn't you know it, the rain stopped as soon as we drove up to the hotel."

Anita Stratton had been hanging back near the door, as if not certain of her right to be there at all. She looked pale and tired and drooped against the wall like a discarded rag doll. A small frown of tension between her eyes was the liveliest thing about her.

Devine went to her and threw an arm around her shoulders. "Anita," he said, "welcome aboard. Come and sit down and tell me what you'd like to drink. We have Scotch and gin and brandy, and I think there's some white wine. Just gallon-jug stuff, nothing special."

Anita let him lead her across the cabin to the settee where she collapsed with a sigh. Then she and Tony both spoke at once.

"A glass of wine for both of us," said Tony.

"I'll have a Scotch. On the rocks," said Anita.

"But, Anita," Tony protested, "you never drink Scotch."

"I do this time," she answered without looking at him.

"Scotch it is," said Leo. "I'll do the honors, Uncle. Gin and tonic for you? Hilda, what's your pleasure?"

"Nothing, Leo. I have some coffee here." She drifted back to the table, indicating to Tony Brand that he should join her. "I'm Hilda Kramer," she said. "It must have been a difficult drive through all that rain. I drove, too, but I got here earlier today before the rain started. Your wife seems exhausted."

"She's not . . ." he began, and then glanced across the room to where Anita listlessly nodded in response to Devine's solicitous inquiries. "I guess she is. She'll be all right in the morning."

Leo, poised in the entry to the passage, surveyed the group and said, "Perk up, kiddies. The night is young, and we've managed to elude the overripe and obnoxious Miss Vulgarity. Cause to rejoice. Drinkies in a minute."

From behind him in the passage, a strident voice clamored. "Who are you calling obnoxious? Ever take a good look at yourself, fruitcake?"

"Whoops!" said Leo, peering down the passage. "Premature elation. Cancel the merriment. The plague is with us. I thought you'd be in beddi-byes, sweetheart. Can I make you a drinkie? How about a nice strychnine and soda?"

"Screw you," said Glory, appearing in the doorway dressed only in Larry's blue bathrobe with the belt knotted loosely around her waist. Leo disappeared into the galley, while his voice trilled back at them in song. "Larry," Glory whined, "you've got to make him stop picking on me. The pansy bastard's been on my case ever since I got here." She undulated into the cabin, her brassy hair floating in a cloud around her shoulders. She bent over Larry, who was crouched on the settee beside Anita, and addressed his ear in a loud stage whisper. "I used your hairbrush. I hope you don't mind." The overlapping folds of the blue bathrobe fell away from the exuberant flesh beneath. Inches away from Larry's nose, pink nipples took aim like snub-nosed pistols threatening his equilibrium. He lurched away and struggled to his feet.

"Not at all," he murmured around a sudden clog in his throat. "Help yourself."

Across the room, Tony Brand sat quietly alert. At the first sound of Glory's voice from the passage, his head had

63

whipped attentively in that direction. He had watched her swarm over Devine and, to Hilda Kramer, it seemed that he was tensely awaiting a similar attack on himself. Anita Stratton, head bent, maintained her air of weary indifference. Hilda smiled with faint amusement as Larry fumbled through the introductions.

"Glory, this is Anita Stratton, Anita, Glory Hayes."

The two women nodded at each other. Glory smirked and adjusted the front of the robe.

"Are you an actress, too?" she inquired, disingenuously.

"Sometimes," said Anita.

"And over here," Larry continued, guiding Glory to the table, "over here is Tony Brand. Tony, Miss Glory Hayes of Hollywood."

Tony got to his feet as Glory fixed him in the speculative beam of her green eyes.

"Tony?" she said. "Tony Brand? I know I've seen you in something. Your face is so familiar. What was it?"

"Off Broadway?" he ventured. His hands gripped the back of his chair and he seemed to by trying, unobtrusively, to maneuver it between himself and Glory. He exhibited all the aplomb of a once-bitten lion tamer. Hilda wondered what was ailing him. He and Anita had brought an unpleasant edge of tension aboard the *Hilda Kay*. And Glory's presence seemed to upset him even more.

"Not unless it was so far off Broadway, it was in Hollywood." Glory spoke as if Tony were the only person in the room, her voice throaty and intimate. "I've never been to New York and I hope to God I never have to go there. I've heard it's a terrible place. The beaches are always full of fat ladies. But I know I've seen you somewhere. Only I can't remember where. Movies? Or television? Oh, well, it'll come to me. Maybe it was somebody else. But I'm pretty sure it was you. I never forget a face."

She turned away and settled herself into the chair that Tony had vacated, sprawling so that the robe fell away exposing a long expanse of thigh. Behind her, Tony Brand seemed about to speak, then glanced across the cabin. For the first time since they had boarded the houseboat, Anita looked directly at him. Their eyes locked. Hilda Kramer, who had the habit of quietly observing the offstage drama enacted by the people she encountered, saw the almost imperceptible jerk of his head and Anita's answering nod.

Glory seemed oblivious to the effect of her entrance on the people in the cabin. She reached for the mug on the table. "Is this my tea?" she asked. "I bet it's cold by now." She sipped and made a face. "It's awful. But we don't want to waste good brandy, do we? Down the hatch!" She swallowed it down and waved her empty mug in Larry's direction. "I'll have another, without the tea. Now we can have a party after all. Sure beats spending the night all alone in that rotten hotel room. Larry, honey, there was something else in the cards that scared me, but it's already come true and it's not as terrible as I thought it would be. Tell you about it later."

Hilda wondered what she meant. The only thing that had happened since Glory had boarded the boat was that the rain had stopped and Tony and Anita had arrived. Well, it was all pretty ridiculous and Hilda had no intention of sticking around to watch Glory Hayes drink up Larry's brandy and become, no doubt, even more complacently self-centered. If that were possible. She stifled a yawn and rose from her chair.

"Good-night, Larry," she said. "I guess I'm just out of the party habit. See you in the morning."

"Hey! Wait a minute!" Glory protested.

"Are you going to the hotel?" Tony asked. "I think we'll go with you. Sorry, Larry. Anita's exhausted and I'm not in such great shape myself. Another time, maybe."

He went to Anita and helped her to her feet. "Come on, babe," he said. "You'll feel a lot better tomorrow. You can sleep till noon."

She clung to his arm for a moment, then pushed him away and walked stiffly to the door. There she paused, turned back to face the room, and without looking at anyone said, mechanically, "Good night. I'm sorry if I seem. . . ." Her voice faded out before she could complete the sentence and she slipped through the door and out onto the deck. Tony Brand followed her, his face clouded with concern.

Devine took Hilda's arm. "I'll walk you back to the hotel."

Hilda was about to protest, when Glory interrupted.

"Hey! What about me? Why are you all walking out on me?" Her voice trembled like a hurt child's and her green eyes swam with unshed tears.

"Shut up, Glory." Devine spoke with sharp exasperation. "You stay here. I'll bring you back some dry clothes. You can't go parading around Duck Creek at midnight in nothing but my bathrobe."

65

"Oh, couldn't I?" said Glory. "This place is really turning out to be Dullsville. I'd do *anything* to liven it up. Try to have a party, and everybody poops out. What the hell am I going to do here for three months? Watch my toenails grow?"

Larry stared at her, then shook his head. "Tell Leo I'll be right back. And don't worry about not having anything to do. Starting tomorrow, I'm going to work your tail off."

Glory grinned lewdly. "Is that a promise?"

Devine fled. Maybe during rehearsals, he could find out what made her behave the way she did. If he was going to get any kind of a performance from her, he'd have to get beyond the facades of whining child and wet-lipped sex object. But suppose he found they were not facades at all; suppose there was nothing at all but that beautiful exterior to work with. "What you see is what you get," he mumbled as he joined Hilda on the dock.

Glory, left alone in the cabin, prowled disconsolately. She poked into cupboards and lockers, and absentmindedly skimmed the titles in Devine's neatly arranged bookshelves. When Leo returned from the galley carrying a tray of drinks, he found her seated at the table flipping the pages of a scrapbook.

"Where is everybody?" he asked.

"I guess I scared them all off," she remarked thumbing through several pages.

"Well, if anybody could . . ." Leo began, but stopped as he noticed the tears rolling down her cheeks. He put the tray down on the table and pulled a chair up beside her. "Have a drink, Glory. It looks like you and I will have to drown our sorrows together. What's making you sorrowful?"

Glory wiped her eyes on the sleeve of the bathrobe and picked up a glass at random. "What's in this one?"

"Scotch, I do believe."

"I hate Scotch." She took a deep swallow and shuddered. "It's terrible stuff, but it'll do the job, won't it?"

"Depends on what job you want done. What are you reading?"

She flipped another page of the scrapbook.

"It's all about Hilda. Is she really as good as they say she is in here?"

Leo peered over her shoulder. "Better. Those reviews only tell what she was like on stage. I've known Hilda since I was a beardless youth." Leo grew uncharacteristically serious.

"She's been a good friend. She helped me over some very rough spots. You could learn a lot from her, Glory. And not just about acting."

"But she's old, Leo, and she's not even pretty."

"What can I tell you, Glory. Watch her. Talk to her. See if you can figure it out."

"Barney told me. . . ." Glory took another deep swallow from her glass, leaving it two-thirds empty. Leo wondered how well she could handle booze. Larry wouldn't be overjoyed if she turned up at rehearsal tomorrow with a hangover.

"What did Barney tell you?" he prompted.

"Oh, nothing." She closed the scrapbook. "That Tony Brand," she mused. "Don't you think he looks mean? Bet he's got a nasty temper. Son of a bitch took off the minute he laid eyes on me. Like I was poison, or something. Who does he think he is?"

Leo sipped at his glass of wine and privately considered that Tony's retreat was undoubtedly well timed. Aloud, he said, "Better get used to him, Glory. You'll be seeing a lot of him this summer. Now finish your drink, and I'll take you back to the hotel."

She drained her glass, set it down, and picked up another one from the tray.

"What's in this one?" she asked.

"That's Larry's gin and tonic. Where is he anyway?"

"He went off with his precious Hilda and his precious Tony and that creepo bitch who thinks she's too good to talk to me."

"You mean Anita?"

"Is that her name?" Glory began working on the gin and tonic.

"Hey! Don't mix your drinks like that. You'll get sick." Leo tried to take the glass from her hand, but she clung to it.

"Who cares," she muttered. "Oh, Leo, I want to go home."

"Well, come on then. Get your clothes. You do have some clothes, don't you? I won't even ask how come you're not wearing them. Just get dressed like a good girl, and I'll take you home and tuck you in and even tell you a bedtime story. How about Goldilocks and the Three Producers?"

"No!" she wailed, and the tears began spurting again. "I want to go *home*. To Los Angeles. I never should have come here. I never should have let Barney talk me into it. Something terrible is going to happen. Well, I don't have to stay. I can leave. First thing in the morning, I can get in that little red car and drive right away from here. I don't have to stick around and wait for trouble."

Some people can cry beautifully, but Glory Hayes wasn't one of them. She blubbered and her nose got red. Her mouth turned into an ugly petulant square. Tears dripped off her chin. Leo watched helplessly, wondering whether he ought to spank her or offer her a lollipop. He was not accustomed to dealing with squalling infants. He compromised by fetching a box of paper tissues from one of the storage lockers, shoving it in front of her on the table, and patting her none too gently on the head.

"Hey, cut it out," he muttered. "If Larry comes back and finds you boo-hooing, he'll think I've been beating you up."

Glory snuffled and produced a lopsided grin. "Are you really into that scene? Leather and all that kinky stuff?"

Leo groaned.

"All right! All right!" Glory plucked a fistful of tissues from the box and mopped her streaming face. "I'll go quietly. Let me just finish this drink."

She gulped down the rest of the gin and tonic, pushed back her chair, and wobbled to her feet. "Shee-it," she moaned. "I should have never had that Scotch. Back home I only drink Brandy Alexanders. They don't make me dizzy. Let's go now. Leo, hold my hand. I don't like the dark and it's dark outside."

"What about your clothes? You can't go like that."

"Have to. Clothes got wet. All wet. It rained on my parade. Leo, why does it *always* rain on my parade?"

She stood, barefoot and forlorn, swaying slightly as she tried to tighten the belt of the bathrobe. Lost in its oversized folds, she looked more than ever like a child playing at being grown-up. Leo, despite his irritation at her maudlin self-pity, felt a sudden wave of sympathy for her. She was loud, vulgar, and bitchily insulting most of the time. And when that back-fired on her, she turned into a whining brat. But somewhere in there, underneath all the fuss and clamor, Leo was certain there was a very frightened kid. What she was frightened of was impossible to guess, and now was not the time to try to find out. Now was the time to get her safely tucked away for the night and hope that she would sleep off the effects of the booze by rehearsal time tomorrow.

Gently he took her fumbling hands away from the belt which she had only succeeded in twisting into a loose tangle. "Here," he said, "let me do that." He knotted the belt firmly around her waist, feeling as if he were dressing a loose-limbed shop window mannequin. From a peg near the door, he took a yellow rubber raincoat. "Now put this on," he said.

Obediently, she thrust one arm and then the other into its sleeves. Leo buckled the metal clasps down the front. The coat was long and stood stiffly out from her body like the carapace of a large clumsy beetle. The sleeves covered her hands. Her long hair was caught inside the collar. Beneath the coat, her bare toes curled as if trying to gain a more secure hold on the floor boards. She looked absurd and vulnerable. Leo put his arm around her and steered her toward the door.

"Leo, you're all right," she babbled. "I didn't think you were all right, but you are and screw Anita Bryant. I'll never drink orange juice again. I'm sorry I was rotten to you."

"Thanks. Be careful. There's a step down here."

"Step down," she repeated as they moved out onto the deck. The rain had stopped but the night sky was still thick with rolling clouds promising more rain to come. The air was fresh and slightly chilly. Glory stood still and breathed deeply.

"Let's push on, old girl." Leo urged her toward the gangplank. "Way to go yet."

"Air's nice," she murmured. "Fresh and nice. Better than no air. S'truth."

"Right you are," said Leo, helping her up the gangplank step by step. "Air's good stuff. You should try some every day."

Glory giggled. "You're silly, Leo." She wavered in the middle of the gangplank, tilting first to one side and then to the other, like a weighted inflated smack-'em-down and pop-up doll. Leo, behind her, steadied her with both hands on her rump and propelled her the remaining few steps to the dock.

Glory was still giggling. "I almost fell in, didn't I? You wouldn't let me fall in, would you, Leo? That Tony Brand, he'd just love it if I fell in and never came up. Then I couldn't tell where I saw him before. Not that I ever would. But he knows where it was. And it sure wasn't on TV."

"Oh?" said Leo. He took her arm and began marching her firmly up the dock away from the *Hilda Kay*. "Where *did* you see him before?"

"That would be telling, wouldn't it? And I'll never tell.

Maybe I'll never tell. Maybe I won't leave in the morning. Maybe I'll stay, just for laughs. It's very funny when you think about it."

Their progress up the dock was slow and somewhat crab-wise. Glory's bursts of giggles were accompanied by erratic footwork. She veered from one side to the other, while Leo held her arm and attempted to steer a true course back to the hotel.

"That's right," he coaxed her. "Just keep putting one foot in front of the other and maybe we'll get there by morning."

"Maybe. And maybe everybody's going to be very nice to me. Just like you are, Leo. I like Leos. Leos are strong. I'm a Virgo myself. Isn't that rikid . . . ridic . . . isn't that funny? Virgos are fussy."

"But I'm not a Leo. I'm a Scorpio. Don't stop." Glory had come to a dead halt, and Leo had to administer an ungentle shove to get her going again. "Just keep walking. I never went in for astrology. But someone once gave me a necktie with little scorpions all over it for my birthday. It was hideous."

Behind them, out over the lake, the clouds rolled away from the face of the moon. Its light silvered the weathered planks of the dock and made a fragile lacework of the gingerbread facade of the hotel looming before them up the slight incline from the marina.

"I don't believe you. You can't be a Scorpio," Glory insisted. "You look like a Leo. You act like a Leo. And your name is Leo. Please don't be a Scorpio. Scorpios are rotten people."

Can't help it. I'm sorry I told you if it upsets you. We're almost there."

They had reached the intersection of the long wooden dock with the paved road that ran behind the marina and the cobblestones of Pier Street. Glory broke away from him and ran up the deserted street.

On one side a cluster of shacks and sheds, which in daylight presented a carnival air, gloomed like a sinister maze where unpleasant surprises might lurk round every bend of the narrow lanes that threaded through them. These were the old fish smokehouses, long diverted from their original purpose except for one that still offered smoked lake trout and other freshwater delicacies. The others had been taken over by local merchants and craftsmen with an eye on the tourist trade, and had been whipped into picturesque shape with gallons of bright paint and yards of cheerful banners and rustic signs proclaiming their wares. Here, in season, the summer visitors were gently urged to buy handwrought jewelry of surpassing ugliness, clumsy handthrown ceramics, oversweet homemade fudge, coarsely handwoven bedspreads and table mats, and minutely exact drawings of the wonders of Duck Creek including self-conscious studies of the fish smokehouses themselves. Over all hung the ineradicable effluvium of smoked fish, and the new inhabitants, evidently on the principle that if you can't rid yourself of a pestilence it's good business to make it part of your charm, had christened their collection of refurbished shanties "Smokehouse Square."

But the season was still weeks away, and only a few of these shops were stocked and ready for business. All of them, at this hour of the night, were deserted. Glory skittered past them as if from their shuttered windows and padlocked doorways might spring the death and disaster she had predicted for herself. To Leo, trudging in her wake and not at all eager to catch up to her, she seemed an erratic and possibly baleful influence on the fortunes of the playhouse. If she had any talent at all, it seemed to be for creating unpleasant alarums and excursions. He wondered what had brought her to the houseboat in the middle of the night, and what it was she had been hinting at that Tony Brand wouldn't like her to tell the world. Probably just a figment of her drunken and overheated imagination. But was she as drunk as she seemed? She had already, on one day's acquaintance, displayed a remarkable flair for gathering attention to herself, and her drunken babbling and scampering through the night might be just another scene played out for the benefit of an audience of one.

Nevertheless, Leo felt responsible for her safety, just as he felt responsible for the smooth operation of everything connected with the playhouse. He admired his uncle and hoped that this season, with Hilda Kramer on hand, would not only be their most successful, but would bring about the reconciliation that both of them seemed to yearn for. Glory Hayes, if she continued to behave like a lunatic child, could ruin that.

At the top of the slope, just a few yards from the hotel entrance, Glory abruptly stopped her flight. She seemed to be waiting for him, the yellow slicker gleaming in the fitful moonlight. The scene was almost surrealistic and Leo, accustomed to viewing life in terms of theatrical impact, appreciated its eerieness. On the one side, the cluster of deliberately ramshackle little buildings leaned against one another as if confiding malicious secrets. On the other, the ornate facade of the hotel writhed in the moonlight, while menacing shadows lurked in its wide pillared porch and on its second floor veranda. Here and there, behind curtained windows, lamplight shone on hidden midnight activities. In the center, the cobbled street twisted away into the misty distance, past the figure of the girl in the yellow slicker, the only spot of color in the prevailing silvery grayness. You could almost expect Dracula to come flapping in from the wings, or the ghost of Hamlet's father to appear on the battlements.

As Leo drew nearer, he noticed that Glory stood as if paralyzed, staring off into the narrow alley that led into the convoluted lanes of Smokehouse Square.

"Hey!" he called out. "What's up?"

Her voice came back to him, uncharacteristically muted. "I don't know. I thought I heard something."

At that moment, a gust of wind swept in from the lake and clouds surged across the face of the moon, plunging the street into darkness. The lights of the hotel flickered once or twice, and went out. A swift slithering sound cut through the night, accompanied by a meteor shower of blue-white sparks and the fresh tingling scent of ozone.

Glory, illuminated by the ghastly flickering light, produced an abortive scream and dropped to the ground. Leo, frozen for a moment by the sight of her terror-stricken face gazing upward, moved forward cautiously. The sparks were now issuing from a spot about a foot away from where Glory lay huddled on the cobblestones. All the rest was darkness. He heard voices raised from the direction of the lightless hotel, and in a moment footsteps sounded on the wooden planks of the porch.

"What's happened?"

"What's going on?"

"Is it a blackout?"

Leo peered through the darkness, not daring to move any closer to the still form of the girl who lay crumpled in the glare of the electrical display.

"I think there's a power line down," he shouted. "Larry, are you there? We need a flashlight. I can't see where the damn' thing is."

"Joe's gone to get one." Devine's deep voice boomed out of the darkness. "Who's that in the road? Glory. . . ?"

72

"Herself," Leo answered. "I can't get any closer until I can see what I'm doing."

The smell of ozone dissipated swiftly, replaced by the acrid stench of burning rubber. Leo pulled a handkerchief from his pocket and held it over his nose. He took a few tentative steps towards the fallen girl, with each one certain that he would be instantly electrocuted. All he could see of Glory was the yellow raincoat, bunched into a shapeless heap and ominously still.

"I'll get my car and turn the headlights on," said another voice from the porch, which Leo recognized as that of Tony Brand. He saw a dim figure run up the street toward the hotel's parking lot.

A powerful searchlight beam burst through the door of the hotel and sprayed the street with its light. Behind it, Joe St. Cloud moved purposefully across the porch, down the steps, and out into the street. "Elena's calling the emergency service crew," he announced. "They'll be here in a few minutes."

He played the searchlight beam on the huddled figure in the yellow slicker. Glory lay with her face buried in her arms, her knees drawn up and only her bare feet visible beneath the hem of the enveloping raincoat. Inches away from her feet, a length of black electrical cable snaked across the cobblestones. Joe St. Cloud followed it with his searchlight, across the street and up to its connection at the top of a pole at the mouth of the alley leading into Smokehouse Square, then back again to where the severed end of the cable spat blue sparks into the night. Behind him, Tony Brand's Volkswagen chugged into position, its headlights added to the illumination of the lurid scene. Tony braked the car and leaped out, hurrying to Joe's side.

"Is she . . . alive?"

"Miss Hayes?" Joe bent over the yellow slicker. "Can you hear me?"

A low moan was the only answer he got.

"All right," he said. "Don't move. We'll have you out of here in a minute."

"You bet your sweet ass I'm not moving!" Glory's voice came stridently from somewhere within the raincoated heap on the cobblestones. "Think I want to get myself fried?"

"She's okay!" Leo exulted. "Praise Allah and whatever saints look after idiot popsies!" He stepped gingerly over the length of cable as far away from the active end as he could get, and hunkered down beside the girl. "Come on, Glory, my old

73

french fry. Let's get you out of this and tucked up where you belong. Tony, can you help me lift her?''

"No!" Glory shrieked, raising her head and fixing Leo with an imploring terrified stare. "Not him! Get Larry! I want to talk to Larry."

"I'm right here," said Devine, moving into the circle of light. "Don't try to talk now. You can tell us all about it later." He knelt beside her and cradled her protectively in his arms.

"Make him go away," she cried.

Devine glanced over his shoulder. Tony Brand shrugged and walked back to his car, where he draped himself over the hood and managed to give the impression that he was the star of the production, temporarily offstage but merely waiting for his cue to return.

Inside the hotel, candles were being lit. Elena St. Cloud appeared on the porch carrying a kerosene lantern. Its soft glow seemed to incite agitated questions among the guests hovering there. Elena issued soothing statements.

"The service truck is on the way. They'll be here very soon. No, this doesn't happen often. Never before that I know of. An accident, I'm sure. The line must have gotten frayed during the storm and then just broke. No, there's no danger of fire."

Hilda Kramer, standing just at the edge of the circle of light, watched Devine comforting the distraught girl. Then her eyes shifted to the live end of the broken cable and remained there as if hypnotized. The sparks had subsided to an occasional blue flicker, while the charred insulation glowed redly whenever fanned by the stray night breeze. Behind her, on the porch steps, Anita Stratton leaned against a pillar, her arms folded tightly upon one another as if she felt a chill. From the shadows she watched Glory Hayes being soothed and comforted. Then she observed Tony, her Tony, displaying what was for him a peculiar kind of disinterest in the proceedings. Something was going on. Something she didn't understand. When they had arrived at the houseboat, she had been weary and depressed, but not so weary that she hadn't caught the hint of something not quite right between Tony and the Hayes creature. Now Glory seemed utterly terrified of him. Anita had every intention of questioning him about it. But not tonight. Not after the tensions of the trip, and not until she got over her misgivings about being there at all. Tonight all she wanted to do was crawl into bed and sleep away the depression and the sense of impending doom that was giving her a bad case of goosebumps.

Indeed, she had been more than halfway to bed, had been brushing her hair in the bathroom, when the lights had gone out. She had groped her way out of the bathroom and out onto the veranda upon which their second floor room gave access through a pair of French windows, where Tony was already viewing the scene in the street below. It was he who had insisted that they go downstairs to help. She had merely followed him through the pitch black corridor, down the stairs and out onto the porch. Once there, there seemed to be nothing for her to do, no reason for her to stand shivering on the steps in her thin cotton dressing gown. Glory was on her feet now, supported on one side by Leo and on the other by Larry Devine. They were moving slowly toward the hotel, Glory stumbling awkwardly and babbling incoherently between the two men. Anita slipped unobtrusively past the people remaining on the porch and went back into the hotel, lit now by candles placed round the lobby. She stood quietly in the shadows as the procession passed on its way into the lounge. She heard Glory Hayes mutter, "It was him . . . the Knight of Wands . . . alias Tony Brand . . . some fucking coincidence . . . the Tower. . . ." Anita took a lighted candle from the row that had been set out on the registration desk. Shielding its flame with her hand, she thoughtfully climbed the stairs to her room.

some of hair colouration that was glebie but a and ...

Indeed, she had apparently then halfway to bed had been
flinging when bed in the bedroom, when the lights had gone
out. She had crossed the passage of the bathroom and out onto
to the veranda upon which that second floor room ran across
through a pair of French windows, were Terry was already
visible she grew. In the street below, it was dark, and so
afraid that the key to ... to him. She had hurry followed
him through the great black corridor, down the stairs and all
onto the porch. Out there, they seemed to be a shine for her
to act, no reason for feeling such shivering on the step, it felt
that action, dressing gown. Glory was on her feet now, one
sprite on one side of it too and on the other by Larry Terror.
They were moving slowly toward the hotel. Glory, stumbling
backwards, and stumbling incoherently, broke on his two arms
in quite a hopeless manner, the people people roaming on all
sides and went back unto one of itself, nearer by, and far back of
round the lobby, she went quietly in on shadows as the mo-
tion passed on its way into the lounge. She stood whis-
tances square ... It was him ... the French, it
would ... Miles long French ... some of the ... The man
dances ... the France ... Anna took a ...
from the moment had begun set out on ... looked she
tremblingly there with her hand, she thoughtlessly thinking
soon to her home.

CHAPTER IX

Brandy," said Glory Hayes. "A double, on the rocks." She lay on a sofa in the hotel lounge surrounded by solicitous faces. She had rejected the notion of going straight to bed, saying that she was afraid to be alone and needed company for a little while. Outside, in the street, the amber light of the emergency service truck revolved, casting its warning flashes through the windows and into the candlelit room, creating an atmosphere of unease. The voices of the repairmen could be heard as they called to one another and communicated the extent of the damage to some central station via two-way radio.

Joe St. Cloud, candle in hand, went to fetch Glory her drink. Larry Devine pulled a hassock over to the sofa and sat beside her, holding her hand. Leo and Elena stood in the doorway discussing the advisability of calling in the doctor. Hilda Kramer stood among the other guests, listening quietly to their speculations. Tony Brand remained outside where his VW was still needed to illuminate the labors of the repairmen.

"Your hand is cold," said Devine, clasping it between his two large ones.

"Damn' right!" said Glory. "I'm chilled to the bone. Wouldn't you be?" She lowered her voice to a whisper. "It came true. The cards don't lie. It was the Tower Struck by Lightning. I could have been killed."

"Nonsense, Glory," Devine protested. "It was an accident. Sheer coincidence that you happened to be there. The cards had nothing to do with it."

"Oh, no?" Glory struggled to sit up and her voice rose hysterically. Her face, in the flashing amber light, twisted into a contorted mask of terrified remembrance. "That thing hit me. It knocked me over. It could have fucking killed me. Don't tell me it was an accident. Somebody or something made it happen."

The watchers in the room drew closer and their whispering ceased.

"Where did it hit you?" Devine asked, hoping to deflect her hysterics by pinning her down to specifics.

"What difference does it make? It hit me. I can't remember where. I ache all over. Where the hell is Joe with that brandy?"

Joe materialized silently at her side, a tinkling glass in his hand.

"Ooh, you do creep up on people, don't you?" She offered him a half-hearted leer by way of thanks, and took a deep swallow of the drink.

"Ah," she sighed. "That helps."

She glanced round the room and for the first time became aware that she had an audience. Still holding the drink with one hand, she disengaged the other from Larry's clasp and patted at her disheveled hair.

"I must look a mess," she said.

Sympathetic murmurs arose from the onlookers. Glory ducked her head modestly and settled down to make the most of the moment. But first she scanned the room again.

"Is *he* here?" she demanded.

"Who?" asked Devine, puzzled.

"Him. Tony Brand."

"No," said Devine. "I think he's still outside."

"Good," said Glory, "because I'd sure like to know where he was when it happened."

"Hey! Wait a minute," Devine protested. "You don't think he had anything to do with this. It was an accident."

"Maybe it was and maybe it wasn't. Maybe somebody just helped it happen."

Devine began to protest again, but Glory overrode him.

"Listen. I was coming back to the hotel. I was a little bit drunk. I admit it. But I felt so bad after you all went off and left me, I guess I had a little too much. Right, Leo?"

"Right, Glory," said Leo from the doorway.

"Boy, there's nothing like nearly being electrocuted to sober you up." She took another swallow from her glass. "Well, Leo said we should go back to the hotel. I think he just wanted to get rid of me. So we started back. I started running. It felt so good. The air was cool and the moon was shining on everything. I almost felt like I was flying, like I could take off and fly back to California all by myself. But I didn't have any shoes on, I left them on the boat, and I hurt my feet on those cobblestones. Besides, I could see that there were still people around in the hotel and I didn't want to walk in all alone wearing this silly raincoat. So I stopped to wait for Leo. He wasn't running, just mooching along. While I was waiting, I thought I heard something. I don't know what it was, a footstep or somebody dropping something. And then I got this creepy feeling, like somebody was watching me. It scared me. Maybe it was nothing, just a noise, but it scared me. I was about to yell for Leo to hurry up, when all of a sudden the lights went out. I mean everything. The moonlight, the lights in the hotel, everything. It was pitch black. And then there was this horrible whistling noise like somebody cracking a great big mother of a whip, and wham! The son of a bitch hit me on the arm and knocked me over."

She held out her arm as if to offer proof of what had happened and then gasped in amazement.

"Holy Christ!" she exclaimed. "Will you take a look at that! I mean, will you just look!"

Devine looked, and everyone else in the room craned to see. Across the sleeve of the yellow slicker ran a brownish-black scar. About the length of a cigarette and slightly wider, it looked like the kind of damage a careless smoker might inflict. But Larry recognized the slicker as his own and knew that no such burn had marred it before tonight.

"You were lucky, Glory," he said. "Did the cards tell you to put on that raincoat?"

"No. Leo did."

"Then I think Leo saved your life. If you hadn't been wearing that coat, you might not be sitting here telling us about it."

"No shit!" Glory exclaimed. "Well, thanks, Leo. You really are all right. Promise I won't call you names anymore."

"All in a day's work," murmured Leo modestly. "And now, my dears, if we've all had enough sensation-mongering for one night, may I suggest that we toddle off and do a little knitting on the ravell'd sleave of care."

"What's he talking about?" Glory queried the room at large. "I don't know how to knit."

"Sleep, my poppet," said Leo, swooping down on her. "Let me lead you to your thrice-driven bed of down. But that's as far as I'll go, so don't get any ideas."

The half-dozen or so of the hotel guests, who had been gathered in the lounge listening avidly to Glory's account, began to disperse into the lobby, candles held high. Hilda Kramer came forward to join Leo and Larry in helping Glory to her feet.

"I'll go upstairs with you," she said. "And if you like, if

you want to have someone nearby during the night, we can leave the doors between our rooms open.''

Glory eyed her quizzically and said, "Thanks."

Elena St. Cloud preceded them through the lobby, lighting their way with her kerosene lamp. "Miss Hayes," she said, "I'm sorry this has happened to you at my hotel. Would you like me to call the doctor in, just to be sure you're not injured? I would pay for it, of course."

"Hell's bells, Elena! Why can't you just call me Glory like everyone else? You make me sound like an old-maid school-teacher. No, I don't think I need a doctor. But I think I could bear to have breakfast in bed in the morning. Poached eggs? You can send Joe up with them about nine o'clock. That would be the best medicine I can think of."

Elena frowned, and Glory exploded with laughter.

"Just kidding, Elena," she said. "You take things too seriously. I really am okay, and I don't blame you or the hotel for what happened tonight. If there's anyone to blame, I think I know who it is. Okay, okay, Larry. I won't say anything else on the subject, but I have my reasons, and you can bet your ass I'm going to be mighty careful where Mr. Tony Brand is concerned, speak of the Devil."

The front door had opened just as Glory had finished speaking and Tony Brand himself stepped into the lobby.

"We should have lights in just a few minutes," he said.

His announcement was greeted with silence, while every head in the lobby turned to stare at him.

"Well, I thought I'd get at least a faint cheer," he said. "What's the matter?"

"Nothing, nothing at all," said Devine, who found himself stepping forward a few paces to stand between Brand and Glory.

"That really *is* good news," offered Leo. "Candlelight's romantic and all that, but not much good for making ice cubes."

"How's the girl?" asked Tony. "Is she all right?"

"I thought you'd never ask," said Glory, stepping around Devine to confront Tony. "I'm a lot better than I might have been. I might have been dead."

And *that's* good news for me," retorted Brand. "I've had a lot of moribund leading ladies, but never a dead one. Keep up the good work."

Glory drew a deep breath, apparently about to unleash a

stream of vituperation, when the lamps in the lobby glowed, flickered, went out, and then came on again in full incandescence. The cheers that Tony had expected to greet his announcement filled the lobby, and everyone began chattering at once. Candles were blown out, and Elena extinguished her kerosene lamp and set it down on the registration desk. The chief repairman swaggered through the front door and came up to her.

"All fixed now," he said. "We gave you a brand new line over to the pole. That old one must have been up there since the year zero. It's a wonder it didn't come down years ago. Oh, well, every storm we have around here, there's a couple or three lines down. Anybody get hurt?"

"No," said Elena, "no one was hurt. Everything is fine. Thank you very much."

"Yeah, sure. Well, you should be okay now unless we have a tornado or something." He turned to go, then spotted Larry Devine. "Hey, you're the guy that runs that playhouse, right?"

Larry nodded.

"Well, I gotta tell you, I come and see all them shows. Sure beats television. Even the wife and kids say so. My daughter, now, she wants to be an actress. She's only sixteen but she's all the time singing. Maybe you could talk to her, tell her what she ought to do to get started?"

"Sure," said Larry. "Send her around. She can watch a few rehearsals."

"And learn about what goes on behind the scenes," said Glory, staring pointedly at Tony Brand.

"Terrific!" said the repairman. "She'll be jumpin' out of her skin when I tell her."

"Tell *me* something, Mr. Electrician," said Glory. "Is it possible that some stupid bastard could have *cut* that line? Never mind why anybody would want to do a dumbass thing like that. Just tell me if it could have happened."

"Oh, gee, Miss. I don't know. Like I said, the line was pretty old. Any little thing could have knocked it down. A tree branch, or a strong wind. Anything. People don't usually go around cutting down power lines. Somebody could get hurt."

"Right. Somebody could. Good-night, all. If I wake up dead in my bed in the morning, you all know where to look."

With a final significant glare at Tony Brand, she swept away up the stairs. Hilda Kramer, after a brief whispered conference

81

with Devine, hurried after her. The repairman returned to his truck, wondering if the blond lady who had questioned him was an actress, and if all actresses used language like that. Maybe he wouldn't send his daughter over after all.

Tony Brand stood in the doorway observing the exodus from the lobby. His handsome face looked weary, but his dark eyes were lively pinpoints of watchfulness beneath his drooping lids. When everyone had left, he slipped out through the front door to return his car to the parking lot. A fine rain began once more to fall.

CHAPTER X

The bus crawled through a gray drizzle, past dank patches of pine forest alternating with an occasional mud-banked pond where despondent ducks floated patiently, here and there a grease-encrusted gas station festooned with dripping Day-Glo plastic pennants gleaming wetly like signposts to oblivion.

Pev Martin brooded out the window of the bus at the dreary landscape. His cream linen suit was stained and wrinkled and his eyes felt like the beach at Coney Island, caked with sand and the debris of generations. He hadn't slept. Beside him, Tina Elliott snored, open-mouthed. He turned to look at her and caught a whiff of stale liquor and poorly digested Howard Johnson. His head throbbed and his stomach heaved. He should never have let her buy those drinks for him. He never could handle booze and he was long out of practice. But she had wanted to celebrate their reunion and he couldn't very well have let her celebrate alone. Besides, he admitted to himself, that first drink had tasted good, so good. And so had the second one. After that, he couldn't remember much about the time they had spent in the dark musty-smelling cocktail lounge waiting for the bus that would complete their journey. A vague recollection of quoting Shakespeare at each other . . . Lear's reconciliation with Cordelia . . . to the raucous enjoyment of the other drinkers at the bar.

Pev Martin groaned. "'I am a very foolish fond old man.'" His lips formed the words but no sound came. "'I fear I am not in my perfect mind.'" How could he have done that before a crowd of leering, smirking dullards swilling beer in a stinking barroom? But was it any worse than the act he'd done years ago on the vaudeville circuit? At least, he had the dignity of age and made a plausible Lear, alas, too plausible. While she, if you closed your eyes and only listened to the kind loving words, you might imagine her a tender ministering daughter. But never with your eyes open. Never, hearing those words and seeing them sprout from violet-painted lips in that pudding of a face, beneath the acidulous orange tangle of hair that gave off a chemical glow even in the smoky darkness of the bar, never could you believe her to be the young and modest princess.

"'Oh, look upon me, Sir,'" she had proclaimed, "'and hold your hands in benediction o'er me.'" And the crowd had quacked with laughter, stomped their feet, and called for more beer. The bartender grinned encouragingly, willing to put up with a little mild lunacy if it was good for business. He set two more drinks before them, refusing payment. "You guys ought to go on TV. You're better than *The Gong Show.*"

"Should I do Portia?" Tiny had whispered to him. "Pa always like me to do Portia."

He had kept her from doing Portia, but he hadn't been able to keep her from the phone booth where, with a fistful of change, she had placed a long-distance call to Tom Elliott, jarring him out of the fragile reveries that were the sole remnant of his life. Pev had stood beside the phone booth, listening to her side of the conversation.

"Hello, Pa. This is Tina. . . . your daughter, Tina. . . . I'm out here in Detroit and you'll never guess who's with me. . . . Pev Martin. . . . That's right, our old touring buddy. What? No, wait a minute. I'm Tina . . . don't, Pa. Please don't call me Mitzi. I'm Tina. I don't even look like her anymore. I just wanted to tell you that Pev and I will be working together, just like old times. Isn't that wonderful? No! No, Pa. Of course, we won't. It's not that kind of a show. Anyway, Pev wouldn't steal your material. Yes, Pa. Okay, Pa. Pa, don't talk like that. Yes, he's right here. I'll put him on."

There was hurt and bewilderment on Tina Elliott's face as she hauled herself out of the phone booth and handed the receiver to Pev Martin. "He wants to talk to you," she said. "He's really off the rails tonight. He thinks I'm my mother. He thinks we've run off together." She looked like a half-deflated vest pocket blimp, sad and saggy.

Martin slid into the phone booth, put the receiver to his ear and said, "Hello, Tom." That was all he got to say. The rest was a replay of a conversation that crossed the miles and spanned the years, almost fifty of them, a conversation that had haunted Martin ever since the first time around with the notion that if only he had acted differently, Mitzi might still be alive. The first time he'd heard it, all those years ago, it hadn't been over the long-distance telephone; it had been face to angry face and he'd taken an active part in it. Now, he only nodded wearily, letting Tom Elliott speak his lines as if they were part of a play that was destined to run forever. When the voice at the other end of the line faltered and grew still, Pev Martin spoke. "That was a long time ago, Tom. It's all over. Mitzi is dead. She wouldn't have wanted you to do this to yourself. And it's making poor Tiny miserable. After all, she had nothing to do with it." He waited, listening to the faint electronic crackle down the wire. After a few moments, the voice came back, papery thin and implacable.

"I have no daughter."

"Have you ever told *her* that?"

The voice laughed. It was like the shredding of old newspapers. "No. She comes to visit me. Nobody else comes. We talk about the old times. We sing the old songs. 'Hello, Central, give me Heaven.' She really breaks them up with that one. Mitzi would be old and fat and ugly by now. What do you want with her?"

"It was a coincidence, Tom." He kept an eye on Tiny, who had gone back to the bar. The bartender was setting up two more drinks. She perched on the barstool, engulfing it like an elephant squatting on a mouse. Her feet, in shiny red slippers, rested primly side by side on a rung of the stool, and she blew her nose into a bright red handkerchief. "We both happened to get jobs at the same place. Do you want to talk to her again?"

"No. It's past my bedtime. Not that I sleep much. Tell me, Pev, old friend, do you sleep well o'nights? Are you fat and sleekheaded? Or do you still have that lean and hungry look? You'd have made a fine Cassius, always ready to stab a friend in the back."

"Do you see yourself as Caesar?"

"I see myself as a decrepit old has-been. I'm glad you're working, Pev. Break a leg. I really mean that." The shredded newspaper laugh rustled in the receiver and then the line went dead. Pev Martin hung up the phone. There had been real malice behind that "break a leg," the old theater slang phrase for good luck. Tom Elliott wished him anything but good luck.

Martin shrugged and walked back to the bar. Tiny had finished half of her gin and orange juice, and had put her handkerchief away.

"Drink up, Pev," she said. Her smile was worse than the

tears he had anticipated. "We still have time to get something to eat before the bus comes. I'm starving."

They had eaten and Tiny had replenished her shopping bag with candy bars from a vending machine. They had boarded the second bus, the one that would deposit them in Duck Creek at daybreak, and Tiny had promptly fallen asleep. Now, in the gray morning, she stirred, groaned, and ran her tongue experimentally over gummy lips.

"Oh, I feel awful." She belched, covering her mouth daintily with a small fat hand. "Are we almost there?"

"Soon."

"In time for breakfast, I hope." She rummaged in her handbag and drew out comb, lipstick, breath spray, mascara, and a small hand mirror.

Pev Martin turned away, unable to watch her at her hopeless repairs, and gazed out the window. She leaned across him to follow his gaze and he held his breath against the stale perfume that rose in musky waves from her hair.

"Where are we?" she asked.

"Upon a blasted heath. It wouldn't surprise me at all if we came upon the three weird sisters around the next bend in the road."

"Ah, Pev. It's not that bad. Look, there's a bunch of cows and a funny little farmhouse. Sometimes, I think, if I could do it all over again, I'd like to live like that. Half a dozen kids and a garden with string beans and petunias."

She sank back into her seat and began combing her hair. Pev breathed more freely.

"You'd hate it," he said.

"Not if I didn't know any different. I never had a choice. Ah, well, I've had some good times along with the bad. I guess I can't complain. Care for a candy bar?"

"No, thanks."

When the bus drew up in front of the Dune Haven Hotel some twenty minutes later, Leo Lemming was on hand to greet them. Splendid this morning in a French sailor's jersey, skintight jeans, and canvas espadrilles, he danced down the porch steps piping cries of welcome.

"Hello, old things! Overjoyed to see you! Have a good trip? Of course, you didn't. How could you on such a prehistoric creature of a bus? But you're here now, and we'll have you all comfy in a minute. Luggage? Oh, Tina, there's an enormous trunk with your name on it. Looks like a relic of the *Titanic*.

We put it in your room. Martin? Just the one bag? Well, come along kiddies. Come in out of the wet, and you can have a lie-down or a bath or whatever suits your fancy. First rehearsal's at two o'clock this afternoon.''

"I could use a nap," said Pev Martin. "Didn't sleep much on the bus.''

"What about breakfast?'' Tina Elliott trudged up the steps still clutching her depleted shopping bag. The bus ground away to complete its circuit of the peninsula. Leo, carrying Tina's overnight case, led the way into the hotel.

"Dining room on the right,'' he said. "Your rooms are back this way. Ground floor with French doors onto the side porch. Very nice. Absolutely awash with lilacs. You can sign the register later. The crew's all busy in the kitchen right now.''

He piloted them through the lobby. Tina peered avidly into the dining room and inhaled, with greedy joy, the scent of bacon as they passed. Pev Martin moved as if in a somnambulistic trance. Leo led them down a short corridor that made a right-angle turn into an ell containing a few guest rooms, Elena St. Cloud's own suite, and a row of storage cupboards.

"Here we are,'' he announced, flinging open two adjacent doors. "Make yourselves at home. I've got to scurry off and see a man about a moose head. I'm in charge of props and a zillion other things. See you later.''

He flitted off up the corridor and skittered around the corner with a cheery wave. Tina and Pev watched him go and then turned to each other.

"Well,'' said Tina, "it looks like we're neighbors for the duration.''

"So it does.''

"I don't mind. I think it's kind of nice. Sort of like old times. Do you remember how you used to take me out for ice cream?''

"I remember.''

"If only Pa could be here it would really be like old times. The three of us together. Wouldn't that be wonderful?''

"There would still be something missing, Tina. A very vital ingredient would be missing. Something we each had once and not one of us has any longer.''

Tina stared at him warily. He looked ill and his eyes had gone strange, as if he couldn't see her at all but something horrid at the end of the corridor. She looked over her shoulder to see what was there. Nothing but a tall mirror in which the two of them were reflected, made smaller by distance. In it she saw his long arms reach out and his bony hands come to rest on her upper arms. She shivered and turned back to stare up into his hovering face.

"What's missing, Pev? What don't we have any longer?"

"A future, my dear." He smiled sadly down at her, shook his head as if to discourage a tormenting gnat, and patted her cheek. "I'm going to sleep now." He disappeared into his room, closing the door softly behind him.

"Silly old coot," said Tina. "He's just as loony as Pa." She went into her own room, smiled when she saw her steamer trunk, and hurried to open it. A clean dress, a more comfortable pair of shoes, and breakfast. The future looked pretty good.

CHAPTER XI

It's funny about this rain. Normally, I'm not affected by the weather. If I'm up, I'm up. And if I'm down, I'm down. And all the rain, snow, sleet, hail, and blue skies smiling at me have not the least effect on my frame of mind. But this drizzle seems to be taking the wind out of my sails. To coin a phrase. When you walk through a storm, keep your head up high and all that. Blow, winds, and crack your cheeks. Everybody's got something to say about the weather. But this isn't even a storm. Just a constant wetness seeping out of the sky. Everything is slimy to the touch. Everything smells of mildew. There are slick pale worms lying torpid in the gutters. The beach is strewn with dead fish, their eyes shiny and sightless. I wonder if it's raining in New York. I wonder if they've found her yet.

I suppose I'll feel better once we start working. There's nothing like work to occupy the mind and keep the dragons at bay. It's an odd group, from what I've seen, but probably no odder than any other gang of poor saps engaged in this so-called profession. Here we all are, young, old, fat, thin, gathered together in this dank little town in pursuit of that sovereign remedy for loneliness—a round of applause. The only trouble with the medicine is that it doesn't cure the disease. And it's addictive. Taste it once, and you're hooked for life. You'll go anywhere, do anything for the sake of a roomful of hands smacking against each other. So, here we are. I wish it would stop raining.

This morning I walked on the beach. I met a child who was collecting pebbles. With his red plastic bucket, he was extraordinarily single-minded, taking no notice of the dead fish in his path or of the alarming vastness of the lake. He showed me some of his treasures.

"These are the best," he said, handing me a smooth gray oval stone covered with lighter circular markings. "Petoskeys. My mom and my sister and me, we polish them and make jewelry out of them."

He tugged at a leather thong that hung round his neck and

from inside his tee shirt produced a pendant. It was one of the stones, flattish and irregularly shaped but highly polished so that the lighter markings showed clearly. They were not truly circular, but crowded together all over the surface of the stone forming a network of tiny polygons. In the center of each polygon was a darker gray spot and from this spot radiated a regular series of lines extending to within a hairsbreadth of the perimeter.

"Very pretty."

"They're fossils," he told me out of his deep knowledge. "Things that used to live in the lake a zillion years ago. It was the glaciers, I guess."

"Will you sell me this one?"

He hesitated. Obviously, the one he wore was his favorite. But he was anxious to please a customer. "Well, I guess so. But I can get you a better one from home."

"I like this one."

"Last summer, I made fifty dollars. If I can find two big ones, we can make bookends. I can sell a pair of bookends for five dollars."

"I'll give you five dollars for this one."

"Well, all right."

He slipped the leather thong over his head and handed the pendant to me. I gave him a five-dollar bill which he folded and tucked into a pocket of his jeans.

"How much longer will it keep on raining?"

"Dunno. Rain is good for finding Petoskeys. You can see them better when they're wet."

He went back to his work, unmindful of the rain, stepping over the small beached fish corpses that were beginning noticeably to stink, stooping here and there to pick up a pebble, examine it, and either drop it into his bucket or hurl it out into the lake.

I went back to the hotel, holding in my hand clean, polished death. Things that had once lived in the lake, transformed into trinkets to hang round tourists' necks. Is *that* the consummation devoutly to be wished? Will our impacted bones in timeless time form quaint gewgaws to deck an alien species come to view our ruins? And aren't you getting just a shade morbidly precious? Come, come. There's work to do. The best panacea in the world, save one, for flagging spirits. But isn't it strange how low I feel, when according to past experience I should be in top form? It must be the rain.

CHAPTER XII

W hat we'll do first," said Larry Devine, "is read through the play quickly. Don't try too hard for characterization right now. We want to let that come naturally once we get on our feet and moving around. But if any of you have any ideas you want to try out, go ahead. Be my guest. I'll be the first to let you know it stinks."

He paused and surveyed the semicircle of actors seated on folding chairs on the bare stage of the Duck Creek Playhouse. A few nervous titters greeted his remarks, emanating from the second row of chairs where the locally recruited extras and bit-part players sat self-consciously mumbling over their lines and casting sheep's eye glances at the occupants of the first row.

"Anybody got any questions?"

Tina Elliott, expansively got up in a wide-sleeved, wide-bodied cerise garment lavishly sprinkled with lime-green dots, shifted perilously in her chair and asked, "What do we do about costumes? Is this one of those scrounge-your-own operations?"

Glory Hayes, who had managed to commandeer a chair in the center of the semicircle between Tony Brand and Pev Martin, snorted with laughter behind a perfectly manicured hand and leaned sideways to whisper loudly in the direction of Tony's ear, "She's right to be worried. The only thing she could hope to scrounge is a smock off a pregnant hippo."

Whether or not Glory had intended her remark to be overheard, the entire company suddenly became exceedingly interested in examining their scripts, with the exception of Glory herself, who gazed in angelic expectation at Larry, and Tina, who flushed to a color approximating that of her dress and seemed about to charge.

Larry slid expertly into the breach. "A good question, Tina," he said. "After rehearsal, we can all take a look at the costume sketches and Emmy will take everyone's measurements."

91

He swung around to peer down into the darkened auditorium. "Emmy!" he called out. "Are you there?"

"Right here, Mr. Devine," came a sweet disembodied voice from the back of the hall.

"Come on up front, Emmy, and show yourself." He turned back to the actors who had been successfully diverted from Glory's vicious slur at Tina and were all watching the center aisle as a short rolypoly gray-haired woman in a ruffled gingham pinafore bobbled down its length and came to a smiling halt at the first row of seats.

"Folks," Devine proclaimed, "I'd like you all to meet Mrs. Emmy Jackson, without whom the Duck Creek Playhouse would have no audience and you'd all go onstage mother naked. Emmy manages the box office and mobilizes all the sewing machines in town. I don't know how she does it, but she's costumed every show we've ever done here, from *My Fair Lady* to *Saint Joan*. And she tells me that opening night is already close to sold out. Say 'Hi!' Emmy."

Emmy dutifully said, "Hi," and blinked up at them shyly over biofocal eyeglasses.

Leo, seated at one end of the semicircle with the prompt script in his lap, began a round of applause and one by one the others joined in. Emmy blushed furiously and ducked her head. When the applause died down, she smiled up at them.

"I've just plugged in the coffee urn, so you can have coffee when you take a break," she said. "Miss Elliott, I have some lovely designs for you. Pale gray satin with a beautiful ivory lace shawl, used to belong to my grandmother. Larry, I'm using some of the gowns we made for *My Fair Lady*. There's lots of wonderful fabric there. So it won't cost so much. See you all later."

She bobbled away up the aisle and disappeared once again into the obscurity of the back rows.

Devine noted that Tina appeared mollified, although she continued to cast venomous glances in the direction of the sublimely oblivious Glory Hayes. Glory, on the other hand, seemed to have gotten over both her electrifying experience of the night before and her aversion to Tony Brand. She had edged her folding chair closer to his, so close that with any encouragement, various enthusiastic parts of her body managed to keep in very close contact with his. Tony did not show any sign of discomfort at this propinquity.

"Ah, well," thought Devine, "better to have them on

friendly terms than at daggers drawn." He wondered where Anita Stratton was. He had wanted to talk to her before rehearsal started, but she had not appeared all morning, nor did she join the group for lunch.

Anita Stratton was, in fact, seated in the very last seat on the left side of the very last row. She had slipped unnoticed into the theater while Devine and the cast were milling about arranging chairs and generally getting acquainted with each other. She, too, had noticed Glory's change of attitude toward Tony and, more to her dislike, Tony's nonchalant acceptance of the intensity of Glory's regard. If it had not been raining, she would have gone to the beach. She had slept late, waking shortly before eleven feeling considerably less exhausted but not very hungry. Tony had already gone out. A note on the tall mahogany dresser explained that he had gone off with Leo to deliver some posters round about the neighboring communities and would see her at lunch. But she had not wanted lunch. She had scrounged a cup of coffee and some toast in the hotel kitchen, chatting with Elena St. Cloud in the lull between meals, and then went back up to the room to unpack. She had brought along a number of books, theater classics that she'd always meant to read or reread, but never seemed to have the time. Shakespeare and Moliere, Shaw and O'Casey, and even the Greeks which she had not cracked since college days. And hoping for sunshine, she unpacked these and her bathing suit.

But the drizzle continued, and when Tony returned from his errands with Leo, he found her lolling dispiritedly in the tall wingbacked chair idly flipping the pages of a thick volume of plays.

"Coming down for lunch?" he asked.

"Not hungry," she replied, pretending to be immersed in the trials of Antigone in the court of King Creon. "I think she's a bit of a manipulator, don't you?"

"Who, Glory?" Tony stood before the mirror fiddling with a reluctant lock of hair that stubbornly failed to take its proper place on his brow.

"Oh, her, too, Every inch." Anita watched him over the top of her book. "No. I meant Antigone. All that business over her brother's body was just an excuse for sniping at the establishment. She says she was after justice, but I think she was really hot for power. And that poor sap, Haemon, got caught up in her political ploys."

"I thought he was in love with her." Tony gave up on the

lock of hair and began inspecting his teeth instead. The mirror reflected back a gleaming imitation of a smile.

"Oh, he was. He was. But she was just using him to get at the king. Oh, well." she slammed the book shut and dropped it to the floor. "I'll probably never get to play Antigone. Or anything else if I keep on lying about like this. I wonder if I could have gotten a job demonstrating vegetable slicers in department stores for the summer."

Tony swung round on her angrily. "Don't start that again. We agreed you were going to have a vacation. Why don't you start having it?"

"And just what do you propose I do? Pitch myself a tent on the beach and look at the raindrops making dimples on the water? Not much joy in that."

"Maybe it'll clear up tomorrow." He came to her chair and bent over her for a kiss, but she turned her head away, feeling both stubbornly resentful and horribly ashamed of herself. He straightened up and strode to the door, his back stiff with hurt pride. "Come on along if you want some lunch," he said.

"No, thanks. I think I'll wash my hair. It might get rid of some of the cobwebs inside my head." She couldn't force herself any closer than that to an apology.

But the shampoo hadn't helped. Now, sitting in the back of the theater, there being no place else to go and nothing else to do, Anita felt even more restless and resentful than before. She eyed Glory Hayes who, ostensibly consulting Tony over something in the script, was pressing close to him with a bare shoulder, a rounded hip scantily covered by blue satin gym shorts, a length of exposed thigh. Besides the gym shorts, she wore only a flimsy halter of a blue tissue-thin material and a pair of wooden wedge-soled sandals with thongs that wrapped and tied around her slender ankles. Anita, who was chilled even in her jeans and quilted Chinatown jacket, wondered how Glory kept warm in such an outfit and shivered as she watched Tony casually drape an arm over the back of Glory's chair.

The reading began, and Anita, listening intently from the back row, hoped for the worst. It was ungenerous of her, she knew, but she couldn't help it. She wanted Glory Hayes to fail miserably. She wouldn't let herself think beyond what that failure might mean, either to herself or to Glory. She knew the play well, having read through it a number of times with Tony, and had arrived at an interpretation of Glory's role, the role that should have been hers. She practically had the lines committed to memory. Now she listened to the words as they came from Glory's lips, and smiled.

Glory read abominably. Her voice was a monotone until she spied an exclamation point on the page, when it rose to a piercing shriek. She missed her cues and stepped on other people's lines. When she had nothing to say for any length of time, she fidgeted, fanned herself with the script, and reapplied her lipstick. Whenever she made a mistake and realized it, she interrupted the reading with breathless excuses before correcting herself. And throughout the entire first act, she directed all of her lines to Tony whether or not his character was the one to whom she should have been speaking.

Anita wondered why Larry Devine permitted the reading to continue without reprimanding Glory once. Anyone can fluff a line at a first reading, and some of the others did. But Glory was behaving in a totally unprofessional manner, which was not lost on the other members of the cast. Anita noticed the puzzled glances that followed some of her more monumental gaffes. But through it all, Devine sat in the front row, slowly turning the pages of the script and jotting notes in the margin.

At the conclusion of the first act, a silence fell. All eyes went to the front row. Devine rose to his feet and stretched.

"Take a break, kids," he announced. And as an afterthought, "Oh, Glory. Come down here for a minute, will you."

Glory jumped up from her chair enthusiastically. "Hey! That was fun!" she exclaimed. "But I don't know how I'm ever going to learn all those lines. Leo, maybe you better start making some idiot cards for me."

"Glory," said Devine, quietly but with meaning. "If you please."

Glory clomped to the side of the stage where a short flight of steps led down into the auditorium. Her wooden sandals set up a booming echo in the hall. At the top of the steps she paused and looked back. "Oh, Tony," she called, "would you be an angel and bring me a cup of coffee. Lots of milk, no sugar."

Tony signaled agreement and went to the side of the stage where Emmy Jackson had set up the coffee urn and supplied a huge tin of homemade cookies. At the back of the auditorium, Anita gritted her teeth at this betrayal, and wished she had a listening device planted in the front row so that she could hear every word of Devine's lecture to Glory. All she could see, after Glory had sat down beside him, was their two heads bent together, Glory's nodding in evident accord with each point that was made. After a few moments, Tony joined them with a cup of coffee in each hand. He handed one to Glory and sat down, casually laying his arm along the back of her chair. Anita craned forward, despising the curiosity that kept her eyes riveted on the trio.

"You do go in for self-torment, don't you?"

She turned guiltily, caught in the act of spying, and unsuccessfully at that.

"Oh, Leo! I didn't see you come up the aisle."

"I didn't. I crept deviously around the side. And what do I find? Another devious person engaged in sordid espionage. If looks could kill, the poor popsie would be writhing in her last agony. But is it personal or professional? Or both? After that reading, I'd like to do her grievous bodily harm, myself. As I'm sure would all the others. What do you think? Wasn't she dreadful?" Leo had sidled along the row of seats and perched on the arm of the chair next to Anita's.

She looked up at him. He smiled encouragingly.

"Of course she was dreadful. But I've heard worse first readings. Anyway, it's really nothing to do with me, is it?"

"Oh, isn't it? Then why, I wonder, is Larry aching to talk with you?"

"Is he? I didn't know that."

"Well, you *have* been making yourself rather scarce, hiding in your room and lurking back here like the little match girl at the feast. But now that I've found you, I hereby deliver the message. Larry is aching to talk with you."

"What about?"

"If I knew that, I'd know a lot. Well, the council of war seems to be breaking up."

Anita followed his glance down to the front row where Tony was standing holding Glory's script and coffee cup while she rummaged in her handbag. Devine was on his feet, too, evidently waiting for Glory to find whatever it was she was searching for. At last, she pulled out a leather case and from it removed a pair of eyeglasses which she put on with an air of sheepish embarrassment.

"Oh, my sainted Aunt Tillie's pongee pajamas!" Leo exclaimed. "The popsie must be blind as a bat and too vain to admit it. No wonder she couldn't read worth a damn. Well, we'll see how she does in the second round. Cheeri-bye, Anita, my lovely. Don't forget. His lordship wishes words with you. Stick around after this is over."

Leo bounded away down the aisle, leaving Anita to settle back in her seat and wonder what Devine could possibly want to discuss with her. She watched as Tony and Glory, followed by Leo, reascended the stage and joined the other members of the cast chatting in small groups.

"All right, people," Devine called out. "Let's get on with it. Act Two."

There was a general movement back to the semicircle of folding chairs. Anita watched as the fat character actress, whom she had not yet met, snaffled a handful of cookies from the coffee table and went back to her chair munching happily. The old matinee-idol type, who was just returning from the wings, passed behind her and, as he did, Anita was jolted by the expression on his face. It passed so quickly and was such a strange combination of emotions, she couldn't put a name to it. Disgust and yearning? Something like that. Something not quite flattering and yet helplessly drawn.

"Oh, boy!" she told herself, "you're really turning into Madame Freud, trying to analyze the old guy's facial tics. It's probably nothing but indigestion. And you're trying to read some kind of angst into a politely suppressed belch."

She watched the old man cross the stage holding himself elegantly erect, and at the same time, out of the corner of her eye, she saw Glory Hayes stoop to pick something up off her chair. A piece of paper, it seemed, or an envelope.

When the group had resettled itself, Larry Devine climbed to the stage and moved into the center of the semicircle.

"I'm glad to see that most of you have at least a nodding acquaintance with the script," he said. "Some of you have even learned your lines already. That's fine. But I want everyone to stay on the script until we get the blocking firmly established. This is a small stage and there isn't a lot of room for improvisation when it comes to movement. If there's time after we read it all the way through, we'll start blocking the first act. And continue this evening after dinner. Okay, people, let's go."

Devine turned to leave the stage and go back to his seat in the front row. The others found their places in their scripts and swallowed the last of their coffee. But before Devine reached the step at the side of the stage, Glory was on her feet waving a scrap of paper.

"Hey! What the hell is *this?*" she cried.

Devine hunched his shoulders and turned to face her.

"What is it now, Glory?"

"Well, look at this! If this isn't the shittiest . . .!" She glared round the stage, red-eyed behind her pink-rimmed glasses. "Somebody here has some fucking funny sense of humor! Well, I don't think it's so funny, and I'm gonna find out who did this. Don't all speak at once."

"Glory, what is it?" Devine repeated impatiently.

"Listen," she said. She raised the piece of paper, adjusted her glasses, and read, "'I took you for that cunning whore of Venice. . . .'" She glared accusingly around the semicircle again. "I've never been to Venice in my life. It's a crummy town, full of creeps, nothing like Malibu."

Devine turned away from her, his shoulders shaking.

"Nice reading," commented Tony with a judicious nod into the stunned silence.

"My dear child," said Pev Martin, trying to draw her back into her seat. "Someone obviously thinks you ought to play Desdemona."

"Oh, yeah? Who's Desdemona?"

"Oh, jes' some honky chick who makes it with a black stud," said Leo, smiling blandly. "An old play. Before your time."

"Fantastic!" said Glory. "What is it, some kind of pimp show?"

"No," said Tina Elliott, "it's about jealousy and murder. She gets strangled."

"Wow!" said Glory, "that's cool. I like shows with lots of action. But I still don't like this part about 'cunning whore.' That's a rotten thing to say to a girl."

"All right. All right," said Devine, shambling to her side. "Give me the note. It's a bad joke, but maybe we'd better forget about it for now and get on with the rehearsal. And remember what I told you, Glory. Take it slow and easy and try to get the sense of the lines. Let's go."

Glory reluctantly surrendered the slip of paper to Devine, who glanced at it briefly, then folded it and put it in his pocket.

"I'm not forgetting it," Glory muttered as she returned to her chair. Peverill Martin leaned across to whisper to her and help her find her place in the script. She smiled at him gratefully and leaned forward just enough to give him a bird's-eye view into her halter.

A thoroughly nice old man, thought Anita Stratton, who had watched and listened with great interest. And a thoroughly appropriate note. She almost wished she had written it herself and wondered who had had the flash of inspiration. From her observation post in the last row, she hadn't seen anyone in the act of scribbling or dropping the note on Glory's chair. She had been chatting with Leo during part of the break, and her attention had been diverted from the stage. At least, it couldn't have been Tony. He'd been sitting with Devine and Glory in the front row. Unless he'd done it when he went to fetch Glory her coffee. Othello was high on his list of coveted roles and he knew the play well. But Tony, if she knew him at all, would say what he had to say for all to hear; he wouldn't engage in anonymous note-dropping. That left the nice old man who seemed to know his Shakespeare and could easily have slipped the note onto Glory's chair, the fat woman who had been insulted by Glory before the entire cast but who seemed to be drowning her rage in an orgy of cookie-munching, Hilda Kramer who remained enigmatically aloof and spoke only when her lines appeared in the script, and Leo. Leo might have done it, just to get a rise out of Glory, or to expose her ignorance. With his eternal clipboard, Leo could be here, there, and everywhere writing notes and no one would think anything of it or remember seeing him do it.

Well, Devine was right. It *was* better to forget all about it and get on with the business at hand. Glory would just have to get used to the backstage jokes actors played on each other. That's all it was. Pretty raw, but Glory had asked for it.

The reading of the second act was well under way, and Glory, with the aid of her eyeglasses, seemed to be doing somewhat better. At least, she managed to come in on cue and make some sense out of the lines. Anita, overcoming her envy, felt a twinge of pity for the girl. She was clearly out of her league and, while she might not know *Othello* from *East Lynne,* she certainly didn't deserve to be hounded with anonymous name-calling. Devine would have his work cut out for him if he expected to get any kind of performance out of her. Maybe he would welcome some help. Maybe, when she spoke with him later, she would offer to coach Glory in the role. Unofficially, of course. It would give her something to do and at the same time, she admitted ruefully, allow her to keep an eye on Tony.

The reading droned on and Anita grew restless in her back row seat. She had gone without breakfast or lunch, and her appetite was finally making itself felt. She might be able to get some food at the hotel, or at one of the little restaurants she'd noticed as they drove through the town late the night before, and return when the reading was over. As she rose and began edging her way across the row of seats, a pair of eyes on stage flickered away from the page, a cue was missed and then picked up after a two-second pause, and the reading went on.

CHAPTER XIII

Barney, you'll never guess."

"Guess what, sweetheart?" His voice came over the long-distance line as if he were in the next room and not half a continent away.

"Who's here."

"Don't tell me. Robert Redford."

"Shee-it, no! What would he be doing here? Barney, it's crazy. Remember the movie, the one you saw me in? Boy, do I wish I had a print of that right now."

"Hot Biscuits and Gravy?"

"Yeah, that one. Well, you won't believe this, but the guy who was in that with me is the leading man in this half-assed operation. Isn't that a gas?"

Barney chuckled. "Small world. From hillbilly porn to summer stock in one giant stumble."

"Boy, did he turn green when he saw me." Glory lay sprawled on her bed dressed only in a pink nylon dressing gown. She cradled the phone with her shoulder and lit a cigarette. From the bathroom she shared with Hilda Kramer came the sound of water rushing into the tub. "He's changed his name and he's scared to death I'll let his dirty little secret out. I pretended I couldn't remember where I'd seen him before. I said to him, 'Oh, haven't I seen you in something?' I swear, Barney, if we'd been alone, he'd have killed me on the spot, he was that shook up. But I had a little talk with him this morning and now we're the best of friends. At least, for the time being. After all, it wouldn't do *me* any good either to have that film cropping up, at least not until I'm already famous. Then it won't matter."

"Listen, kid. I gotta run. Gotta meet some people for drinks in a few minutes. Glad you're having fun. Keep in touch."

"No, wait, Barney. I have to tell you something else. I almost got killed last night."

"What!"

"Well, it was an accident. There was a storm and a power

line got knocked down and it hit me. At first, I thought *he* did it. You know, to keep me quiet. But I guess that's kind of far-fetched, isn't it? Everybody here says it was an accident, so I guess it was. Barney, do I really have to stay here?''

"Are you all right?''

"Well, yeah. I mean, I wasn't hurt or anything. Just scared. And everybody's being supernice to me now. *Almost* everybody. There's this old geezer who wants to tell me the story of his life in show biz. A sweet old guy, really. And there's the most fantastic-looking Indian stud here at the hotel.''

"How's Hilda?''

"She's taking a bath right now. She's in the room right next to mine with the bathroom in between. She doesn't say very much, but she's always watching. It's a little creepy some-times.''

"Give her my love. I've really got to go now, Glory. I'll be back in L.A. tomorrow night. Call me then, okay?''

"Barney, wait. There's something else.''

But the line had gone dead. Glory felt abandoned. She wanted to tell him about the horrible note that had been left on her chair. Devine had assured her after rehearsal that it was only a joke, and that it would be giving it more importance than it deserved to try to find out who had done it. Best to forget about it, he'd told her. And at the time, she had agreed. But now, alone in her room, with the connection between her and Barney broken, she felt vaguely threatened by it. There was no threat in the note itself, but someone at the rehearsal had said it was from a play about murder. Everybody seemed to know what the play was about, everybody but her. Well, so what! She couldn't know every play in the English language. Barney was always giving her books to read, but those old plays were so long and took forever to get to the point. He'd made her go and see the movie of *Romeo and Juliet* and that was fun because it was so sexy and sad. She'd cried at the end. But when she tried to read it, she fell asleep before she ever got to the good part.

Behind the closed bathroom door, she heard the sound of water gurgling down the drain. Maybe she'd have time to take a bath before dinner. She wondered if Hilda Kramer had writ-ten the note. It didn't seem likely, but she din't really know any of these people. For all she knew, they were all loony. She got up from the bed, crossed the room, and rapped on the bathroom door.

"Yes?"

"It's me, Glory. How's the hot water?"

She heard the bolt on the other side of the door being drawn back. The door opened and Hilda Kramer stood there wrapped in a faded old flannel robe, her dark hair a mass of damp curls.

"There's plenty of it, and I'll bet you'd like to use some of it. I'm just about finished. Isn't this a magnificent old bathroom? I haven't seen a tub like that in years."

She stepped back into the bathroom which, like so much else about the Dune Haven Hotel, was a relic of the last century. The tub was huge, half again as long as a modern bathtub, and encased in mahogany paneling. The sink was marble and stood on a gracefully curved pedestal, with an enormous gilt-framed mirror hanging on the wall above it. The toilet, also encased in mahogany, stood upon a marble platform raised about six inches from the hexagonal tiled floor. The tall single window displayed a pair of leaded-glass lovebirds perched on a cornucopia spilling jewel-like fruit within a frame of many colors.

While Hilda gathered up her belongings, Glory debated asking her about the note. If she had written it, she certainly wouldn't admit it. But if she hadn't, she might have some idea who did. And with her habit of always watching people, she might have noticed who had put it on the chair.

"I hope I don't get any more of those notes," she began.

"It wasn't very pleasant, was it?" said Hilda. "I meant to tell you before how much better your reading was in the second act. Larry is rather a genius at getting past people's inhibitions."

"You mean about the eyeglasses?"

"If you need them, you should wear them. No one will think anything of it."

"They're so ugly."

"Only if you think they are. Now I must get dressed. Be sure you don't fall asleep in that tub. It would be so easy to drown in a tub that size." She opened the connecting door on her side of the room.

"Hilda, wait. Do you know who wrote that note? Did you see who put it on the chair?"

"No, my dear. I don't and I didn't. And you really would

be wise not to pursue it any further. Let Larry deal with it. We don't even know that it was meant for you, do we?"

"Who else? It was on my chair."

"Did it have your name on it?"

"No."

"You see. It might have been dropped by accident. It might not have been a message at all. Just a reminder of a line in a play."

"How come I'm getting all these accidents all of a sudden? Last night was an accident, okay. Maybe it was. I'll accept that. But not the note. That was intended for me and nobody but me. It's spooky to get a note like that. It makes me feel like somebody's watching me."

"Does it?"

"Hilda, Barney told me a lot about you. How he tried to help you when you were out on the Coast. And where you went from there."

Hilda paused with her hand on the doorknob. Her voice changed to a husky snarl. "He shouldn't have told you that. Even Larry doesn't know that. Barney and Leo were the only ones who knew. And now you. What, excactly, did he tell you?"

She came back into the bathroom and faced Glory with an intense probing gaze that made her falter and step backward. Glory realized that the door to her own room had swung shut behind her, and she groped frantically for the knob.

"Hey, wait a minute. Lots of people have a problem with booze. He said you were one of the lucky ones, to be able to go away to a nice sanitorium and get dried out."

Hilda swung away from Glory and gazed at her reflection in the tall old mirror. "He told you that?"

"Yeah. And he didn't tell me it was any deep, dark secret. Only that he was glad you were all over it now and getting back to work. He said you were too good to pour yourself into a bottle and pull the cork in after you."

"He said that?" Hilda shrugged and went back to the door on her side of the room. "Why are you telling me? Why don't you run straight to Larry with this fascinating bit of gossip? Why don't you shout it from the stage on opening night? Hilda Kramer is a reformed lush, but watch out, she might fall off the wagon and make a spectacle of herself. Or did you think that I wrote that silly note and you could get me to admit it by this crude piece of blackmail?"

"No! No! I didn't mean it that way! I only meant that you had a problem and you got help. Barney helped you. And now I've got a problem. Somebody around here is out to make trouble for me. Barney's miles away. Everybody says, 'It was only a joke. Forget about it.' But it's not very funny and I can't forget. I'm afraid. And nobody here will listen to me. I just thought maybe you. . . ."

Her voice trailed off and she gripped the doorknob so she could make a quick retreat if Hilda turned nasty. But Hilda remained thoughtfully silent and for a few moments the only sound in the humid bathroom was the rain beating against the stained-glass window while the two women stood, each at the door leading to her own room, looking at each other warily. At last Hilda spoke.

"You poor kid," she said. "How old are you? The truth, now."

"N-n-ineteen. I'll be nineteen in August."

"Barney should have known better than to throw you in with this group of maniacs. Actors are always sniping at each other, Glory. Playing silly little jokes, trying to break each other up on stage. That's why no one takes that note seriously. I grant you, it was ugly. But maybe you invited it by the way you talk and the way you dress."

Glory had been listening quietly, but at Hilda's last words she bridled.

"What's wrong with the way I dress?"

"It leaves very little to the imagination."

"If you got it, flaunt it. That's my motto."

"That's fine. But if you flaunt it, you have to expect someone to take up the challenge. And in ways you might not like." Hilda opened the door to her own room. "Now, I really must get dressed. Will you sit with Larry and me at dinner?"

"Oh, thanks. But that old geezer, Pev Martin, asked me to sit with him. He's kind of sweet, don't you think? He's been telling me about vaudeville and we're only up to 1932. Ancient history! Hey, you don't think *he* wrote the note?"

"Don't think about it anymore." Hilda vanished into her room and closed the door behind her.

Glory began filling the tub.

CHAPTER XIV

Oh, the cunning whore! She's pretending that she didn't get the message, that the significance of the note was lost on her. Anyone but a cretin would understand. Yet there she sits, smiling, laughing, chewing her food. Ye gods, it doth amaze me! And makes me lose my appetite as well.

Or is it this headache? This heaviness in my head, not an ache precisely, but a weight that drags me down into regions of intolerable despair. So soon? And deeper than before? A pit of hopelessness so deep that I will never scale its sides, never see sunlight again? No matter. I, too, must smile and laugh and chew my food, although I choke on every morsel. We are such a happy group here. The room is full of chatter and the tinkle of busy silverware. On all sides, mouths, lips, teeth, tongues in the act of devouring. If viewed from a certain perspective, eating is an obscene act and should be done in private with the curtains drawn and the door locked. Yet here I am, forced to witness the wholesale mastication of parts of dead animals, of things that sprout and ripen on the corruption of the earth. We feed on death. We thrive and grow fat on death. Why, then, should death alarm us? It is our friend and nurturer.

Look at her then, eating death. Her lips are greasy with it. How daintily she lifts her napkin. False delicacy. Will she be so dainty when she is the food for worms, the very worms that enrich the earth that grows these lovely strawberries? How will she laugh then?

"What? Oh, no. The food is fine. It's only that I seem to have a headache. Herb tea? Why not? I've tried everything else. Tell me, is it still raining? It is? Fine weather for Duck Creek. Ha-ha!"

The Indian woman is very fine-looking. And kind. I wonder why she saddles herself with this worn-out hotel? There's no future in it. There's no future in anything, and all of her herb teas won't cure that. I know the best medicine for what ails me. The only question is . . . when.

CHAPTER XV

Dawn.

Fog and a dank chill slid in at the open window, sifting wraith-like through the limp net curtains. But at least the rain had stopped. A foghorn groaned nearby and another farther up the lakeshore answered faintly. Anita Stratton crept quietly out of bed and groped, shivering, for her clothes. She found her jeans where they'd been thrown the night before, across the back of a chair. From her half-packed suitcase she took a clean shirt and underwear, all the while murmuring to herself, "Please don't let him wake up. Please let me get out of here without another argument."

As she tiptoed around the room, the old boards creaked beneath her feet. She winced, glancing over her shoulder at the sleeper sprawled in the other half of the high old-fashioned double bed, his black hair tumbled on the pillow, his left arm cradling his head while his right, even in sleep, seemed to be reaching out possessively for her. Outside, on the veranda, chattering birds set up a shrill complaint. Anita pulled the French window closed on their commotion, wishing they would take their quarrel elsewhere. She had plenty of her own.

In the bathroom, she dressed quickly and washed as quietly as she could, allowing only a trickle of water to escape from the tap as she splashed her face awake and brushed her teeth. Everything this morning was coated with a greasy dampness and the smell of mildew hung in the air. She peered into the tarnished mirror above the basin, searching her face for signs of last night's anguish. She felt as if tears had carved deep channels down her cheeks and that the print of Tony's hand, where it had struck her, would be blazoned in sullen red.

It had been a terrible night. Her talk with Larry Devine turned out to be a tactfully worded but nonetheless unacceptable request that she take on the job of understudy to Glory Hayes. She refused, stiffly polite and so shocked and dispirited by the offer that she forgot her resolve to be kind to the girl and coach her in the role. Instead, she decided that the only thing she could possible do was to leave Duck Creek. It had been a mistake to come along. She'd felt that from the very beginning. Now all she wanted to do was get away.

But when she'd tried to tell Tony of her decision, he refused to listen. At dinner, he was moody and distracted, his attention constantly wandering to the table where Glory sat with Peverill Martin. The old man was animated and garrulous and Glory appeared to hang spellbound on his every word. At another table, Larry Devine presided over a laughing, chattering group consisting of Leo, Hilda Kramer, and the fat woman, Tina Elliott. Already the camaraderie of working together on a show was taking hold, and she was excluded. She felt that Tony longed to be a part of it but was hampered by her presence. Well, not for long. As she would let him know as soon as she could get him alone for fifteen minutes.

But she was not to have those fifteen minutes. As soon as the coffee cups had been cleared away, Devine herded everyone back to the theater to work out the movements for the first act. He pointedly ignored her, and she was left in the deserted dining room among the crumbs and the used napkins.

"Some fresh coffee?"

Joe St. Cloud had come noiselessly into the dining room and was beginning to strip the tables of their white cloths.

She shook her head, pressing her lips together against kindnesses from any source. "What time does the next bus leave?"

"In the morning." He came and sat in Tony's vacated chair. "About eight-fifteen. Will you be leaving?"

"Yes."

"I'm sorry."

"Why? Why should you be sorry?"

"Are you happy about leaving?"

"I'm relieved. I'll be happy once I get away from . . . here."

"Back to the city?"

"Yes."

"And what will you do there?"

"I'll be busy. I'll look for work. I'll find something to do. And I'll have my friends."

"What will you leave behind?"

"Tony? He'll never know I'm gone. No. That's not true. He'll be relieved, too. He won't have to worry about whether or not I'm enjoying my vacation. And he'll be free to play whatever game he's up to without me peering over his shoulder."

"And that's all there is to it? You're running away because you're jealous and don't know what to do about it?"

Anita pushed her chair back angrily. "I'm not jealous. And I'm not running away. I'm simply going back where I belong. All I wanted from you was the bus schedule, not a psychiatric examination. And an amateur one, at that."

Joe leaned back in his chair and laughed. "Not so amateur. But I'm sorry for practicing on you without your consent. You can call me Doctor Joe if it'll make you feel better. All my patients do."

"Doctor!" Anita sat down again puzzled. "You mean you're a . . .?"

Joe nodded. "I shrink heads instead of scalping them. You seem surprised."

"Well, I am. Why are you wasting your time clearing off tables in this . . .?

"Dump? Oh, don't be embarrassed. We know the hotel is a losing proposition. But Elena loves it, and it's therapeutic for me to do a little manual labor now and then. Besides, if my patients see me doing some of the same kind of work they do, it makes it easier for them to talk to me. I even go out cherry-picking once in a while."

"Your patients?"

"Did you think the white man held a franchise on mental illness?"

"I guess I never thought about it. Do you have an office and a . . . ?"

"A couch? In a manner of speaking. Would you like to see it?"

"Where is it?"

"Upstairs."

Anita hesitated. The man sitting across the table from her exuded a kind of calm purposefulness. Already, her hurt and anger seemed slightly ridiculous. Still, she would not be swayed from her intention of leaving in the morning. Not even a tall dark handsome native American psychiatrist could keep her off that bus. She examined his face for signs of carnal intent. He smiled. She shrugged.

"Why not," she said.

He led her up the stairs, past the second floor where her suitcase waited to be packed, on up to the third floor where, beyond the rooms occupied by Hilda Kramer and Glory Hayes, another narrow enclosed staircase ascended to the top floor of the old hotel.

"There's an outside stairway, too," he said. "It's a little like a fire escape, but many of my patients prefer to use it. It makes them feel as if they're climbing a sacred mountain to consult the shaman who lives on top."

"Do you have many patients?" Anita asked, wondering how many Indians with psychiatric problems there could be in the rural area surrounding Duck Creek.

"Not a lot. But word is getting around and some of them come because they've heard that I use the old medicine. They expect magical cures for all kinds of ailments, not just mental disorders. Elena helps out there. She's boned up on the old herbal remedies. Some of them are medically very sound."

"And you? Do you really use the old medicine?"

"You'll see."

They had reached the top of the narrow staircase, and Anita found herself in a large open space illuminated only by the fading daylight that filtered in through dusty dormer windows set into the far wall. The center of the space was occupied by a jumble of discarded furniture. Broken rocking chairs and splintered wicker porch chaises leaned sadly against each other. A cumbersome wardrobe gaped hollowly, its door hanging ajar on warped hinges. Two bentwood hatracks groped toward the rafters, lost in gloom and cobwebs. Around their curved feet swirled an accumulation of odds and ends, somber paintings in chipped gilt frames, small tables and large umbrella stands, unmatched bits of china, a hoard of derelict objects that had outlived their usefulness.

"Elena's treasure trove," said Joe, with a dismissive sweep of his arm. "One day, she's going to hold an attic sale and get rid of it all. But somehow, the day never comes. This way."

He led her down a corridor where a double row of closed doors indicated a series of small rooms on either side. Joe explained. "In the heyday of the Dune Haven Hotel, whole families used to come up by train from Chicago. Lots of children, cousins, impoverished maiden aunts, nursemaids. These rooms were for the servants and the poor relations. We don't use them much now. Once in a while, backpackers or kids on bicycle trips come by looking for cheap rooms, and we put them up here."

He opened a door at random and Anita peered in on a small

monastically furnished room: bed, dresser, and chair, a row of brass hooks on the wall in lieu of a closet. The ceiling was low and sloped down toward the tiny window.

"When I was a child," Anita remarked, "I always wanted a room under the eaves where I could be alone."

Joe closed the door. "Now," he announced, "we come to the lair of the savage. The tepee of the great medicine man. Are you ready?"

Anita smiled and followed him to the end of the corridor where the last door, no different in size than the ones they had passed, had been painted with symbolic figures in bright red, yellow, and gleaming black.

"I guess you could call this my shingle," he said, pointing to the stylized figure of a fierce-looking animal with an alarming number of teeth and claws streaking across the top of the door beneath a crescent moon with upward-pointing horns. "My tribal name is Wolf Runs in the Night. And this," he said, indicating another animal figure, "is the Great Bear, a very powerful sign. But let's go in. I'll show you how my medicine works."

He pushed open the painted door and stood back to allow Anita to enter. She passed through the door, expecting to find herself in a room similar in size to the one she had seen down the hall, but fitted out as a consulting room.

"What do you think?" Joe St. Cloud closed the door and stood grinning at her astonishment.

"It's a little overpowering," Anita murmured, "especially to a paleface. I suppose it has a slightly different effect on your clientele."

"It seems to work." Joe watched as Anita took a few tentative steps into the room which was really three of the small rooms knocked into one. The low ceiling had been removed to expose the rafters and the rough sloping boards of the underside of the roof. In the long outer wall, the small dormer windows had been replaced by slanting panes of glass that gave a panoramic view out over the lake.

"It's much better when it's not raining," said Joe. "You can see the islands, and when it's very clear, all the way over to Wisconsin."

But Anita was not drawn to the view which, in any case, was limited because of the rain and the gray twilight closing in. She went instead to the far end of the room where a tepee stood, its flaps pinned back invitingly.

111

"Is this it?" she asked. "Your version of the psychiatric couch?" She peered into the tent where two low blanket-covered pallets were placed on either side of the entrance.

"If a man comes to me," said Joe, "and his spirit is depressed and making him ill, we might sit in the tepee and smoke for a while. We might blow the smoke to the four corners, and when the pipe is finished, he might say to me, 'Wolf Runs in the Night, I am troubled in my heart.' Then he might or he might not tell me what the trouble is. He might tell it straight out, or he might invent some story to carry his message. He might choose to remain silent and leave without saying a word, having used the time to gain some peace and think his own thoughts. It could be that he's angry with his wife, or unhappy about the direction his life has taken. And, believe me, Indians have a lot to be unhappy about in that direction. But whatever the trouble is, the tepee represents the old ways and the old values, and it seems to be a comfort to people who feel they've been dispossessed and disinherited. When I first put it up, I wondered if I were practicing medicine or showmanship. I guess it's a little of both.

"A man came to me once who was miserable because his wife had a job and he didn't. He didn't put it quite that way, though. He'd had severe pains in his stomach, and he was convinced that his wife was poisoning him. The doctors down at the clinic couldn't find anything wrong with him. So they suggested he come to me. We sat in the tepee and we smoked for maybe twenty minutes. Then he told me a story. He said it was one that his grandmother had told him in a dream. It seems that once a great warrior married the daughter of a chief. The chief had no sons and so he had raised his daughter to hunt and ride like a man. When she married the warrior, she promised to give up her rough habits and behave like a proper wife. But she soon grew restless and wanted to be out riding with the men. When she discovered that a baby was to come, she became even more unhappy because she realized that never again would she mount her horse or shoot her arrows at a running deer. So one night, while her husband was asleep, she cut open her belly and took the baby out and cut open his belly and put the baby in there until it should be time for it to be born. But the warrior's belly was hard and muscular and there was no room for the baby to grow. The woman didn't care because now she was free to ride and hunt, which she did all day, while her husband stayed home with a great pain in his belly. When

112

it came time for the baby to arrive, the warrior's pain increased because no matter how the baby twisted and struggled, there was no way for it to be born. He was maddened with the pain, and when his wife came home to the tepee that night carrying over her shoulder the deer she had killed, he picked up the deer-skinning knife and plunged it into her heart. When the baby heard what was going on, he struggled harder than ever and burst his father's body open and leaped out, crying, "Wah! I have no mother and no father. How shall I live?"

"That's quite a story," said Anita. "Do you mind if I sit inside the tepee?"

"No. Go right ahead. Would you like to smoke a pipe?"

"No, thanks. I don't smoke. Only sometimes a little grass." Anita bent her head to enter the tepee and settled herself on one of the pallets. It was dark inside the tent, and while she could see that there were objects hanging from the tentpoles, she couldn't make out what they were. Joe followed her into the tepee and sat crosslegged on the other pallet.

"What happened to the man? Did he want to kill his wife?" she asked.

"Not really. But he might have taken to beating her up." Joe took a small skin-covered drum from one of the tentpoles and began tapping it softly with his fingertips. "First I sang him a song in the old language. He didn't understand a word of it. Not many people do anymore, but I've been learning it from an old man. I told him it was a song to start his purification, and that the purification would take a long time. I told him he should come to me once a week and tell me any more of his grandmother's stories or any other dreams he might have, and that he should think over his past life to see when it was that the bad spirit could have entered his stomach. And I gave him some of Elena's sassafras tonic to take when the pain was bad."

"Did it work?"

Anita found herself nodding drowsily in time with the soft tapping of the drum.

"He doesn't have any more pains in the stomach." Joe stopped drumming and hung the drum back on the tentpole. "And he's working down in Manistee at a sawmill."

Anita shook herself awake. "Don't you ever feel as if you're practicing witchcraft?"

Joe laughed. "At first I did. After my very expensive education in dealing with the white man's craziness. But I quickly

113

found out that very few white people were crazy enough to trust their troubles to a redskin. Even one with a haircut and a vested suit. I spent a very unproductive year in Detroit, mostly driving a cab. When I came back here, I started studying the old ways, finding old people who remembered some of the songs and stories. And I began putting the old and the new together."

Joe got to his feet, "It's getting dark. Come on, I'll show you the other side of the coin."

Anita followed him out of the tepee. Through the windows, she could see the lights of the marina and the outlines of two or three boats. The lake itself was a smear of darkness beyond the raindrops trickling endlessly down the glass. Joe flicked a switch, bathing the room in light and turning the window into a dark mirror reflecting the tepee and Anita standing before it. He beckoned her to the other end of the room, where crammed bookshelves stretched to the rafters and a long worktable piled with papers and recording tapes stood against the wall. Beneath the window on that side of the room was a low platform bed piled with cushions.

"This," said Joe, "is where Wolf Runs in the Night turns into Dr. Joseph St. Cloud, scientific investigator of the psychology underlying such legends as he can collect. Maybe one day he'll write a book on the subject."

"If he does, I'll read it. If he'll send me a copy." Anita prowled the office end of the long room, a puzzled frown lingering in the wake of her now dissipated resentment. "Why have you told me all this," she asked, "shown me this side of you? I didn't need to know that you were anything but a good-looking busboy."

"Believe it or not, I don't know," Joe replied. "You seemed to want something. I thought it might amuse you. No, that's not right. Or not all of it. You didn't look very happy at the table with your friend tonight. I guess I thought I could make you feel a little better." He smiled, "I'm as clumsy as the next guy about my own feelings. Is it safe to say I like you?"

"Oh. What are these?" Anita picked up a small basket filled with smooth polished gray pebbles that was sitting on top of a pile of papers on the desk.

"What? Oh, those. Petoskey stones. The lakeshore is full of them. It's a pretty fair cottage industry around here. Everybody polishes Petoskey stones and sells them to the tourists. Mostly in the form of jewelry. One of my patients gave me those."

"Pretty," said Anita, fingering one of the stones. "Well, I guess I'd better go pack. Thanks for the quiet time."

"You'll still be leaving in the morning?"

"Yes. But only because I'm as out of place here as you were driving a cab."

"I'll walk downstairs with you."

CHAPTER XVI

My feet are wet. I'll probably have a cold in the morning. I should have brought an extra pair of shoes along. Now I've got a chill, as well as a headache. The tea didn't do a bit of good. Not that I expected it to. All *her* fault. Everybody jammed into her car. "Come on," she said, "it's raining. I'll drive over." Fine. And then park right next to a puddle. A puddle! Damn' thing was ankle-deep and three feet across. And me, the first one out of the car. If she wasn't such a stupid twit, I'd think she did it on purpose. Never mind, we'll take care of her later.

But look at her now. Prancing around the stage like a bitch in heat. At least, she's got some clothes on tonight. If you can call that transparent blouse and those skintight pants clothes. And speaking of clothes, what was it she said about the costume sketches this afternoon? "Just don't make me look like Martha Washington." Asinine. It's a period play, but not that period.

Cue coming up. It's hard to concentrate on what I'm doing with the pounding, pounding, pounding in my head. Don't think about it. Just give the line, walk across the stage, write down the direction, cross downstage left, and turn. And. . . Oh, Christ! What's she doing now? Screaming. Climbing a chair. What is it?

A spider? Is that all? Quick. Step on it. There. No more spider. It was rather large. Did you hear it crunch? "A tarantula? No, I don't think so. Just a spider." Wipe up the mess with a piece of newspaper. Everybody laughs, nervously. She gets down from the chair. Shaky. Pale. She comes over to thank me. "I can't *stand* spiders." A kiss. Oh, my. It was nothing.

Nothing. I can still feel the softness under my foot. The slight and frantic squirming as I put my weight on it and then twist and twist. Lovely. She'll squirm soon. Wait and see. Now back to work.

CHAPTER XVII

The bag was packed, unpacked, repacked until by two in the morning Anita fell exhausted on the bed. Tony hadn't returned, and the hotel was silent. Earlier there had been footsteps, comings and goings. Each time she heard someone outside the door, Anita had prepared her speech.

"I've made up my mind, Tony. I can't stay here. I'm leaving on the bus in the morning. Please don't try to stop me. It's better this way. We'll be so glad to see each other in September."

But each time, the footsteps passed by and other doors opened and closed down the hall. By midnight, she had rehearsed the speech so many times, it no longer sounded right. She examined her decision to leave and found it lacking in honesty. She *was* jealous, just as Joe had suggested. Miserably jealous. If she ran away, she would be acting like a child. What was so horrible about being an understudy? She'd done it before. What hurt was being asked to understudy a person like Glory Hayes, who not only had small talent and no concept of the role, but was also climbing all over Tony to his evident enjoyment. And she was going to leave, slink away without a fight? Oh, no. She put on her Chinese jacket and was actually out in the corridor on her way to the playhouse to tell Devine that she had reconsidered and would take on the understudy post, when she heard voices in the lobby below. One was unmistakably Glory's.

"Well, come on up and we'll have our own little party. Boy, that Larry's a slavedriver! I need a little relaxation after that workout."

The other voice or voices, Anita couldn't tell how many, were low-pitched and making shushing noises. If Tony were there with Glory, she didn't want him to find her lurking about in the hall, spying on him. She ran back to the room and quickly unpacked her suitcase, stuffing the clothes into the drawer helter-skelter. Then she waited again for Tony to appear, ready to tell him the good news.

But he didn't come.

By one o'clock, the suitcase was packed again and the drawer empty. Anita tried to read, but the words on the page gave way to a scenario that played and replayed itself in her head. Glory and Tony. Tony and Glory. Drinking, laughing, falling all over each other up in Glory's room.

She considered storming up the stairs and bursting in on them. But the thought of what she might find was sickening. At last, she collapsed on the bed, fully dressed, still with her book in her hand and open to the same page she'd been staring at for the past hour. When the door finally opened, she had fallen into a doze, but she woke instantly.

"Tony? Is that you?"

"Shh. Of course it's me."

He closed the door and locked it, and then slouched wearily across the room and slumped down on his side of the bed.

"Where have you been? Do you know what time it is?" Anita realized that she sounded grimly possessive, but she couldn't help it. All of the calm assurance that she'd gained from her visit with Joe St. Cloud had deserted her.

"Late," Tony muttered. "Very late. Too late."

"Too late is right." Anita climbed off the bed and came around it to stand in front of him. "I tried to tell you before, but you wouldn't listen. And the funny thing is, I even changed my mind, but you weren't around to hear about it. Oh, no. You were too busy playing games upstairs and downstairs and in my lady's chamber. Don't think I don't know you were up in her room tonight."

"What did you say?" Tony's head swung up to face her. "Up in whose room?"

Anita was stunned at his appearance. His eyes glittered between lids that were puffy and reddened, as if he had been crying. His nose seemed pinched and his cheeks hollow. His mouth had lost its sardonic self-mocking quirk, and his lips were drawn down in a grimace of disgust. His shirt was soaked and his dark hair was wet and plastered flat to his skull.

"I was waiting for you," she whispered. "I heard Glory come in. I thought you were with her."

"Well, I wasn't." He spat the words as if they were a mouthful of acid. "Get that through your head. Oh, God, I'm tired."

He fell back across the bed and covered his eyes with both arms.

"Tony."

"H-m-m."

"Tony, I have to tell you something."

"Can't it wait?"

"No, it can't. Because if it waits any longer, I won't be here to tell you."

"What?"

"I'm leaving. In the morning. I'm going home."

"No. You're not."

"On the bus. It leaves at eight-fifteen. I might not see you again before I go."

"*You* are not going anywhere. *You* are staying here. Get back in the bed."

He had lifted his arms so that they lay across his forehead and his eyes gleamed at her from the shadow cast over his face. They looked like the eyes of a wild animal peering out of a cave, both wary and menacing. Anita backed away from the bed, feeling naked and defenseless although she wore her usual jeans and shirt. Her sleeves were rolled up, and she realized, with a jolt, that the hairs on her arms had lifted and she felt suddenly very cold. She reached once more for her Chinese jacket and started to put it on.

"I'm *not* staying here," she blurted. "In fact, all I have to do is close that suitcase and wait downstairs for the bus. I can sleep in a chair in the lobby."

He was off the bed before she had pushed one arm into the sleeve of the jacket. He grabbed the other arm and swung her around to meet the crack of his open palm against her cheek. The slap knocked her off balance and she staggered backward. Her rump struck the arm of the oversized chair, but she slid off it and landed on her hands and knees on the floor. He was beside her in an instant, crouching, repentant, and begging her to get up.

"Oh, Anita, babe. I'm sorry. I didn't mean it. Come to bed. I'll make it up to you. You can't leave now. I need you. Here. Please don't go."

Then he was helping her to her feet, stroking her head, wiping her tears with the damp tail of his shirt, holding her gently, so gently. And then he was undressing her and carrying her to the bed, and covering her up to the chin with the thin summer blanket, kissing the hurt away as if she were his well-beloved child. All the while, murmuring, crooning his penitence, telling her she mustn't leave him. And then he was beside her, over her, around her, inside her, pleading with his insistent body that she stay. There was a terrible urgency about it that she didn't understand, that kept her from losing herself in pleasure shared. This was no pleasure. There was something pitiful and frightened about him, something terribly wrong. Long after he fell away from her exhausted, she lay awake wondering while the silent tears streamed down her face.

CHAPTER XVIII

Well, come up and we'll have our own little party.''

Was ever an invitation like that one issued before, in such innocence? Usually that kind of thing is said in the general vicinity of Eighth Avenue and 42nd Street. But here? In the late night lobby of the Dune Haven Hotel, family accommodations and outdoor fun for all? And by her? That's not so surprising. But she is certainly innocent of what *this* party might mean in the way of fun and games.

"Sure. I'll come up. But keep it quiet, Glory. It's midnight. People are sleeping. We don't want to wake them up."

So, tiptoe up the stairs. She is, after all, lonely. Sent home to bed all alone, her Act one scenes finished. The others, with still at least an hour's work to do, have no time for party-time. I, myself, must return for my final scene. I'm taking a chance, I know, that no one will miss me. But this won't take long, and there is an important scene to play here. *Her* final scene. I follow her up the stairs. How quiet it is. All these good people, safely in their beds, dreaming of sunny days on the shores of Gitchee Gummee. I hope the sun does shine tomorrow. I could use a little sunshine in my life.

She, too, is hoping to shine. Like all the rest of them. And she could probably do it. She's just brash enough, tough enough on the outside, underneath lonely and frightened. Just like I was. Was I? I don't know anymore. I can't remember. It's too long ago. But she's beautiful. Is she? Again, I don't know. Beauty changes with the weather. She's right for today's market. Tomorrow she might be the wrong piece of merchandise. But, lucky girl, she won't have to face that sad day.

Here we are. She opens the door. "Sit down," she says. "Make yourself comfortable." But the chair is heaped with bits and pieces of her wardrobe. "Oh, wait a minute." She picks them up and tosses them on the floor behind the chair. "I've got to get out of these clothes," she says, and begins to

123

do so. While I watch. While I watch. The lean, taut belly behind the unzippered pants. "There's a bottle of brandy on the dresser. Help yourself." The words are muffled. She's pulling her blouse over her head. Her breasts peer at me, placid, unconcerned. I can wait. But not too long.

This headache, now. More than a headache. Long, slow waves of heat alternating with a deadly chill. I shiver and sweat. "They told me I was everything; 'tis a lie, I am not ague-proof." The good king knew what pits of corruption they all are. It made him mad. Lear-mad. Leer-mad. Loony. But not me. Only a pain in the brain, soon relieved.

"Thanks for killing that spider. Don't they scare you? I hate crawly things. Especially spiders. They absolutely panic me."

See her now. Impossible for a man or woman to remove a pair of trousers without looking ridiculous. She does it standing up, first on one foot and then the other. A little hopping about, breasts jouncing merrily. She's wearing only a sheer web of a nylon triangle, barely containing the darkness of her secret parts. Tiny dark curls escape.

"I can't stay long," I warn her. "I have to get back."

"Boy, that Larry. Son of a bitch doesn't know when to stop. But I'm glad he didn't make me wait around until everybody else finished up. 'Get a good night's sleep,' he said, 'we start bright and early in the morning.' Where the hell is my bathrobe? Did I leave it in the bathroom?"

She goes to the door. Opens it.

"Glory, I have a present for you." My hand is in my pocket, fingers twined around the leather thong attached to the stone pendant.

She stops. "Oh, yeah? I love presents. What is it?"

I walk to where she stands, greedy and naked. "Something. Nothing much. Just a souvenir of Duck Creek."

I take it from my pocket and, holding the thong with both hands, slip it over her head. She runs to the mirror. The gray stone hangs between her breats, heavy with time and the weight of glaciers.

"What is it?" she asks again, staring at her reflection. "Some kind of rock?"

"I'll show you."

I come up behind her. My own face appears in the mirror. Smiling. My fingers touch the thong where it curves around her neck and disappears beneath her hair. And quickly pull, and tightly twist and twist and twist! Oh, doesn't she wriggle!

Just like the spider beneath my shoe, before the crushing weight smashed it to pulp. Feel, just feel how she struggles. Her hands. Look out! Slapping, flapping, scratching, clawing. Knocking things over. I don't like a mess. Now there's glass shattered all over the floor. Ugh, smell the perfume. Thick, musky, sickening. Her eyes. In the mirror, surprised. Green lights submerged. Green light for go. Time to go? She sinks. She falls. But don't let go yet. An extra twist or two. A string of drool hangs from her lips. And what's this? A yellow puddle on the floor? Poor baby, she's wet herself. It's all right. It could happen to anyone. The gray stone now is tucked beneath her chin, peeping out like a tiny frightened mouse. And the phone is ringing.

Goodbye, Glory. I have to leave you now. But don't worry. There's still work to do. And now I'll do it well.

CHAPTER XIX

Anita crept down the stairs, her suitcase in her hand. It was much too early in the morning for the bus, but she preferred to wait for it in the lobby where she would be safe from any more of Tony's moods. She'd left him still sleeping and, with luck, she would get on the bus and be gone before he woke up. The man was an emotional basket case, and she wasn't much better. Was that the attraction they had for each other? The ability each had to bring out the other's weaknesses? And call it love? Did she secretly enjoy being slapped around as a prelude to sex? Her hand went to her cheek and she felt a slow flush rising. No, she did not! It was humiliating. Even the memory of it was sickening. Yet another reason why she had to get away, get her head together.

When she reached the lobby, she heard a desultory clatter from the back regions and the smell of fresh coffee drifted past her nostrils. She hesitated. A cup of coffee would be very nice. Maybe Joe was up and about.

She put her suitcase down beside the registration desk and walked through the dining room where the drapes had been drawn across the tall windows leading to the side porch and the tables stood shrouded in ghostly ranks. As she neared the service door that led to the kitchen, she heard voices.

"But, my dear, you simply must realize that these people are afflicted with a form of lunacy." Anita recognized Leo Lemming's malicious piping. "They're not normal. If they were, they wouldn't be actors. You have to be a little bit crazy to want to be in the theater in the first place, and if you're not, the life soon makes you crazy. Be patient with them."

"I am patient, but there have already been complaints." The deep contralto belonged to Elena St. Cloud. Anita stood still in the shadowed doorway and listened. "First there comes a call from the family in the room beneath Glory Hayes. Bottles are being thrown around, smashing on the floor. The noise woke their baby up. This was around midnight. I telephoned, but there was no answer."

"Oh, dear," said Leo. "Temper tantrum, I expect. May I help myself to another cup of your wonder brew? It may make a man of me yet."

"That's not all," said Elena. "Later, I'm not sure what time it was, the phone rang again. This time it was Mrs. Cully, one of my old-timers, a widow, a very nervous woman. She was frightened to death, whispering. Something is going on next door. A woman is crying. There are thumps and bumps. She's sure someone is being killed and her turn is next. Her room is next to Tony Brand's. Leo, you must talk to them."

"Me!" Leo's shriek of mock dismay brought another flush of mortification to Anita's face. "Can it be," he inquired melodramatically, "that Mrs. Cully has forgotten, if she ever knew, that the transports of animal passion can sound like bloody murder? And you want me to be a spoilsport? At risk of life and limb, you want me to ask our star-crossed lovers to turn the volume down? There *will* be a murder if I do. Mine. And you'll be accessory before the fact."

"Leo, don't be silly," Elena began to protest, but Anita did not linger to hear the rest. She turned and ran back through the dining room to the lobby and, without stopping, out through the double front doors into the fog that blanketed Duck Creek.

Running. Away from the hotel. She couldn't see more than three feet in any direction. Away from Elena St. Cloud and Leo Lemming laughing in the kitchen. Away from Tony, Joe, all of them. Running down the cobblestoned street. The fog swirled around her, filling her mouth and nose with the choking odor of rotting fish. The street sloped downhill and she ran with the slope, her feet sliding on the wet stones. She slipped once and almost fell, catching herself just in time. Ahead, the foghorn groaned its warning. She remembered that the street led down to the marina. Boats. The houseboat. Larry Devine. No! Not that way! She wanted to see no one. To be where no one could see her. She turned off the cobblestones and found herself walking on sandy ground between clumps of coarse grass. The grass was tall enough to catch at her arms as she hurried past, its edges sharp enough to draw blood. She put a hand to her mouth and tasted salt.

A path. And somewhere, not too far away, the muffled sound of the lake slapping against the shore. She followed the path, treading cautiously, shying at small furtive movements in the grass. When it seemed that the path would go on forever

128

leading her deeper into endless fogbound sand dunes, a dark shape loomed up on one side and then another. The scent of wet pine needles billowed up at her and the path twisted its way among prickly branches that snatched at her hair. Above her head, the trees rustled and creaked unseen. The fog was even denser here, and the path difficult to follow as it wound around tree trunks and skirted the occasional boulder. Anita felt deprived of air. She took long gasping breaths but seemed not to be able to fill her lungs. A sensible notion urged her to turn back, that foggy mornings were not meant for aimless strolling, especially not in strange territory where she might fall off an unseen precipice or stumble into some unknown danger. She imagined eyes among the trees watching her, but she continued.

The trees ended as abruptly as they had begun. The path ran up to the edge of a rise and then dropped over. Although the fog still crowded thickly around her, she had a sense of standing on the verge of limitless space. Below, the lake splashed gently. Anita tried to guess at the height of the dune, the steepness of the descent. Impossible. She couldn't even see the water, although it sounded quite close by. How high could it be? Not as high as Everest. With a shrug, she launched herself down the side of the dune. After a brief sensation of stepping off into nothingness, she found herself sitting down with a thump at the bottom, sand in her shoes and out of breath. She was on the beach. Alone.

A good place to think. She got up, brushing the damp sand off the seat of her jeans, and walked toward the water's edge. The fog had taken on a yellowish tinge and was beginning to shred into tenuous wisps, swept by a faint breeze. If Tony needed her so much and demanded that she stay on in spite of her own wishes, then why had he spent a good part of the night with Glory Hayes? Anita had no doubt that he'd been part of the midnight commotion that had roused the sleeping baby on the floor below. After all, hadn't she heard Glory come in? And wasn't there someone with her? It must have been Tony. She cast her mind back to the night they had arrived, and Leo had insisted they go to Larry's houseboat for a drink. As tired as she was, she'd noticed Tony's edginess when Glory appeared on the scene. He'd become tense and wary and hauled her off to the hotel before the drinks had come round. Then later, after Glory had escaped safely from her encounter with the broken power line and the lights in the hotel had come back on, Tony had come to bed moody and uncommunicative. But Glory, when they brought her into the lounge, had been muttering something about Tony, something that was far from friendly. Then, oddly, the next day, yesterday, they'd both done a complete about face and were thick as thieves. At dinner last night, he couldn't keep his eyes off her. And later, when he finally did turn up, well after midnight, he looked as if he'd been in a brawl. Up in Glory's room. Some brawl.

Anita trudged along the waterline, brooding over the near certainty that Tony had leaped from Glory's bed to hers. Not that she expected utmost fidelity from any man. Life just wasn't that way anymore. But at least a little breathing space between. She, herself, was inclined to conduct her affairs one at a time. Maybe Tony wanted to spend the summer alternating between the two of them. Not if she could help it. Not another night.

The fog was beginning to lift and the yellow glow carried a hint of warmth. Anita raised her face gratefully to the sky where a concentration of light indicated that the sun was trying to break through. Along the beach, objects were becoming visible. She spotted a driftwood log a little distance away and halfway between the shore and the dunes that marched in undulating ranks into the hazy distance. She ran to it. It would be good to sit and rest for a while and let the sand out of her shoes. Somewhere a dog barked.

She dug her bare feet into the sand and gazed out over the lake. The steady lapping of the water against the shore had a soothing, almost hypnotic, effect and Anita began to feel calm and drowsy. She hugged her knees and rested her chin on them. It would be so easy to fall asleep, especially since she hadn't slept the night before. But she mustn't miss the bus. Ten minutes more and then she would start back.

But hardly five minutes had passed before she realized that she was staring at something at the water's edge, something that was all wrong in the still morning. Had it been there all along, hidden by the fog? Was it, indeed, what it seemed to be? She got up from the log and walked reluctantly across the sand down to the water. It's another piece of driftwood, she told herself. It just looks strange because it's been in the water so long. It's pale and smooth because the water's been working at it, and that long part lying out of the water is really a branch with a cluster of twigs at the end that only looks like a hand.

But it is a hand, and an arm, and there's the head and the rest of it still in the water and oh, God!

Running again! Back the way she had come. Wanting to scream but choking on it. Falling on her knees in the shallow water to vomit. Retching and shaking her head like a dog that had swallowed a bone. Then, weakly rising, turning to look back down the beach. A mistake? No. No mistake. But dead? A dead person? Maybe not dead. Oh, Lord! Running off like that when maybe help. . . . Back again. Grabbing the arm. Cold and wet. Pulling. Get the head out of the water. The body, face down, slithering and sliding in the lake's mild swell. How? Fell off a boat? An accident in the fog? What happened? Who? Up on the sand. Heavy. The skin so white. No clothes. Turn it over. A woman.

"Glory?"

Anita wiped her hands on her jeans. No help. No hope. Dead. Drowned. But how? Glory lay on her back on the sand, her green eyes staring up at the sky where a high haze was all that remained of the fog. Anita wanted to walk away, but she couldn't. She wanted to climb the dune, go back to the hotel, and get into bed beside Tony. She wanted never to have seen this beach, this lake, this thing lying half in and half out of the water. She wished the fog would come back and blot it all from her sight. But it didn't, and her eyes refused to give up examining what lay before them. The mouth set in that horrible grimace, the whole face blotchy and puffed, the ugly bruise on the jaw, the long pale throat with the narrow red line that ran from one side to the other and looked as if it might continue on around to the back of the neck. Why the bruise? Why that line? What had happened to Glory?

She forced one foot to take a backward step. And then another. Slowly, she backed away from the water, keeping her eyes on the long white shape as if it might float away or evaporate if she didn't watch it every moment. Suddenly, her heel struck something hard. She leaped and spun around, expecting, irrationally, to be surrounded by squads of policemen aiming riot guns at her. There was only the driftwood log and her shoes. All up and down the beach, there was nothing. No one. No curious accusing faces watching from the top of the dunes. No flotilla of boats pressing in from the open lake to see what she had seen. Only the wide water and the empty sand. To one side, the long bleached stones of the breakwater with the squat lighthouse at the end guarding the sheltered moorings of the marina. To the other, a high point of land fingered its way into the lake. She picked up her shoes and walked away.

The fog had thinned rapidly and now the sun, unveiled at last, appeared as a circle of hot white radiance pasted to the morning sky. She felt its heat on her face and on the soles of her bare feet as she trod the quickly warming sand. Absurdly, she thought, "I should bring her some suntan lotion. She has the kind of skin that burns."

The dune was not so high nor the walk so long as it had seemed in the fog. Among the pines, cool shadows and furtive rustlings. She hurried along the path, letting the branches snatch at her and scrape at her face, hoping the stinging needles would shock her mind into knowing what to do.

"What if Tony. . . ?" she thought. "Wouldn't it be better if I told him first? He might have. . . ."

No! It must have been an accident. Glory was unpredictable, impulsive. She may have decided to go for a midnight swim. Alone. Got into trouble. But it was raining last night. Nobody, not even Glory, goes swimming in the rain. And what about the bruise on her chin, the mark on her throat? Easy. She fell off the pier, struck her chin, got fouled in a mooring line. Then how did she get free to wash up on the beach? Oh, why couldn't she just ignore the whole thing, let someone else find Glory, get on the bus at eight-fifteen and be miles away before the questioning begins? Because, what if Tony. . . ?

At the inland edge of the stand of pines, she sat on a boulder to put her shoes on. Across the field of coarse grass and weeds, she could see the line of shanties that was Smokehouse Square. To her right, the rear fence of the marina, an ugly affair of shiny chain link with a frosting of barbed wire on the top, evidently designed to keep the land-bound summer people away from the polished decks and Styrofoam beer coolers of the boat folk. To her left, the peaks and gables of the hotel roof, its three stories and attic making it the tallest building in the town with the single exception of the Methodist Church steeple in the village square. She spotted the slanted glass panes of Joe St. Cloud's aerie and wondered if he were up there looking down on her.

What would it be? Raise the alarm, spread the news, broadcast her discovery to the proper authorities? Or warn Tony and see what his reaction would be? Or run away from this, as from everything else?

132

There was a side entrance to the hotel, a door that led off the side porch past some ground floor guest rooms to a back staircase used by the maids. Maybe she could get back up to the room without being seen. She got up from the boulder and walked away across the field, her head bowed and her hands automatically wiping themselves against her jeans. Behind her, the pines swayed and rustled and the soft crackling of quick footsteps on the fallen needles faded away unnoticed toward the beach.

CHAPTER XX

"Good morning! Isn't it a beautiful morning? Sunshine at last. I wonder if they have some of that delicious smoked trout for breakfast. I could eat a ton of that."

The fat woman waddled up the corridor, beaming like an overabundant ray of the sunshine that she extolled. This morning, she was all in golden yellow, a difficult color for most people and singularly unbeautiful on Tina Elliott. Her loose-fitting dress was the color of marigolds, her orange hair was bound in a yellow and red African style turban perhaps intended to make her look taller, and on her feet were yellow plastic mules. She carried a large yellow straw handbag.

Anita edged past her. "Yes, it is nice out. I've just been out on the porch."

"If you're going upstairs," said Tina Elliott, "would you tell Glory I have her script? She left it at the playhouse last night. Can't imagine how she's going to learn her lines if she leaves her script around like that."

"Sure," said Anita. The back stairs were only a few feet away. Anita started up them and then looked back over her shoulder. The fat woman was sailing past on her way to the dining room, a look of greedy anticipation on her face. Anita went on up the stairs.

Carry messages to Glory. Oh, sure. That was one message Glory would never receive. That was one script poor Glory would never have to learn. She hurried down the hall to her room. Hers and Tony's.

Tony wasn't in bed.

The imprint of his head on the pillow was cool to the touch, and the bedclothes had been flung back as if he had risen in a great hurry. The jeans and shirt he'd worn last night, still damp, were lying in a heap on the floor where he'd dropped them. But his shoes were nowhere in sight.

She opened the bathroom door and looked in. It was and looked no different than it had when she had her own unhappy face in the mirror. Was it only

135

She touched his towel and felt the bristles of his toothbrush. Both damp. His electric shaver lay on the shelf below the mirror, its cord plugged into the wall socket. But there was no sprinkling of black shaving crumbs in the sink basin. The shower curtain and bathtub were both dry. Therefore, he had washed and dressed quickly, just as she had done, and gone . . . where?

Aimlessly, she wandered about the bedroom, and then began picking up Tony's scattered clothes. She hung his damp shirt over the back of a chair. The jeans really needed to be washed. They were caked with a mixture of sand and mud. Maybe there was a launderette in town. She probed the pockets to be sure they were empty before washing. Three of them were. In the fourth, her fingers touched something hard, with a cord attached. She pulled it out. It was a polished stone, exactly like the ones she had seen up in Joe St. Cloud's room, but larger and this one hung from a leather thong. Joe had told her about the jewelry the townspeople made from the stones. Tony must have picked it up as a present for her and forgotten to give it to her. She slipped it over her head and went into the bathroom to study the effect in the mirror. It was a clumsy thing. The stone was too large and the thong too long. But the pattern of the stone was interesting. She held it away from her chest to examine it more closely. There was something caught in the metal prongs that gripped the stone and provided a loop for the thong to pass through. It looked like a piece of thread, or a hair. A hair. Golden blond. Just like. . . .

Anita heard the bedroom door open and close. She ripped the pendant from her neck and quickly stuffed it back into the pocket of the jeans which she then hung on a hook behind the bathroom door.

"Anita?" His voice was low and questioning.

"Right here." She came out of the bathroom. He was standing just inside the door, holding her suitcase.

"Where have you been?" he demanded. "And what's this all about?" He strode across the room and tossed the suitcase onto the bed.

"Tony!" She ran to him and clutched his arm. "It's all right. I'm not leaving. Forget about last night. I'm on your side."

"Well, good," he said slowly, "because you may have to stand in for Glory."

"Oh," she said, puzzled. "I never thought of that. Have

they . . . did you . . . did someone find her already?"

"Find her? She was never lost. She's locked herself in her room and won't come out. Says she has laryngitis and can't rehearse until she gets over it. Where did you go this morning?"

Anita backed away from him and sank into the plush armchair that stood like a throne beside the cold fireplace.

"I went for a walk," she said. "On the beach. To think things over." She paused for a moment, staring at him. "Tony, did you see her? This morning? Did you actually set eyes on Glory?"

Tony stretched and yawned and threw himself down on the bed. "No," he said, "but she woke me up at the crack of dawn. The telephone rang and there she was, croaking into my ear. You weren't here. I thought you'd run out on me." He punched his pillow into a plumper shape and then did the same to hers. "Hey, come on back to bed. It's still early."

Although she longed to do exactly that and pull the covers over her head, Anita stayed where she was. "You're sure it was Glory on the phone?" she asked. "I mean, couldn't it have been someone else pretending to be Glory?"

"No, why would anybody do that?" Tony smiled at her. "Don't worry about it. She's probably faking, but even if she isn't, she'll get over it. Laryngitis is hardly ever fatal. Anyway, I brought her a cup of tea and some orange juice, and left her to her misery."

"Then you *did* see her?"

"No. I told you. She won't open the door. I left a tray on the floor outside. I asked her if she wanted to see the doctor, but she said she didn't. I think if we all ignore her she'll get very healthy very quickly."

Anita pulled herself out of the chair and went to the bed, where she knelt on the floor beside Tony and let her head droop onto his chest.

"Oh, Tony," she whispered. "You can tell me. I won't tell anybody. Whatever you did, I'm sure you had good reason for it. But somebody's going to find her. Just like I did. And they'll go to the police and then there'll be all kinds of questions about how she died. I didn't *want* to be the one who found her."

"Hey, wait a minute!" Tony gripped her shoulders and held her upright, staring into her face. "What are you talking about? Glory's not dead. She's up in her room on the next floor enjoying ill health and creating a nuisance for everyone else."

"No, Tony. She's not," Anita insisted. "She's down on the beach, and she's dead. I thought she was drowned, but when I pulled her out of the water, I saw . . . I saw . . ." Anita began shaking. Her hands covered her mouth and her eyes lost focus as she visualized the scene on the beach.

Tony sat up and swung his legs over the side of the bed. He held her tightly and lifted her to sit beside him, cradling her in his arms. "Baby," he crooned, "don't upset yourself. But get this straight. Glory's upstairs. So she can't be down on the beach. She's not dead. She's very much alive and making a pain in the ass of herself. Now, I don't blame you for wishing her dead. After all, she did steal your job out from under your nose. But I think you just dreamed this whole thing, and the sooner you forget about it the better. Nobody's going to find her and nobody's going to call the police. Okay?"

Anita shook her head. "You're telling me I'm crazy. You're telling me I didn't really see what I know I saw." Her voice sank to a whisper. "I touched her, Tony. I'll never forget how it felt. Her arm was cold. Not like ice. Colder. I don't know how to explain it, but my hands feel like they'll never be warm again. It was real. Tony, I'd never seen a dead person before. Don't try to tell me I imagined it."

"Okay, you saw it." Tony stroked her hair tenderly and spoke softly. "Why didn't you scream, yell for help, call the police?"

"How do you know I didn't?"

"Did you?"

"No."

"Why not?"

"Oh, Tony," she sighed. "I'm so ashamed. Last night I was waiting for you. Along about midnight, I decided to go over to the playhouse. I started out, but before I could get down the stairs, I heard Glory come in. Someone was with her. I thought it was you. I didn't want you to think I was spying on you, so I ran back to the room. I sat here expecting you to come in any minute. But you didn't. So I guessed you were with her. When you finally did turn up, you were in one of your rotten moods and I was in no shape to be understanding. If I could have left last night, I'd be miles away by now. And I never would have gone to the beach this morning. But I did, and I saw her, and I thought . . . Tony. Tony was with her last night. That's why I didn't tell anybody. I wanted to tell you first.''

Tony laughed. ''Well, now you've told me. What do you want me to do about it?''

Anita shook her head, puzzled by his laughter. ''I don't know.''

He got up from the bed and pulled Anita to her feet. ''Come with me.''

''Where are we going?''

''Upstairs. You're going to talk to Glory and hear from her own lips that she's a poor sick creature suffering bravely for her art. Maybe we can even get her to open the door. Then, if you're still convinced you found a body on the beach, we'll just have to let the police find out who it is and how it got there. Maybe it's someone else, someone who just looks like Glory.''

Anita hung back, mutely shaking her head.

''What's wrong with that?'' Tony demanded. ''All I want you to do is get it through your head that Glory's alive and if not well, at least kicking.''

''I won't go up there,'' Anita muttered. ''Glory is dead. I think she was strangled and thrown in the lake last night. I don't think you did it, but I don't know where you were last night. If there's someone upstairs pretending to be Glory, then that someone is likely to be the killer and doesn't know the body's been found. Why don't you come down to the beach with me and see for yourself?''

''All right, I will,'' said Tony. ''And as for where I was last night, it's very simple. We rehearsed until almost one o'clock. I walked back from the playhouse with Hilda Kramer and we got to talking about . . . things. I spent about an hour with her in her room. Perfectly innocent. And not a peep out of Glory, who, as you may recall, lives right next door to Hilda. But she couldn't peep very loudly if she'd been strangled and dumped in the lake, as you so fervently wish. You didn't, by any chance, do it yourself, did you? Is all of this some round-about way of confessing that you've done in your arch rival?''

''Tony, it's not funny.'' She went to the door. ''Let's go. It wouldn't surprise me if there were hordes of people on the beach by now, all milling about and staring at poor Glory.''

Tony followed her out into the corridor, locking the door behind him. ''Either way,'' he remarked, ''dead or alive, it looks as if you'll have to take over for her. That ought to remove some of your gloom. I hope you don't mind that I carted your suitcase back upstairs. Unless you're still planning to make a getaway."

It occurred to Anita to ask him why, if he'd spent an hour or so in Hilda Kramer's room, he was drenched to the skin when he came to bed. And what about the stone pendant in the pocket of his jeans? Where had that come from? And how did it happen to have a long golden blond hair caught in it? Too many questions. Anita wasn't sure she wanted to know the answers.

At the landing, they met Hilda Kramer on her way down to breakfast. Tony greeted her affectionately, with a peck on the cheek and a quick hug.

"Morning, Duchess. You're looking gorgeous, as usual. What's the latest on our invalid?"

Hilda shrugged. "Not too sick to play the radio at top volume."

As they descended the stairs, Anita caught Hilda's arm, letting Tony go on before them.

"Did you see her this morning? How does she look?"

"See her!" Hilda exclaimed. "I don't need to see her. I can hear her. Rock music! My ears are still hurting."

Tony stood waiting at the foot of the stairs. In the dining room across the lobby, breakfasters were gathering. The doors to the side porch were open, and Leo Lemming stood at one of them chatting with Peverill Martin. Tina Elliott was already seated at the large center table, busy with knife and fork. Other early-rising guests of the hotel were dotted about. The only absentees were Glory Hayes, who was either skulking in her room or lying dead on the beach, and Larry Devine, who always breakfasted aboard his boat.

"Will you join me?" asked Hilda, nodding toward the dining room.

"Thanks," said Tony, "but we're going for a little jog on the beach. Nothing like exercise to perk up the appetite."

"And beachcombing," Anita added. "You never know what you'll find on a beach after a rainstorm."

Anita watched the older woman closely for any reaction to her statement. If anyone ought to know what had happened to Glory, her next-door neighbor should be the one. But Hilda merely shrugged and smiled.

"Enjoy yourselves, children," she said. "For me, getting up each morning is exercise enough."

As Tony and Anita went through the lobby toward the front

door, Joe St. Cloud looked up from the newspapers he was stacking into a rack beside the registration desk. He beckoned to Anita.

"Message for you," he said.

As he went behind the desk, Anita was strongly tempted to lay the whole problem on his blue denim shoulders. But Tony was waiting for her at the door, and the lobby was a little too public to discuss real or imagined bodies on beaches.

Joe took an envelope from a numbered mail slot and handed it to her. "The bus is due in a few minutes," he remarked.

"I think I'm going to miss it."

"Good."

"You think so?"

"As my ancestor said, 'If you run from the Bear, his shadow is long and will reach your lodge before you do.'"

"Smart ancestor."

"Thanks. I just made it up."

"Smart you. Oh, by the way, you know those stones you told me get made into jewelry? If I wanted to buy some, where would I go?"

"Petoskeys? Most of the shops in Smokehouse Square have them. And almost any kid in town is a dealer. They set up on street corners the way kids in other towns set up lemonade stands."

"Petoskeys. Thanks." Anita glanced at the envelope Joe had handed her. On it, her name was scrawled in red marking pen, the thick script trickling across the white paper like a trail of blood.

Tony was waiting for her on the porch. She went out to him and showed him the unopened envelope.

"Do you suppose it's a fan letter?" she asked.

"Or an invitation to a pow-wow from the friendly savage. What was that all about? Should I be jealous?"

"Shopping hints. Local artifacts. Souvenirs of carefree days in Duck Creek." She turned the envelope over, but there was nothing on the back. "Who would be writing me letters? I don't recognize the handwriting. Do you?"

"Why don't you open it and find out?"

"Not a bad idea."

She ripped open the envelope and drew out two folded sheets of paper. Both sheets were covered with the sprawling red script. She turned away from Tony to read.

"Dear Anita," the first page began. "It's only fair that you

141

should be the first to know. I'm leaving. I only came out to this dreary hole because I had nothing better to do. Well, now I have. My agent called last night to tell me that I'm up for a very important movie role. Hallelujah! So it's home to Hollywood for little me, and you're welcome to fuckass Duck Creek and all it's rural charm. I know you really wanted the job, and that's why I'm letting you know first. So you can just jump right in when they find out I've skipped. I appreciate your keeping it under your wig unitl after I'm gone. I'm going to have a bout of laryngitis so I can get packed and out of here without going through a long taradiddle with Devine about broken contracts and other boring details. Hope you don't think I was after your Tony's delicous body. Tempting as it is, he's a little too broody for my taste. Your friend (?), Glory Hayes.''

Anita folded the pages and replaced them in the envelope, which she stuffed into the pocket of her Chinese jacket.

''Let's go down to the baech,'' she said.

''What is it?'' Tony eyed her quizzically, a smile flickering around his wide mouth. ''A mash note? Obscene suggestions? Blackmail?''

Anita shook her head. ''Tell you later.''

The fog had completely burnt away, and the sun sparkled brilliantly on the lake. Anita expected at any moment sirens would wail and a fleet of police cars and ambulances would converge on the dunes above the beach. Surely by now someone would have gone down ot the water's edge and seen the same pitiful sight that she had seen earlier. But the morning remained tranquil as she led Tony across the grassy field and through the stand of pines.

When they raeched the rim of the dune, Anita hung back and let Tony go first. He stood on the rise overlooking the lake and shaded his eyes against the glare of the sun on the water.

''How far up the beach did you go?'' he asked.

''Not far. It seemed a long way in the fog. But when I came back, it was no distance at all.''

Anita stood slightly behind him and looked down at the beach below. Curving away to the north, the shoreline stretched untenanted except for a dog that romped in the distance. His barking reached their ears as a faint disturbance of the clear bright air.

''I don't see anything,'' said Tony. ''Do you?''

''No.''

"Well, let's go down and take a closer look."

Tony led the way down the slope, moving in long sliding strides. Anita followed less eagerly. Something was wrong. The beach was as vacant as if it had just been created. At the bottom of the dune, Tony took her hand and they began slogging through the sand to the water's edge. The lake lapped peacefully at the shore. Far out on the water, a freighter hung motionless. A clutter of shore birds, annoyed at their presence, squawked angrily and then flapped off to a more private pecking ground. They walked slowly on the wet sand.

"You pulled her out of the water. Is that right?"

"Yes. And I turned her over and saw her face."

"So she ought to be right at the water's edge. Can't you remember anything to mark the place?"

"I wasn't thinking about landmarks. Tony, do you suppose she could have floated out into the lake again?"

"Possible. But the water's pretty calm. Was it still foggy when you found her?"

"Some. It was beginning to lift. I sat on a log to let the sand out of my shoes. When I looked up, she was there. At first, I thought it was just a piece of driftwood."

"Are you sure it wasn't?"

"Of course, I'm sure. And there's the log." Anita broke away and ran up the beach away from the water. When she reached the log, she turned triumphantly to Tony, who followed slowly looking thoughtful. "Here's where I sat and took my shoes off," she announced, "and there's where I found her." She pointed down to the water.

"Anita. There's nothing there. Look."

"No. You look. She's got to be there. Look in the water. She didn't get up and walk away."

Tony took her hand. "Anita, babe," he said, "let's go back to the hotel. I'll bring you breakfast in bed. You take it easy today. Tomorrow you'll feel better."

Anita wrenched her hand away. "Don't treat me like an invalid!" she flared. "I know what I saw!" She ran away from him, straight to the water's edge and into the lapping wavelets.

"Here! Here! Here!" she screamed, plunging her arms into the lake. In the knee-deep icy water, she flailed about, searching for the object she knew must be there. Her hands met nothing but the chill resistance of the water. She waded deeper, feeling the tug of the lake at her sodden clothing, but nothing else. No body. Nothing but sand and pebbles beneath her feet. At last, she stood still, shivering. The water reached her waist. Tony, waiting patiently on the shore, was looking at her with an expression of great sadness on his face.

"Come out now," he said.

Slowly she came out. Her arms and legs felt leaden as she surged through the few feet of water to the shore. She let him guide her away from the lake and across the sand back the way they had come. Neither one spoke. At the foot of the dune, she stopped and looked back.

"She was there, Tony."

"Sure, babe. Can you make it up the hill?"

"She was there. And now she's gone. Someone moved her."

"Christ, Anita! You really are crazy! If the facts don't fit your story, you just invent some new ones. Can't you hear how crazy it sounds? Who in their right minds would cart a corpse around in broad daylight? It just doesn't happen. Now let's get back to the hotel and get you into bed. Your clothes are all wet. I don't want you catching a cold."

She made it up the hill and back to the hotel with Tony hovering protectively every step of the way. As they walked through the lobby, Anita was conscious of the water dripping from her clothes and of Leo Lemming eyeing them curiously from the dining room where he lingered over his clipboard and coffee cup.

"Rehearsal at nine o'clock, Tony," he called.

Tony nodded and shepherded Anita up the stairs. On the second floor landing, they met Elena St. Cloud on her way down from the third floor with a tray in her hands.

"Miss Hayes has no appetite this morning," she remarked.

"She's not feeling well," said Tony.

Anita glanced at the tray which held a cup brimming with cold clouded tea and an untouched glass of orange juice. She said nothing. Tony's arm tightened around her shoulders.

"We've had a little accident," Tony offered, when he saw Elena pondering the trail of wet footprints that followed them up the stairs.

"Yes. I stupidly fell in the lake," Anita added. "Sorry about the mess."

"It's nothing. It will dry," said Elena. "Are you all right? The lake is still very cold at this time of year."

"I'll live," said Anita.

"She's just chilled," said Tony. "We'll get her out of these wet clothes and into bed for a while. That should do it.''

Elena nodded and continued on her way downstairs. Tony propelled Anita along the corridor to their room. Once inside, he deposited her in the mammoth armchair and knelt at her feet to remove her shoes. The wet laces were difficult to untie, and while he struggled with them she leaned forward to place a cold hand on his arm.

"She's not in her room, is she, Tony?"

He made no answer.

"She's not in her room and she's not on the beach. Where is she, Tony?"

"Don't ask me." He pulled off one shoe and began working on the other. "She was there earlier."

"Where? On the beach or in her room? Who's crazy? Me or you?"

"Don't ask so many questions." The other shoe was off and the dripping socks followed. "Stand up, now. We'll get you out of this gear and into something dry."

"My robe is in the suitcase."

As Tony went to fetch it, Anita stood up and began struggling with her wet clothing. She was trembling with chill, fatigue, and nerves, and with the certainty that Tony was somehow involved in whatever had befallen Glory Hayes. Despite his insistence that she was alive and barricaded in her room, Anita was convinced that he knew what had happened to her and where her body was hidden. It was so obvious, now that she thought about it, that someone had removed the body from the beach. It must have been Tony. But if Tony had moved the body, why had he let her go through the awful charade of searching for it? Just to make her doubt the evidence of her own senses? But why? What would he gain from that? Had he, or someone else, been skulking about in the fog and seen her pull Glory from the lake? Oh, it was too confusing, and right now all she wanted to do was get these dratted shirt buttons unbuttoned and get into bed where it was warm and dry.

Tony came back to her with her robe slung over his shoulder.

"Let me do that," he said. And in minutes, she was bundled into her robe and tucked snugly into bed with two pillows behind her head and the promise of breakfast on a tray as soon as the kitchen could be moved to provide it.

"Don't bother, Tony," she said. "I don't think I could eat, and you shouldn't be late for rehearsal."

"The show must go on, mustn't it," he said drily. "Right you are. I'm off. You rest, babe. And no more questions. Okay?"

Anita, feeling very much a chastened small child, allowed him to adjust the blanket and plant a small kiss on her brow.

"Want something to read?" he asked.

"No, thanks. I'll try to sleep."

She watched him tiptoe from the room, closing the door softly behind him. For a while, she lay still, just as he had left her, listening to the obscure noises of the old hotel. There were quick, muffled footsteps overhead. Through the open window, she heard Leo Lemming prattling his way off to the theater, a short walk up the lane that ran behind the hotel. The entire company of the Duck Creek Playhouse would be gathered at the theater at nine o'clock sharp. Everyone but Glory Hayes. According to Tony's bedside travel alarm clock, it was now five minutes before the hour. She lay still while around her plumbing gurgled faintly, distant clashes from the kitchen told her of pots being scrubbed, and a shaft of sunlight crept slowly across the floor. When the shaft of sunlight struck the leg of the armchair, she got out of bed and got dressed.

CHAPTER XXI

Some people will do anything to gain a little notoriety for themselves. Climb the World Trade Center, go over Niagara Falls in a barrel, swim the Hellespont, confess to a murder they didn't commit, confess to a murder they *did* commit.

That's not my way. But it would certainly get results. I can just see the headlines, hear the voices of the television newscasters oozing my name from coast to coast. Instant fame and somewhat dubious glory. Oh, that's a good one.

"Why did you do it?"

"For the dubious glory."

With stunning repartee like that, I should at least be able to get on the Johnny Carson show.

And why not? Anything would be better than this continued nonentity. Anything? Think about it. The sequence of events. First, the highly dramatic confession scene. Everyone astounded. Dramatis personae: The police chief or sheriff or whatever they have in this backwater, and his minions. Bet they've never had to deal with a confessed murderer before. The entire company of the Duck Creek Playhouse forming a kind of Greek chorus to comment on the action. Next, the sordid incarceration scene, the squalid cell, the monotonous diet, the sadistic guards. Sad and dreary. Ah, but then, the trial scene. Everyone loves a courtroom drama. I wonder if they would allow the TV cameras into the courtroom. At least the newspaper photographers. If not, I want Hirschfeld to do the sketches. I've always wanted to be caricatured by Hirschfeld. And afterward? Prison? Could it be any worse than the treadmill of endless auditions to get one stinking job? I could organize my fellow prisoners into a theater group. We'd be so good, they'd let us out to perform for the public. We'd be written up in newspapers and magazines. Maybe Truman Capote or Norman Mailer would write a book about me. All very nice, but not precisely the kind of notices I once hoped for.

In the meantime. In the meantime, it's business as usual.

Until, as Hamlet said of Polonius, they nose her as they go up the stairs. Hamlet was driven mad by murder and murdered in his madness. But was he mad or feigning madness? I have no convenient ghost to cry "Revenge!" and urge me on to bloody deeds. But isn't it revenge all the same? Revenge upon the future because it has no place for me?

In the meantime, open the script and get on with it. Here's Leo, bursting with news. An announcement is about to be made. Prepare to be astounded.

"Glory is unwell this morning."

Unwell!

"She appears to be suffering from laryngitis."

A very sore throat.

"She's resting today, and if you all can bear the shock, I'll walk through her part so we can finish the blocking."

Rest in peace.

"Second act beginners on stage. Everybody else, stand by."

Standing by. Don't do anything rash. The script is taking an unexpected direction.

148

CHAPTER XXII

The third floor corridor was deserted, but there was no telling how long it would remain that way. Anita tiptoed down its length to the door of Room 304 where a "Do Not Disturb" sign dangled from the doorknob. She knocked softly and listened.

There was no sound from within. She knocked again, harder. Still, there was no response. Tentatively, she tried the doorknob, turning it first one way and then the other, and pushing slightly at the door. It remained firm. Locked.

Feeling ridiculous, she called out, "Glory? Glory, are you there?"

It was insane to be calling on a dead woman to open the door, but Anita felt she had to give Tony the benefit of the doubt. Two nights ago, Glory had practically accused Tony of trying to kill her by somehow causing the power line to fall just as she was passing beneath it. Anita had dismissed the idea as hysteria, the need to blame someone for what was obviously an accident. But what if there were some truth in it? This morning, after Tony had left for rehearsal, Anita had gone out onto the veranda where Tony had been standing that night when the lights went out. Their room was at the end of the second floor, a corner room, and the veranda came to an end just beyond the French window that gave access to it. She stood at the railing and looked across the street to where the new power line was attached to its pole. Following the line back to the hotel, she saw that it stretched over her head and was connected to the corner of the building in a series of insulators that could easily be reached by a tall person standing on the veranda railing. Tony was a tall person.

But that was absurd. In the first place, why would he do it? And in the second place, how could he be sure that the line would fall in just the right place and at just the right moment? Still, if Glory hadn't been wearing that rubberized raincoat. . . . Everyone said it was an accident. Everyone but Glory, and even she came round after the initial shock. But

149

suppose it wasn't an accident? Suppose Tony *had* cut the wire? Suppose he'd been out on the veranda waiting for her to return to the hotel? But what had he cut it with? He would have needed some kind of insulated wire-clippers, and there was no such thing, as far as she knew, in their combined luggage, and no opportunity for him to find one. But suppose the line was frayed, and only a quick tug or a sharp blow with a stick was enough to rip it from its connection? No, that wouldn't work either. It had been dark when they arrived. Tony'd had no chance to see that the line was there, let alone that it was frayed. No, it had to be an accident.

All right. But suppose the accident had put the idea into someone's head. Not necessarily Tony, but someone who wanted Glory out of the way. Like herself. Now that really was ridiculous. All these suppositions and suspicions led to false conclusions. *She* hadn't murdered Glory. Of that, at least, she was positive. But someone else might reach the same false conclusion based on the fact that she alone, out of all these people, had been done out of a job by Glory Hayes. Murder had been done for far less, and even Tony had hinted, jokingly, that she might have wanted Glory dead.

It was then that Anita decided to go up to Glory's room. If there were someone in there, whether or not they opened the door, she would know that Tony wasn't lying to her. If someone answered from behind the closed door, she could simply walk away, curiosity satisfied. Or if Glory herself opened the door, she could pretend she was there to inquire about her health. But how could she? She was dead. So, if no one answered, she would try to get into the room and find out whatever she could.

So it was that after twisting the knob and calling Glory's name with no result, she took from her pocket the large old-fashioned iron room key tagged with her own room number, and slotted it into the keyhole. Sometimes these old keys worked interchangeably. At first it refused to turn, but after a bit of jiggling, all the while glancing nervously over her shoulder and listening for footsteps on the stairs or the opening of another door down the corridor, she felt a slight amount of give, twisted the key quickly, and heard the tongue of the lock click back. She pushed the door open and, standing in the doorway, tried to remove the key from the lock. But no matter how she twisted and turned, the stubborn piece of iron remained snugly lodged in the keyhole. Perhaps she had bent it while trying to open the door. Leaving the key in place, she closed the door. She felt uneasy about not being able to lock the door while she searched Glory's room. Anybody could walk in on her. But at least there was no one on this side of the door. That had been obvious at first glance.

No one. And no sign of anyone having occupied the room. No suitcases, no personal belongings on the dresser. The bed was neatly made. Quickly, Anita went to the closet and opened it. Only empty hangers hung on the rod. She opened the dresser drawers one after the other, with the same result. Nothing. In the bathroom, there were two towel bars with towels draped over each. Only one set was damp. An ancient flannel robe hung from a hook behind one door. Certainly not Glory's style. The hook on the other door, the one through which she had entered, was empty. She remembered that Hilda Kramer shared this bathroom with Glory. One toothbrush, one tube of toothpaste, and a jar of cleansing cream in the medicine chest. On the rim of the huge bathtub, a container of Vita-Bath. But the bathroom smelled faintly of a heavier flowery scent. Nothing there to account for it. As she went to try the other door, the door to Hilda Kramer's room, she felt something gritty underfoot.

She stepped back and looked down. The tiny hexagonal floor tiles swam dizzily before her eyes, creating an optical illusion of pyramidal steps, come climbing toward her and then, as she blinked, reversing themselves and plunging away. She knelt to see what she had stepped on, and was rewarded by a sharp pain in her right knee. When she lifted the knee from the floor and examined it, she found embedded in the blue denim of her jeans a tiny sliver of glass. She picked it out and laid it in her palm. Nothing much to be learned from squinting at it, but broken glass was one of the hardest things in the world to clean up thoroughly. Maybe there was more of it.

Remembering the baby on the floor below who had been woken at midnight by the crash of breaking glass, Anita bent to a closer examination of the tile floor. She had assumed that the breaking of glass had meant a party for two in progress, booze bottles dropping from hasty hands in a sudden surge of drunken passion. Bad enough, if Tony happened to be the passionate drunk. But what if it meant a struggle, here in the bathroom, and the breaking glass had been tumblers, bottles of bath oil, jars of whatever Glory used to anoint her sumptuous body, all swept crashing to the floor while Glory gasped for

151

breath with a tightening cord around her throat. A cord. The thong. The leather thong in Tony's pocket attached to the Petoskey stone pendant with the golden hair embedded in its metal prong.

Oh, God! No wonder he insisted that she was still up here, alive and well except for a bad case of laryngitis. No wonder he was so positive that there would be no body on the beach. Of course not. He'd moved it. He must have been right behind her in the fog. He must have hidden in the grove of pine trees and gone down to the beach as soon as she'd left. But where? Where can you take a body, a naked body, with the sun burning away the fog and at any moment an early-rising Duck Creek resident liable to come moseying along on a morning ramble? And above all, why? Why had Tony, for now it was no longer a vague suspicion, why had Tony killed Glory?

Her head buzzing with unanswered questions, Anita groped behind the pedestal of the sink, tentatively, fearing cobwebs or, worse, the soft scuttling of insects that live in dark damp corners. Her fingers encountered something hard and sharp-edged. She picked it up and drew it from its hiding place. It was a curved piece of glass, jagged at one end, but at the other a double thickness of a perfect oval shape no more than an inch and a half across its long diameter. Undoubtedly, the bottom and part of one side of a small bottle. She sniffed the fragment. A heavy sweet scent clung to it. Impossible to remember if the scent was one that she could associate with Glory.

The voice blared out of the silence of the empty bedroom. "Glory? Are you there?"

Anita leaped to her feet, clutching the shard of glass. She hadn't heard the outer door open, but now she heard soft footfalls and a harsh wheezing in the other room, then the sound of drawers opening and closing and the clicking latch of the closet door. Someone was searching Glory's room, just as she had done. Soon the searcher would try the bathroom. The only way to avoid being caught was to slip out through the other connecting door into Hilda Kramer's room. She moved swiftly, and she hoped soundlessly, to the opposite door and turned its knob. Locked. From the other side. No way out and nowhere to hide. The only thing left for her was to brazen it out, think of some acceptable excuse to be snooping around in a room where, in all probability, a murder had been done. But so far, she was the only one who knew about it. She and the killer. Tony. The bathroom door shivered open.

Anita gasped with relief. "Oh, it's you."

"Well, where is she? I came all the way up here to give her her script and she's not here." Tina Elliott was breathing heavily and looking extremely put upon. "It's no joke, let me tell you, for me to climb all those stairs. What did she do, change her room? Wasn't this one good enough for her? Larry wants her to study the script while she's recovering from her laryngitis. Laryngitis, my foot. If you ask me, she's got a bad case of swollen head."

"I don't know where she is," said Anita. And *that's* the dismal truth, she commented to herself. "She certainly seems to have cleared out of here."

"I can see that for myself," said Tina Elliott. "Here, what did you do to your hand? You're bleeding all over the floor."

Anita looked down. She was, indeed, bleeding all over the floor, and the blood kept on welling out from between the fingers of her clenched hand. She opened her hand and the shard of glass fell with a tinkling sound onto the tiles. Until that moment, she had not felt any pain, but now the open cut stung unmercifully.

"Well, don't just stand there," said the fat woman. "Put it in the sink. Run some cold water on it. Don't you have a handkerchief? Never mind. We'll use one of these towels."

Anita did as she was told, while Tina fetched a towel and held it ready to bind up the wounded hand once the blood had been rinsed away.

"Thank you," said Anita, after the towel had been securely wrapped and fastened with a safety pin which Tina magically produced from somewhere inside her voluminous garment.

"Hold it up, so the bleeding stops. You ought to put some antiseptic on it, and a bandage. I don't think it needs stitches. What on earth were you doing to yourself?"

"It was just . . . I found a piece of broken glass. I was going to throw it away. Where did it go?"

Tina Elliott stooped with surprising agility for her size. "This it? I'll just toss it in the wastebasket."

She returned to the bedroom and made straight for the wastebasket at one side of the small writing desk. Anita followed with her swaddled hand held stiffly upright.

"Ho!" said Tina. "What's this?" Again, she stooped with a quick bird-like movement and scooped something from the wastebasket. A fat fistful of crumpled papers. "Well, now.

Here's something. Let's see what we have here."

She smoothed the papers out on the desk. Even without going any closer, Anita could see that they were covered with sprawling red handwriting. The same handwriting that covered the two sheets of paper that were folded in the pocket of her Chinese jacket.

She watched as Tina Elliott pored over the papers, not daring to seem too interested in what was written there. Abruptly, Tina gave a hoot of laughter and crumpled the papers up again.

"Oh, the idiot child. Would you believe that she was practicing her autograph? That's what it looks like. Nothing but Glory Hayes, Glory Hayes, over and over again. Well, good luck to her." Tina stuffed the wadded papers into a pocket where they disappeared without a trace among the ample folds of her dress. "I'll get rid of them downstairs. And now," she turned to Anita, "what did you say you were doing here?" Her eyes were shiny black buttons perched on top of the pillows of her cheeks.

"I came to see if I could . . . if she needed anything. What about you? Aren't you supposed to be at rehearsal?"

Tina plopped herself down on the bed and picked up the play script that was lying there. "Oh," she said, "I don't have much to do in the second act. But I've been carting this around since last night." She fanned the pages, and Anita caught glimpses of marginal notes done in red marking pen. "She's got a lot of lines to learn and Larry wanted her to be working on them while she's ill. Can you imagine just going off and leaving your script behind after the first rehearsal? He asked me to see that she got it. Now I don't know what to do with it."

"I'll take care of it, if you like," Anita offered. "If she did change rooms, I'll find out downstairs and see that she gets it. Or maybe she moved over to that new place on the other side of the marina. Maybe she just up and left. What do you think?"

"Frankly, my dear, I don't give a damn." Tina chuckled and got up from the bed. "Always knew I'd have an occasion to use that line. It's a great line, and in this case, it's the absolute truth. If she has left, good riddance. I'm sure you, of all people, will agree."

Tina waddled to the door, handing the script to Anita in passing. "If you don't find her, hang onto it. You may need it.

154

I don't think we can stand many more rehearsals with Leo camping his way through her part. Take care of that hand. You don't want to get blood poisoning." Tina left.

"Thanks," Anita called after her.

As the fat woman trundled away down the stairs, Anita took one final look round the empty room. Glory Hayes might never have existed for all the impression she had made on it. Lordy, if only that were true. Now the problem was Tony. How to let him know that she wasn't going to do anything to threaten him. That she would lie for him and tell the world that he was with her from the moment he left rehearsal last night. That she loved him enough to perjure herself if necessary. If she could produce some firm piece of evidence that he had been in this room last night, then he would have to tell her the whole story including why he'd done it and where he'd hidden the body. If only Tina Elliott hadn't pocketed those scraps of paper, she could have compared them with the note she had received that morning and with Tony's handwriting. Obviously, someone had been practicing Glory's signature on those scraps. Still, she now had Glory's script and could compare the note with the marginal jottings and at least prove that they came from two different hands. Even if she couldn't prove that Tony had forged the note.

But first she had to get back into her own room, the key to which was firmly stuck in the keyhole of Room 304. Well, she'd got it in and opened the door with it, and now she was damn' well going to get it out. She stood in the corridor outside Glory's room, twisting the key this way and that. It wouldn't budge. She could neither lock the door nor remove the key. Nor could she just walk off and leave it there.

"Can I help you?"

"Oh, my God! I wish you wouldn't creep up on people."

"Can't help it. Some people got rhythm. Indian walks in quiet moccasins. What's the trouble?"

"Key's stuck." She glanced up at Joe St. Cloud, daring him to ask her what she was doing getting a key stuck in a door that wasn't her own, and gave the key a final despairing twist. It turned in the lock and slid smoothly out into her hand. "Well, what do you know? Now it's unstuck."

"How is Miss Hayes? I heard she wasn't feeling well."

"Oh, ah, she'll be all right. She's sleeping now." Only half a lie, Anita thought. She won't ever be all right, but she's certainly sleeping.

"Good," said Joe. "Elena was a bit worried. She gave Tony some red clover tea to take to her this morning. Later, she came up to see if she could do anything else. But no one answered the door, and the tea hadn't been touched. She's been telephoning off and on, but still no answer. She asked me to look in and see if something is seriously wrong." Joe dangled a master key from a ring of other important-looking keys.

"Um, no," said Anita. "That won't be necessary. It's only that she can't talk and she doesn't want to see anyone. I wouldn't disturb her now. She's resting quietly." How easy it is, she thought, to tell these little half-truths, these not-quite-lies. You'd think I'd been practicing all my life. But now I've committed myself to Tony's big lie. And now, Tina Elliott knows that Glory's not in her room. I wonder how quickly *that'll* get around. We'll have to come up with a good story to explain that.

"You're sure there's nothing I can do?" Joe asked.

"Positive."

"What's wrong with your hand?"

"Oh, it's nothing. Just a cut. I'm afraid I'm bleeding all over a hotel towel."

"Don't worry about it. Come on upstairs and I'll bandage it for you. I'm qualified to give first aid."

"No!" Anita avoided his questioning eyes and edged away from the door. "I mean, all it needs is a Band-Aid. I think I've got some in my room."

"Okay."

Joe stood in the middle of the corridor, watching her run toward the head of the stairs. Before she could start down, he called to her.

"Anita!"

She turned.

"If you need help, remember where the doctor's office is."

She ran down the stairs.

CHAPTER XXIII

Leo, have you seen the key to the prop room?"

Emmy Jackson bobbled up the center aisle, her arms full of flowing satin and rich velvet.

"Is there one? I never knew we kept our treasure house locked. There's nothing up there worth a bean."

"Well, that's just it." Emmy lowered herself into one of the front row seats beside Leo and almost disappeared beneath the enormous heap of fabric. "It's never been locked before as far as I can remember, but when I went up there just now, I couldn't get the door open. I wanted to get out some of those old fans and parasols."

"Maybe the door's just warped and stuck. It's been awfully damp in this part of the world."

"Maybe," said Emmy, "or maybe somebody locked it by mistake. How do you like this velvet? Isn't it pretty? 'Course it's really only velveteen, but it looks so scrumptious. Can't you just see it on Glory?"

"Scrumptious is the word for it, Emmy, darling. And wouldn't I look fetching in a plum velvet gown with ecru lace cascading o'er my heaving bosom? I think I could play this role every bit as winsomely as Miss Glory Hayes. If she doesn't watch her step, I may just snatch it away from her the way she snatched it away from Anita Stratton. Do you think the audience could tell the difference?" Leo thrust forward his thin chest and arranged his mouth into a wet-lipped pout.

Emmy Jackson's own motherly bosom heaved with stifled laughter. "Leo, you're naughty. You shouldn't make me laugh at the poor girl when she's so sick and all."

"Ah, well," sighed Leo. "You'll probably dress me up in sober black broadcloth and make me look like an undertaker. Can't I at least carry a parasol?"

Emmy giggled. "How about a walking stick? I think we have a few of those upstairs."

"How about a sword cane? Then I could puncture her bustle every time she goofs up. She'll look like a pin cushion before the summer's over."

"Well," Emmy struggled to her feet. "I want to get this stuff home and start cutting on it." She pulled a full-skirted gray satin gown from the bundle and held it up. "Seems a shame to cut this up. I remember when we made these. Six of them, all alike. But I guess it's a good thing we have six. It may take all of them to make one gown for Tina."

Leo leaped to his feet in mock dismay. "Horrors!" he exclaimed. "Is that my own sweet Emmy darling uttering words of sordid sarcasm? My virgin ears are blushing pinkly."

"Oh, Leo!" Emmy's cheeks turned the color of ripe tomatoes. "I didn't mean . . . well, what I meant was. . . . Oh, fiddlesticks, we really will have to use all of them, what with the sleeves and all. I really like Tina. She's good-hearted and she can't help it if she's chubby. She told me it was glandular. Anyway, I'm leaving now, but I'll be back later this afternoon. You will try to find that key, won't you?"

"Oh, sure." Leo settled back down with his clipboard and made a note. "There we are. Find prop room key. I vaguely remember some kind of mystery key box that we inherited with the place. It might be in there. I'll poke around the office and see what crops up. If worse comes to worse, I'll batter the door down for you with my own brute strength."

"Oh, Leo!" With a final barrage of giggles, Emmy Jackson toddled away to organize her sewing ladies.

158

CHAPTER XXIV

Back in her room, Anita pulled the towel from her hand. The bleeding had stopped, but the cut was in an awkward place on her palm and every time she opened or closed her hand, it began oozing again. Fortunately, it was her left hand, so it wouldn't prove to be too much of a nuisance. There were no Band-Aids in the room, despite what she had told Joe St. Cloud, but Tony had a supply of brand-new handkerchiefs. She took one from his drawer and managed to tie it around her hand, using her teeth to pull the knot tight.

Then she looked around the room for her Chinese jacket. Not in the closet, not thrown over a chair. She remembered that Tony had helped her undress after the abortive trip to the beach from which she had come back soaking wet. Soaking wet! She ran into the bathroom. The jacket was hanging from the shower rod, dripping into the tub. Some of the drips were pale pink and the pocket of the blue jacket was stained an ugly purple color. With her good hand, she reached into the pocket and pulled out a sodden square of paper. The envelope was streaked with red and when she unfolded it, its flaps opened out like wings where the glue had lost its sticking power. The two pages inside were blotched and blurred. It was evident that words had once been written there. Among the blotches, there were peaks and valleys and rounded trails of bright red. But not a single word was legible. All had rippled and flowed into a senseless red blur. The letter was no more readable than the towel she had removed from her bleeding hand. She dropped it into the sink.

She remembered only too well what the note had said—that Glory was only pretending to have laryngitis until she could make her getaway back to Hollywood where there was an important movie role waiting for her— but now there was no chance of comparing it with Glory's handwriting in the script. Evidently, Tony was trying to make it look as if Glory had split without a word to anyone. Except for the note. Which she, Anita, was supposed to produce on cue and then everyone would write Glory off as a deserter. And there would be no further inquiry into her disappearance. Except when she didn't reappear somewhere else. And that could take weeks.

Not a bad plan, except for two things. Glory herself had spoiled it by getting herself washed up on the beach. And she had stupidly ruined the note by plunging into the lake in search of a body that wasn't there. No wonder Tony had looked exhausted when he finally turned up in the small hours. No wonder he had struck her when she insisted that she was leaving in the morning. She imagined, yet again and in further gruesome detail, the events as they must have taken place up in Glory's room. Tony, the leather thong, the struggle, the crash of glass on the bathroom floor. And then, Tony creeping through the silent hotel carrying the limp, lifeless body. Would he at least have wrapped her in a blanket? And then what? Down to the lake. Would he have walked all the way, or used the car? Probably the car. Less chance of being seen with his dreadful burden. She pictured Glory doubled up in the tiny backseat that she usually occupied. Then finding a sufficiently lonely spot from which to consign the body to the deep. Only the deep hadn't been deep enough. Then back to the hotel to pack up Glory's belongings and make it appear as if she had skipped. What had he done with them? And what about Glory's car? Was it still in the hotel parking lot, or had he managed to get rid of it, too? The only thing that Anita's imagination refused to tell her was, Why? What had Glory done to cause Tony to attack her? Anita felt she had to know that before she could decide what to do. And there was only one way to find out. She would have to confront Tony with her suspicions.

She plucked the two sodden sheets of notepaper out of the sink, handling them carefully with her fingertips so they wouldn't tear. She blotted them gently with wads of toilet tissue, preserving as much of the blurred scrawl as she could. Then she carried them into the bedroom and placed them flat on the dressing table. If necessary, she would help Tony reconstruct the note so it could be produced at the right moment.

She glanced at her bedside clock. Almost lunchtime. The morning's rehearsal would be breaking up soon, and they'd all come trooping back to eat. Tony would undoubtedly come straight up to see how she was. She would be ready for him.

From the pocket of his jeans, still hanging in the bathroom, she once again took the Petoskey stone pendant. Why, she wondered, hadn't he simply left it in place around Glory's throat? Or thrown it into the lake after her? It would have sunk to the bottom and stayed there. In a few minutes, she would ask all those questions and, depending on his answers, would help him plan his next moves. Or. Or what? She placed the pendant on the dressing table beside the sheets of note-paper.

As she stood back to consider the effect, she heard, through the open window, familiar voices approaching along the side lane that led to the playhouse. Larry Devine's deep baritone and Leo Lemming's shrill laughter were there. An occasional clear tone from Hilda Kramer. Anita pictured Tony walking, moodily silent, among them. She sat down in the overstuffed armchair to wait for him.

CHAPTER XXV

The boy squatted on the furthermost boulder of the breakwater, his fishing rod secured in a crack between the tumbled stones. His line hung straight and his bobber bobbed placidly in the still water. There was no activity in the depths and the noon sun beat down on deserted beachfront and lake. Everyone was home having lunch. The boy munched a thick sandwich of cheese and bologna liberally smeared with mustard, and sipped warm orange soda from a can. In the canvas bag lying on the stone beside him, along with his meager fishing tackle, were another sandwich, this one of peanut butter and grape jelly, and a package of potato chips, all part of the lunch he had prepared for himself early in the morning.

Now that school was out and the tourist season about to begin, his mother and sister started polishing Petoskeys first thing in the morning. The boy liked to leave the house early and stay away all day if he could. He didn't mind collecting the stones, that was fun, but polishing was boring. Fishing was kind of boring, too, unless it could be done from a boat out on the open lake where at least he would have a chance at catching something big. The boy chewed his sandwich and dreamed of the boat he would own one day, as soon as he'd saved enough money, and of the giant lake trout he would catch all on his own, bigger than anything those charter boat people had ever seen. He looked up when the shadow fell across his lunch.

"Oh, hi," he said. He got politely to his feet, clutching his soda can. The last bite of cheese and bologna stuck in his throat.

"Hi. Catch anything?"

"Nope." He swallowed hard. "Can't catch anything here. Only stupid little suckers. Anyway, they're all sleeping this time of day. Down at the bottom."

"How come you're not collecting those stones?"

"Aw, they got enough of them up at the house. They'll be polishing from now till Christmas."

163

"How big do they get? As big as this?" The visitor had stopped to pick up a hefty-sized rock from the jumbled stones that filled in between the boulders.

"I never seen one as big as that. Mostly they're little, but sometimes as big as a muskmelon. That's the biggest I ever seen."

The boy took a sip from his soda can, wondering whether he ought to offer it to his visitor. He was sure his mother wouldn't want him to pass on any mouth germs.

"I'll bet you're a good swimmer."

"Pretty good. Ain't won any prizes, but I can make it from here to the marina if the water's not too choppy. I'd show you, but my mom don't like me to swim alone."

"Hey! What's that?"

The boy turned to look out over the lake.

"I don't see . . ."

Nothing. The word never left his lips. Nothing turned into an explosion of pain on the side of his head, followed by an enveloping coolness that felt so good. Deep within his ebbing consciousness, something told him to breathe. He opened his mouth and the coolness flowed in. He gagged, choked, and didn't try again. He drifted to the bottom of the lake. A large stone plunged past him and reached the bottom before he did. His canvas bag followed more slowly. The soda can bobbed on the surface for a while, then gradually sank and came to rest a few feet away. His fishing rod floated out into deeper waters of the lake.

The sun shone brightly on the deserted breakwater.

CHAPTER XXVI

"**O**kay! So she's dead! But I didn't kill her. My God, Anita! What really happened is bad enough. But I swear I didn't kill her and I didn't move her body from the beach."

Tony paced the room like a caged cheetah, his muscles twitching nervously beneath his skin and his eyes shining with a feral gleam. Anita crouched in her chair.

"Tell me what really happened," she whispered. "You said you were with Hilda Kramer."

"I was. We worked pretty late. I'm not sure what time it was. Glory had finished her scenes, and Devine told her not to wait around. So she left. Alone. I think that was a little before midnight. The rest of us were off and on through the rest of the first act. When we finally finished, we all walked back up the lane together. Devine said good-night and walked off down to his boat. That left Leo, Tina, Hilda, and Pev Martin. And me. Everyone was pretty tired. We all trooped into the lobby together. Tina and Pev went straight to their rooms. I remember thinking the old man was probably too old for this kind of life. He looked like a walking corpse."

Anita covered her face with her hands. Tony stopped his pacing and bent over her.

"I'm sorry, love. That's not the best choice of words. But he did look awful. Anyway, Leo made some flip remark about how Glory was developing in our scenes together and flitted away up the stairs. Hilda and I followed, and as soon as Leo was out of earshot, she asked me if I could spare her a few minutes to discuss something that she thought was important to both of us. I asked her if it couldn't wait till morning, but she said it was urgent, so I went on up to her room with her. First she asked me if I'd known Glory before. That surprised me. I asked her what gave her that idea.

"'The way you reacted when you saw her for the first time down on Larry's boat,' she answered. 'There was a tension in the air all out of proportion to a first meeting. And then the way she accused you of having something to do with that broken power line. She was distraught, but the accusation had to come from something more than an instant personal dislike.'

"Well, she was right, of course, and I told her so. You might as well know, too. A few years ago, I was in Hollywood, broke and no job in sight. Some sleazy character approached me with a way to pick up a few bucks. Porno movies. Pretty hardcore stuff. I used a different name, but nevertheless, that's me on that piece of film. Me and Glory Hayes."

Tony had moved away from Anita and stood staring into the empty fireplace. Anita reached out to touch his arm.

"That's not so horrible," she said. "We all do things we're not so proud of, just to stay alive. I worked as a topless dancer when I was broke. I got fired, though. I wasn't really the right shape for the job. Not enough jiggle, I guess."

Tony went on with his story. "I admit I was surprised to see her here. She's bleached her hair and changed her name. I can't even remember what she called herself then. But the voice was still the same. And the mannerisms. I wasn't too happy about the idea of spending the summer working with her, and I guess I showed it that first night. The next morning, we had a heart-to-heart talk and got it all out into the open. Glory always had a tendency to blow things up all out of proportion. If you didn't love her, you hated her. Nothing in between. So, because I didn't fall all over myself to greet her as a long-lost buddy, to her that meant I was out to get her. With the added reason that I wouldn't want it to get around that I'd done that movie with her. Hell, I wouldn't. But these days, nobody cares. I haven't got that much of a career to ruin, and I'm not out to be Pat Boone in white buck shoes. If I were that squeamish about it, I wouldn't have made the damn' film in the first place.

"Well, I finally convinced her that she wasn't in any danger from me. But she was still nervy and frightened about something. Granted, that little episode with the power line was enough to set anyone's nerves on edge, but she seemed to be fatalistic about that. Said it was in the cards. Said she'd done a Tarot reading that told her to be careful of the people around her. I laughed at her and told her it was a lot of superstitious nonsense. But, as it turned out, I guess she was right.

"Anyway, I told Hilda all about my past encounters with Glory, and then she said a funny thing. She said, 'Do you think she's capable of blackmail?' Well, I suppose anybody's capable of blackmail, in one form or another. But as far as out and out criminal blackmail for profit, I didn't think Glory would go to all the trouble involved. She was a creature of the moment, everything right now, happy or sad or angry or frightened, with never a thought for the long run. But I gathered from the question that Glory had somehow got hold of some skeleton in Hilda's closet.

"Well, all of this was pretty thirsty work. We'd been talking for about twenty minutes and I was tired and needed a drink. I asked Hilda if she had anything on hand, and she apologized and said all she could offer me was a glass of water. I said fine, and she got up and went to open the bathroom door. Now, as you know, since you've been up there snooping around . . ."

"I wasn't snooping," Anita protested. "I was trying to find out what happened to Glory."

"As you know, Hilda and Glory shared a bath between their two rooms. The doors each have a sliding bolt on the bedroom side and another on the bathroom side. Hilda slid back the bolt on her side and opened the door, still talking to me. She was slightly behind the door as it swung open, so I got a clear view into the bathroom before she did. The light was on and the farther door into Glory's room was open.

"I said, 'Hilda, wait a minute!' and leaped out of my chair to get in there before she did. But, of course, by that time she'd seen what was there and rushed in to help Glory. At first, we thought she'd fainted or fallen or had some kind of attack. We did everything we could—cold water, artificial respiration. But then we found that thing around her neck and realized there was nothing we could do for her.

"My first thought was that you had done it. I'm sorry, babe, but you were pretty angry at her for taking the job away from you, and you've certainly been less than your usual cheerful self lately. Besides, you were the only one in any way associated with Glory who was in the hotel when she came in."

"But that's absurd!" Anita sprang out of her chair and gripped Tony's arm in protest. "I didn't kill her! I heard her come in last night, and there was someone with her. I thought it was you."

"Well, that's absurd, too." Tony led her back to the chair and sat himself down on the bed facing her. "I was on stage in full view of everybody from the time Glory left the playhouse until we finished rehearsal. After that, we all walked back together, and I was with Hilda until we found the body."

"How do I know you and Hilda didn't do it together?" Anita asked. "From what you've just told me, Glory could have been blackmailing both of you."

"Don't think that didn't occur to us. That's why we decided to get rid of the body, and make it look as if Glory had skipped out. Not a very wise decision, after all. But last night, it seemed to make sense. We wrapped her up in a sheet from Hilda's bed, and Hilda helped me carry her down the back way. We were both terrified that someone would hear us, or that Joe would come creeping up on us in that soft-shoe way of his. But we managed to get out to the parking lot without anyone seeing us. We put Glory in the trunk of Hilda's car. Not a very pleasant business, I can tell you. I don't know about Hilda, but the only way I got through the whole thing was by pretending it was just another role in a blood-and-guts movie.

"While I drove off looking for a secluded place to pitch poor Glory in the lake, Hilda went back upstairs to clean up. There was broken glass all over the floor . . ."

"I know," said Anita, holding up her injured hand.

". . . and we had already decided to pack up all her paraphernalia and shoot it over to the airport in Traverse City. I didn't want to spend all night driving around with Glory in the trunk, and remember, it was raining like a DeMille version of the Deluge. So I drove down toward the marina and found a side road that went past the breakwater and out onto that point of land you can see from the beach. It was a dirt road and I didn't dare drive all the way out in case the car might get stuck. So the last bit of it, I had to carry her. It was pitch dark. I couldn't very well leave the car lights on, and I had no idea how far out into the lake the land projected, or how deep the water was.

"Finally, I just couldn't carry her any further. I walked over to the edge, where there seemed to be a drop. I put her down and rolled her out of the sheet. There was a splash. And that was the last I saw of Glory Hayes.

"When I got back, Hilda had all the suitcases packed, the bathroom cleaned up, and, as a further refinement, had produced that note to you. She was the one who invented the laryngitis. It would have worked, too, if I'd been a little more careful about disposing of the body and you hadn't gone charging down to the beach this morning."

"Someone else would have found her," Anita reminded him.

"Evidently, someone else did. But who? Believe me, Anita, it wasn't me."

Anita closed her eyes and laid her head against the back of the chair. She was silent for almost a full minute. When she spoke her words were carefully chosen and her tone calm and rational. Her eyes remained closed.

"If what you've told me is the truth . . ."

"Don't you believe me?" Tony interrupted.

"Never mind that for now. If what you've told me is the truth, and neither you nor Hilda went down to the beach this morning, then it stands to reason that whoever found the body and moved it is the murderer. Otherwise, why hide it? Why not simply call the police?"

"That's what we should have done last night." Tony shook his head ruefully. "But we were both afraid of being implicated. And there was still the possibility that you were involved."

"It's not too late. I think we should call them right now. Frankly, Tony, I don't feel too comfortable knowing there's a strangler on the loose who might have seen me pull Glory from the lake. You'll have an awful lot of explaining to do, but your scenario is already falling apart. Tina Elliott knows that Glory's room is empty." Anita opened her eyes to guage Tony's reaction to this news.

"What the hell!" he exclaimed. "Did you tell her? Who else did you spout off to?"

He looked angry enough to strike her, but this time Anita didn't care. He must have sensed her detachment; he turned and slammed his fist down on top of the dresser, knocking his hairbrush to the floor.

"No one else," said Anita. "And I didn't tell her. She walked in on me while I was looking around up there." Anita got up, walked over to the dresser, picked up the hairbrush, and put it back in its place. "Tony, you've explained everything very neatly, but there are still one or two things that bother me. For instance, why did you hang onto this?" She picked up the stone pendant and held it swinging from its leather thong.

"I don't know," he answered. "I truly don't know. I remember that we took it off her neck when we were trying to revive her, and then I must have stuck it in my pocket and forgot about it. Incidentally, what is it? I've never seen a stone like that before."

"I never had either, until I saw some up in Joe's office. It's a Petoskey stone."

"Joe! Do you think he . . . ?"

"No!"

"What makes you so sure? You're ready and willing to suspect me, but not some Indian hotel flunky. He could have had something going with Glory. How do we know . . . ?"

"Petoskeys are a dime a dozen around here. Anyone could pick one up. They sell them in all the shops and kids peddle them on street corners."

"Then all we have to do is find out where this one came from." He snatched the pendant from her hand. "We'll take it around to everybody who sells these things and ask them who bought this particular one."

"Tony. The police will take it around and do the asking. They'll ask some other embarrassing questions, such as what did you do with her luggage and the car?"

"The luggage is in a locker at the airport. We left the car in the parking lot outside the rental office. We were going to buy a ticket in her name, but the ticket office was closed."

"Shall we go now?" Anita picked up the still-damp sheets of notepaper and held out her hand for the pendant.

"Wait a minute," said Tony. "Don't you think we ought to let Hilda know what we're up to? Don't forget, she's just as much a part of this as I am. If she doesn't want to get the police into it, I don't think we should go ahead without her."

Anita hesitated. "I guess you're right. But, Tony," she glanced up at him questioningly, "is there any way she could have done it, and then arranged the whole discovery scene as a cover-up for herself and to get you to help her get rid of the body? You said that Glory had something on her. Did you find out what it was?"

"No. I was only guessing. I would have asked her, but that's when we found Glory. We were too busy after that, and the subject never came up again. But I don't see how Hilda could have done it. She was at the theater, just like all the rest of us. You have a very suspicious mind, love. First you think it was me. Then Hilda. You'll wind up suspecting the whole cast and crew. Maybe we all ganged up on her to rid the world of a no-talent pest, and if you don't stop poking around, we'll get you, too."

Tony made as if to drape the leather thong around Anita's

170

neck. She screamed and stumbled backward, her face distorted into a mask of panic. Tony laughed.

"What's the matter, babe? Lost your sense of humor? Am I not a 'fellow of infinite jest, of most excellent fancy'? You used to laugh at me sometimes. Don't worry. I'm not going to strangle you on an empty stomach. Let's go get some lunch. We'll talk to Hilda afterward. Okay?"

Anita nodded, unable to speak.

CHAPTER XXVII

"Oh, my dear girl! You've no notion how absolutely glad I am to see you!" Leo welcomed her effusively with a lavish display of hugs and hand-pattings. "It was a great lark for me to waltz through Glory's scenes this morning, but I think your Tony found it a bit off-putting. He didn't say anything, but there were negative vibrations shooting off all over the place. He wasn't at his best. Very subdued. He's not coming down with something, too, is he?"

Anita smiled reassuringly and said, "No."

Leo chattered on. "And how is our popsie this afternoon? I meant to look in on her, bringing cheer and chicken soup or at least a small nosegay, but what with one thing and another I didn't have a minute to spare. Believe it or not, I miss bandying words with her. Oh, mute inglorious Glory! What shall we do if she loses the power of speech entirely? The question is rhetorical, my dear. Don't bother to reply. The only possible answer is, 'Very nicely, thank you.' Are you all ready to carry on? Yes, of course, you are, you good little trouper, you. Script in hand and a properly attentive attitude. Larry will be delighted. I don't mind telling you he was monumentally pissed off this morning. Ready to ship her bag and baggage back to the sinkhole from whence she sprouted. It may come to that yet, if she doesn't shape up. So just show yourself willing and all may yet be well. If you know what I mean."

"Yes," said Anita, after the flood of prattle had abated. Across the stage, Tina Elliott was elaborately mouthing words at her which she translated as "Did you find her yet?" Anita shook her head and opened the script she had brought with her. Glory Hayes' script.

Emmy Jackson scurried onto the stage. "Oh, Leo!" she burbled. "You'll never guess! The Women's Literary Club just called up to reserve a block of thirty seats for opening night! We'll definitely have a sellout!"

"Wunnerful! Wunnerful!" said Leo. "I won't have to hawk tickets door to door and give away hams as courage-in-the-face-of-facing-a-night-of-nonelectronic-entertainment prizes. Not that they won't get a fair serving of ham right here. Larry always accuses me of overacting. I can't imagine why.''

"Oh, Leo. You never did that," said Emmy.

"Thank you, Emmy. My one true fan. In an age of stark and ugly realism, it's nice to know someone appreciates a touch of style and grace.''

"I meant you never had to sell tickets door to door.''

"Rats! Shot down again. And by my trusted cohort. Off with you, woman! Back to your curmudgeonly bookkeeping! You have no sense of grandeur.'' Leo waved her away with grandiloquent gestures.

Emmy giggled and retreated a few paces, but she bounced back almost instantly to clutch Leo's arm and ask, "Did you ever find that key? I'd really like to get into the prop room soon.''

Leo sighed and raised his eyes to the spotlight-strewn heavens. "The woman has no mercy,'' he proclaimed. "No, I haven't found the key. And no, I haven't even looked for it yet. But if it will make you happy, I'll come and look for it right now.''

Together, Emmy and Leo descended the steps at the side of the stage and, chattering to each other, made their way through the auditorium to the office at one side of the lobby. Behind them, the actors gathered onstage and waited for rehearsal to begin. A hand dipped casually into a pocket and fingered the flat piece of metal that rested there. A pair of eyes flickered up the aisle following the retreating figures before dropping onto the first page of the third act.

At one side of the stage, Anita Stratton felt the old sense of excitement and renewal that accompanied each new role she played. She had been reluctant, under the circumstances, to attend the rehearsal, wanting to go without any delay to the offices of the town police. The slender local telephone directory featured a handy map which indicated that those offices were located conveniently nearby, on one side of the picturesque village green. She had been all for walking over there immediately after a lunch of grilled trout and red leaf lettuce salad which she had been unable to eat. But Tony had insisted on waiting until they'd had a chance to consult privately with Hilda Kramer.

The chance had not presented itself during lunch, and now it seemed they must wait until an opportune moment during the rehearsal. Hilda, at the moment, stood at the rear of the stage deep in conversation with Larry Devine. Pev Martin wandered forlornly about the stage, while Tina Elliott had settled down in her usual chair next to the cookie tin. Tony himself paced back and forth, muttering silently while slowly turning the pages of his script. The backstage area bustled with busy extras who were also drafted into scene-painting chores. It all felt good and normal to Anita, who was tempted to forget the events which had brought her there and lose herself in the creation of the character whose words and emotions, so far, existed only on paper.

Larry Devine strode to the front of the stage, calling, "Third act! Places, people, if you please."

Anita cleared her throat, took a pencil from her pocket, found her place in the script, and walked to stage center.

CHAPTER XXVIII

"**N**o! Absolutely not. I will not have anything more to do with it. Last night was horrible. That was enough." Hilda Kramer's hand shook as she raised her Styrofoam coffee cup to her lips.

"But, Hilda," Tony argued, "the plan isn't working. The body washed up on the beach. Anita saw it. And the note that was supposed to explain her disappearance has been destroyed. We have to go to the police, before they come to us."

Larry Devine had called a twenty-minute break in the afternoon's rehearsal. The three of them, Hilda, Tony, and Anita, sat in the middle of the auditorium, well away from overhearing ears, sipping Emmy Jackson's coffee and talking in whispers.

"No," said Hilda. "I'll write another note. We'll carry on as before."

"It's too late for that," Tony objected. "Anita's right. This is something for the police to handle. We should have gone to them last night."

"Anyway," Hilda pursued, "how do *we* know the body really did wash up on the beach? Forgive me, Anita, but you're the only one who saw it. And you're the one who destroyed the note. Even Tony thought you might have hated Glory enough to kill her. Why are *you* so eager to go to the police?"

Hilda pointedly emphasized that she and Tony were allies in the events of last night, while Anita was an interloper, and suspect at that. Tony, sitting between the two women, clasped Anita's hand and squeezed it encouragingly.

"I'm not the only one who saw it. Tony says he didn't move it from the beach, and I guess I believe him. But how do I know that *you* weren't lurking about in the fog this morning? It would be hard work for a woman, but you could have gotten a rowboat or something and simply dumped her back in the lake. I'm not saying I think you killed her. Tony's positive that you couldn't have. But if neither you nor Tony moved the

177

body from the beach, then someone else did. And whoever it was is probably the killer. And *that's* why I want to go to the police. I don't feel exactly safe knowing there's a Duck Creek strangler on the loose. Do you?"

Hilda's hand crept to her throat. "Maybe you're right," she said. "Maybe we should have gone last night instead of trying to make it look as if she'd left." She shook her head despondently. "Larry still doesn't know. I couldn't bear to tell him. Can you imagine what the publicity would do to the playhouse? It would ruin him. Oh, God!" she groaned, "I wish I had a drink."

Tony sprang to his feet. "I'll get you one. There must be something around here. Maybe Leo has a bottle stashed away in the office."

"No! Don't!" Hilda clutched at his arm. "I mean, don't bother right now. I'll be all right." She pondered for a moment. Then she asked, "If you do go to the police, do you have to tell them the whole story? Can't you just say that she's missing and we're worried about her?"

"What good would that do?" Tony asked. "Sooner or later, the whole thing's bound to come out. Especially if the body turns up. We're going to be in enough trouble for trying to conceal it in the first place. But it'll be ten times worse if we start out by pretending she's just missing, and then have to admit we knew she was dead. We'll be lucky if they don't arrest all three of us. I don't know about you, Hilda, but jail is definitely not my idea of a run of the play contract."

"All right," said Hilda. "You go. But don't expect me to go with you. If they want to ask me about it, I'll tell them exactly what happened last night. But that's all. I don't know anything about beaches or fogs or what Anita says she saw this morning. Someone ought to tell Larry what's going on. You both realize, don't you, that this is liable to close down the playhouse?"

"Do you want me to tell him?" asked Tony.

"No," said Hilda. "I'll tell him. I've run away from a lot of things in my life, but I'm not running away from this one. If I'm responsible for destroying his playhouse, he's going to hear it from me. I owe him that much."

"Hilda," said Anita, "don't blame yourself. The only thing you did was to try to keep this horrible thing quiet. It may have been a mistake, but surely Larry will understand that you had the best interests of the playhouse at heart."

178

Hilda rose from her seat with a sharp bitter laugh. "Not bloody likely," she said. "It was Hilda Kramer's own best interests that made me do it. I think I can say the same for Tony Brand. Isn't that true?"

Tony nodded.

"In a way," Hilda continued, "we're all accomplices in Glory's death. She was frightened and we laughed at her. She was loud and vulgar and we all found her a ridiculous nuisance. We all lost sight of the fact that she was only a kid doing the best she could in an environment that she must have found pretty hostile. None of us really liked her, and somebody disliked her enough to kill her. The police are quite likely to suspect the three of us. And with good reason. How do you propose to convince them that someone else may have had a better reason?"

"We'll tell them the truth," said Anita. "They'll have to believe it. If we were guilty, we certainly wouldn't go to them with such a crazy story."

"Good luck to you," said Hilda, edging out of the row of seats. "I'll go find Larry now. And I'd better get in touch with Barney Gross. For all we know, the poor kid has some family who ought to be notified. Will you bring the storm troopers here to question the suspects, or take them first to the scene of the crime?"

"I think we'll have to leave that up to them," said Tony. "Come on, Anita. We might as well get it over with."

While Tony and Anita turned one way to leave the theater, Hilda Kramer walked thoughtfully toward the stage. Larry Devine was nowhere in sight. Leo Lemming sat in the front row hunched over his clipboard and the prompt script. As she passed him, Hilda asked, "Have you seen Larry?"

Without ceasing his scribbling, Leo answered, "I think he's gone up to the hotel to read Glory the riot act. Either she gets her dimpled tushie down here and gets to work, or she's fired. Somehow, I believe my omniscient uncle senses a fine case of malingering."

"She's not malingering," said Hilda.

"Well, then, I hope whatever she has isn't contagious. Where would we be if the whole gang wound up ill and cowering behind locked doors?"

Hilda reversed her direction and headed back up the aisle. "I think I'll go meet him," she said.

"Tell him to hurry," Leo called after her. "We can't afford to get behind schedule."

CHAPTER XXIX

Tony and Anita sat side by side on a hard wooden bench in the small anteroom of Duck Creek's police station. Across the room, a tall dusty window looked out on the parking lot where the town's fire engine was being lovingly washed and polished by a pair of teenaged boys in cutoff jeans. The police and fire departments both occupied space in the rambling old Municipal Building, as did the Mayor's office, the County Health Department, a small infirmary, the ASPCA, and the Duck Creek Museum, which offered displays of arrowheads, Petoskey stones, and yellowing photographs of historic shipwrecks. Tony and Anita had peered into the Museum's dim and frowsty display hall while looking for the police chief's office. The custodian, a serious young person with lank yellow hair, directed them down the hall and to the right, adding with a disdainful sniff, "They have a separate entrance through the parking lot."

They found the pebbled glass door without any trouble, but the police chief was out. Everyone was out except a very junior policeman who sat at a desk behind a scarred mahogany counter and spoke laconically into a telephone. He'd obviously heard it done that way on television. The area behind the counter contained several other desks, all of the heavy yellow oak variety and all cluttered with stacks of paper, manila folders, coffee mugs, and the assorted detritus of officialdom. Along the inner wall of this area ranged a number of doors leading into private offices. The opposite wall featured more tall dusty windows and an uninterrupted view of the parking lot. Between the windows stood groups of green metal filing cabinets. On top of one of these, a large fish tank with a bubbling aerator provided intermittent flashes of gold. The young policeman put down the phone and came to lean over the counter.

"Chief'll be back soon," he said, "but he's likely to be pretty busy. Been a drownin' down by the lake. First one of the season. If it's a fishin' license, I can fix you up." He pointed

181

to a sign on the counter that advised that fishing licenses were necessary and could be obtained on the spot.

"No," said Tony. "We'll wait."

Anita rose from the bench and walked to the counter. Her legs trembled as she leaned against the sturdy wooden bulwark. "I guess you get a lot of that," she said. "Drownings?"

"Not too many," the young man answered. "Mostly, people are pretty careful."

"This one," Anita pursued, "is it a man or a woman?"

"Said it was a kid. Didn't say who. Hey, you folks ain't missin' a kid, are you?" He sounded almost hopeful.

Anita shook her head.

"Well, good." The young man swallowed his disappointment. He would have relished for once being part of the action instead of always being left behind to answer the phone. "It happened down by the breakwater. Got the call about an hour ago. Somebody out walking on the breakwater looked down and saw the kid lying on the bottom. Water's not too deep out there. Chief says they'll be comin' in pretty soon. But I don't know if he'll be able to see you. Unless it's pretty important."

"It's important," said Tony. "We'll wait."

Anita returned to the bench and sat down, slipping her hand into his.

"Okay with me." The young man walked over to the fish tank, picked up a small container of fish food, and sprinkled some on top of the water. "One of these days, I'm gonna get me a couple of those Siamese fighting fish," he remarked. "They say they're mean little buggers. Fight like tigers. Sure would beat firecracker patrol on the Fourth of July. You folks ain't had a robbery or anything like that, have you?"

"No," said Tony.

"Didn't think so. We don't get much of that. Nothin' much ever happens here. Exceptin' once in a while a drownin' like today. Chief always notifies the next of kin hisself. I expect that's what he'll be doin' soon's he gets back." The young man drifted back to his desk and lowered himself listlessly onto his chair. "Could take a while. You sure you want to wait?"

"I'm sure," said Tony.

Anita got up and wandered restlessly around the small anteroom. She helped herself to a paper cup of water from the water cooler, gazed out the window at the gleaming fire engine, and returned to her seat on the hard bench beside Tony.

"Maybe we should come back later," she whispered to him.

"If the chief's anything like his fish warden, he may not be able to handle more than one thing at a time."

Tony frowned. "We stay," he hissed back at her. "We stay until we can unload this whole bundle in the lap of whatever powers there be in Duck Creek. I don't want to give Hilda a chance to have second thoughts about it. Or myself, for that matter."

"Are you having second thoughts?" Anita tried to catch his eye, but he avoided looking directly at her, letting his gaze wander around the room.

"I sure as hell don't want to be the patsy in this number. I don't care if they never find out who did it, just so long as they don't decide it was me."

"Or me," said Anita in a small voice.

"Or you," Tony agreed.

"Nice of you to include me on your list of those you don't suspect of murder. You're about as convincing as John Travolta trying to play Hamlet."

"What's that supposed to mean?"

"You're a fine actor, Tony," she told him, "but it's going to take more talent than you've got to con your way out of this one. And you're not going to do it by making me the guilty party."

"What!" he shouted. "What the hell are you talking about?"

"Ssh. Keep your voice down." She glanced across the counter at the young policeman. He was sitting at his desk, deeply engrossed in a paperback book with a brightly colored photograph of tropical fish on its cover. "What I'm talking about," she whispered, "is that I think you told me the truth, up to a point. All that about dumping the body in the lake and making it look as if she skipped out. I think that's true. But you also planned to use me to make it look good. And now that it's not looking so good, you just change the plan a little to make it look as if I killed her. You said it yourself. I was the only one who was in the hotel when Glory came back last night. Outside of a dozen or so other guests and the hotel staff, none of whom had any reason to want her dead, everybody else was at the theater. But don't forget, I heard someone come in with her. I thought it was you. Who do *you* think it was?"

Tony shrugged. "How should I know? I wasn't there. Listen, babe . . ." He tried to put his arm around her, but she pulled away, sliding along the bench to the very end. "Believe me," he pleaded, "I'm not trying to make you look guilty. Why on earth would I want to do that? I want both of us completely out of this whole mess. And Hilda, too. I want to let the police worry about who killed Glory Hayes."

"You must have some idea who did it," Anita persisted. "You can't just find a body lying around and not wonder how it got there."

"Oh, babe, I don't know." Tony leaned wearily back against the institutional green wall behind the bench. He stared at the ceiling. "I don't want to think about it. Maybe she went somewhere after she left rehearsal, a roadhouse or a bar, and picked up some screwball who didn't like the way she wore her lipstick."

"You didn't think that last night."

"No. And I guess I don't really believe it."

"Then you *do* think it was one of us. Which one?"

Tony reached for her, sliding along the bench until she had to let his arm surround her or get up and walk away. She didn't get up. "Anita, will you, for God's sake, stop picking away at it! All I'm really sure of is that she didn't strangle herself. You're the one who wanted to get the police in on it. Now that we're here, you're working yourself into a panic. You've got to calm down; otherwise they really will think you killed her."

Anita shuddered. "I'm afraid," she whispered. "I'm afraid because I don't know whether or not you could do a thing like that. I've lived with you for six months, and I don't really know you very well. For all I know, you could be some kind of homicidal maniac, with dozens of strangled victims behind you. You could be a real nut case, and how would I know?"

Gently, Tony pressed her head down onto his shoulder and with his other hand began rhythmically stroking her hair. "Do you really believe that?" he asked.

"No." Anita closed her eyes as the tears began seeping out and dripping onto Tony's shirt. "But somebody killed her. And if it wasn't you or me or Hilda, it has to be one of the others. I keep wondering which one. And I keep thinking of him following me in the fog this morning and watching me find the body. I must have walked right past him when I went back to the hotel. He could have killed me on the spot. But instead, he let me go by and he hid the body somewhere." She lifted her tear-streaked face. "Tony, maybe we ought to try to

184

find the body and come back later. We don't really have very much in the way of evidence to back up our story. The first thing they're going to ask is where is the body. And we can't tell them.''

Tony fished a handkerchief out of his pocket and began mopping Anita's face. She took it from his hand and blew her nose vigorously. "Thanks," she murmured. "Sorry to be such a stupid crybaby. And sorry about calling you a nut case. I know you're not. I guess my nerves are just out of control.''

Tony smiled and kissed her softly on both eyelids. The young policeman's eyes flickered over the top of his paperback book. He'd been straining to hear their whispered conversation, but was only able to catch a few words, not enough to determine what their problem was. He didn't recognize them. They weren't regular summer people. Maybe they were just passing through. Maybe he was an FBI man pursuing dangerous radical terrorists and he wanted to check in with the chief and ask for his assistance. But what about the girl? Did the FBI have female agents? And if they did, would they send them out on such a dangerous mission? They'd been behaving like a married couple having an argument. But come to think of it, wouldn't that be a perfect cover? Maybe the chief would assign him to be their guide around the countryside. There were plenty of places where radical terrorists could be holed up. Plenty of summer cottages that wouldn't be opened up until after the Fourth of July, overgrown orchards where the trees had died of exhaustion and no one would notice a tent or a camper on a bit of waste ground. The young policeman stared at a color photo of *Betta splendens.* but saw himself, service revolver held at the ready, leading the two unlikely looking FBI agents on a surprise midnight attack on the band of weirdo radical terrorists hiding out in the abandoned lighthouse at Crow Point.

The door to the anteroom clattered open and a tall, stoop-shouldered man shambled through. He was a gray man, with silver-gray hair and a grayish cast to his lined face, dressed in a rumpled gray uniform shirt and trousers. If it were not for the very businesslike-looking gun holstered on a wide leather belt that drooped from his thin hips, he could have been mistaken for a school custodian close to retirement age.

He was followed by two somber-faced younger men, both in neatly pressed uniforms, escorting a small weeping woman.

The young policeman behind the desk dropped his tropical fish book and leaped to his feet.

"Chief!" he excalimed. "That's Alberta! What's she doing here?"

The chief pushed through the swinging gate that separated the anteroom from the desk area. He laid his gnarled hand on the young man's shoulder and sat him down again.

"Kenny," he said softly, "I want you to get in touch with your brother and get him down here right away. Alberta needs him. We've already called the drug store, but he left a while ago. Alberta thinks he may have gone down to Benson's Hardware to pick up a new lawnmower. Start calling around."

The young policeman sat mutely in his chair staring up at the chief with pleading eyes.

"That's right, son," the chief said. "It was young Jerry we pulled out of the lake. Now get busy."

The young policeman swallowed hard and made a halfhearted attempt to get out of his chair. But the look of despair on the face of the woman as she was being led into the chief's office forced him back down, and he drew the telephone close to his chest as if he could gain some solace from it. The chief turned away. If he had noticed Tony and Anita sitting against the wall, he gave no sign.

Tony sprang up and pushed his way through the swinging gate. "Chief," he called, "I want to report a murder."

The chief stopped in the door of his office and turned his sad face toward Tony.

"Who are you?" he asked.

"My name is Tony Brand."

Gray eyes probed Tony's face. "Who's been murdered?"

"One of the actresses at the playhouse. Glory Hayes."

Anita ran forward, giving herself a sharp crack on the knee as she burst through the swinging gate. She stood beside Tony, grasping his arm and glancing from his pallid face to the chief's.

"We can't find her. That's the problem." Anita heard herself enunciating each word distinctly as if trying to explain herself in a foreign language. "She's dead. We know that. We both saw her. But she's disappeared. Off the beach. This morning. We need you to help find her."

"Can't you people leave him alone!" The young policeman had dropped the phone and stood hunched over it like a loyal dog guarding his master's hearth. His eyes flamed and his

186

voice shrilled out of control. "What is this? Some kind of publicity stunt? You want headlines? 'Actress Missing, Feared Dead'? Then at the last minute she turns up and you sell lots of tickets? Don't you realize it's *his* grandson who drowned?" He collapsed back into his chair and buried his face in his hands.

"Hush, Kenny, hush." The chief went to him and stroked his heaving shoulders. "It's all right. They couldn't know. Now you get back on the phone and find your brother."

Kenny looked up, his face smeared with tears.

"Nothing wrong with crying, son," the chief went on tenderly. "But Alberta sure would feel better if she had her husband at her side right now. And if these folks have a problem, they're entitled to my help. And yours."

"Yes, sir," Kenny snuffled, and went back to his telephoning.

"The chief walked slowly back to where Tony and Anita stood pressed against the wall just inside the gate.

"Kenny's upset," he told them. "You have to understand Duck Creek's a pretty small town without the summer people. Those of us who live here year-round know each other pretty well, and a lot of us are related. The drowned boy was Kenny's nephew. My daughter Alberta is married to his brother, Jack. Helps a little if you know the background. But I'm curious. Would there be any truth at all in what Kenny just said? Are you, by any chance, trying to drum up a little sensational news to help sell tickets?"

"No," said Anita, shaking her head vehemently.

"I wish it were as simple as that," said Tony.

"Okay," said the chief. "I've known Larry Devine since he started here, and he's never done anything out of line. How come he's not down here with you?"

"He didn't know about it," said Tony. "We sent someone to tell him."

"Now let me get this straight," said the chief. "Three of you knew about a murder that happened this morning, and you're only just now reporting it to the police. Is that correct?"

"No," said Tony. "It happened last night. It's a long story."

"Seems like," said the chief. "In that case, we maybe ought

to be better acquainted. My name's Welles. Young lady, I don't believe you've told me yours."

"Anita Stratton."

"And you're with the playhouse?"

"I . . . I guess so. I've been standing in for Glory."

"Sort of a permanent job, isn't it? If what you tell me is true."

"It's true," said Anita. "I found her body on the beach this morning. I went to get Tony, and when we went back, she was gone."

"If she was drowned, what makes you think she was murdered?"

Tony took a deep breath and pulled the Petoskey stone pendant from his pocket. "She wasn't drowned. She was strangled. With this." He held the pendant dangling from its leather thong.

The chief examined it closely without taking it from Tony's hand. Then he called out, "Alberta, would you come here a minute?"

The small, disheveled woman appeared in the doorway of the chief's office. She had stopped crying, but her face remained drawn and dulled with grief. "Yes, Dad," she murmured thickly.

"Take a look at this," he said, indicating the pendant. "Ever seen it before?"

She looked, gasped, and stumbled forward, reaching for the stone. "It's Jerry's!" she cried. "It was his favorite. He wore it all the time. Where did you get it?"

"Hold on, Alberta," said her father. "All in good time. Now think back a minute. Was he wearing it this morning?"

"Oh," said Alberta. "That's right. He sold it a few days ago. He came home and told me he got five dollars for it. And he asked me to make him a new one. I told him he'd have to make one himself if he wanted one so badly." Her eyes went blank with memory and fresh tears began spilling down her cheeks. "He hated the polishing. He loved prowling the beach and finding them. And he liked to set up his display outside the hotel and pretend he was a big businessman. But he hated the polishing. Said it was boring. I wish I'd made him a new one when he asked me to." She looked everywhere but at Tony. "Did he sell it to you? I'd sure love to have it back." Whatever else she might have said was lost in a fresh burst of tears.

Chief Welles took the pendant from Tony's hand. He put

his other arm around his daughter's shoulders and guided her back into the office. "We'll talk about that later, honey," he said. "You go back in there now and wait for Jack." She went, and he closed the door behind her.

"I sure hated to do that to her," he said, as he returned to Tony and Anita. "I thought I recognized it, but I had to make certain." He held the pendant up, the stone swaying gently at the end of its thong. "Now suppose you tell me exactly how you happened to come by this."

"It was twisted around Glory Hayes' throat," said Tony. "I took it off."

"I thought you said the body was gone from the beach by the time you got there."

"It was. This was last night at the hotel. Look, Chief Welles, I told you this was a long story, and I'd like to start from the beginning if it's going to make any sense at all."

"I'd like that a whole lot," said Chief Welles. "Suppose you two just make yourselves comfortable in here for a bit, while I tend to Alberta." He led them to an office adjacent to his own, furnished mainly with a looming soda machine and an assortment of vinyl covered chairs that matched only in their shabbiness. "Machine takes quarters," he said. "Afraid there's only Coke and Vernor's ginger ale." At the doorway, he paused. "Funny thing about young Jerry. Seems like all his gear fell into the water when he did. And he's got this terrible-looking bruise on the side of his head. Must be he slipped and hit his head on a rock. Wonder who he sold that Petoskey to, don't you?"

The chief left. Tony and Anita drifted to opposite sides of the room and sat, staring at each other.

CHAPTER XXX

W ell," said Leo, squatting back on his thin
haunches and peering disconsolately into the empty cigar box,
"this is certainly 'the door to which I found no key,' and my
apologies to the old tentmaker. I'm sure Omar the K. never intended his words to apply to anything so mundane as a locked
door."

Beside him on the floor was a pile of keys, which he had one
by one tried in the lock of the prop room door, without success. He scooped them all back into the cigar box.

"Oh, dear," said Emmy Jackson, hovering over him, atwit-
ter with apprehension. Does this mean you're going to break it
down?"

"I could do that, of course," said Leo, rising to his full five
feet seven and taking a weight-lifter's stance.

Emmy giggled. "You look like a praying mantis."

"But if I did," Leo went on, ignoring her remark, "I'd only
have to get someone in to repair the damage. So I think I'll
save myself the trouble and call a locksmith in the morning.
That is, if you can wait that long for your fans and parasols."

"Oh, Leo, of course I can. And I'm sorry to be such a
nuisance."

"No apologies, Emmy, my love. It's a nuisance all right, but
it's not your fault. Now, let's get downstairs and see what's
holding up rehearsal. Larry should have gotten back by now."
Leo picked up the cigar box and headed for the narrow rickety
staircase that led down to the backstage area.

But Emmy Jackson stood musing before the locked door.
"You know, Leo," she said, "I could swear that the key
always used to be there, just sticking out of the lock. It's not
the sort of thing you really pay any attention to, especially if
you never lock the door. But I'm almost positive it was always
there. And if that's true, then somebody deliberately locked
the door and took the key away. Now, who would do a thing
like that?"

Leo shrugged. "How should I know? Maybe those junior

college extras have been using the prop room for sex and cocaine orgies and have their dope stashed in there."

Emmy skittered to his side. "Ooh, Leo! Do you really think so? My goodness! I've known most of those kids since they were tadpoles. Never thought they'd do any such thing. What should we do now?"

Leo squinted his eyes menacingly and hissed at her through clenched teeth. "Body search! I'll do the boys; you do the girls. Unless you'd rather have it the other way around. First one finds the key yells, 'Open Sesame!' and we all join hands and dance naked."

Emmy clutched his arm and exploded with laughter. "I didn't believe you for a minute," she chirped. "Not for a minute. You ought to be ashamed, teasing someone who's old enough to be your grandmother. Still and all, it's funny. For the door to be locked, I mean."

From below, a voice roared, "Leo! I want you!"

"Uh-oh," said Leo, "it sounds like my revered uncle is in a lather about something. If I were you, Emmy, I'd lurk up here until the storm passeth." He started down the stairs at a run. "Coming, Uncle!" he called.

Emmy stood hesitantly at the top of the stairs, torn between a desire to hear what was going on and her stern Methodist upbringing which told her to get herself down the hall and into the costume room where it would not be possible to eavesdrop. Curiosity won. In any case, she could not have missed Larry Devine's opening salvo.

"What the hell is going on here?" he demanded as Leo reached the foot of the stairs. "You're the stage manager. You're supposed to know these things. Tell me, if you can, why Hilda is up in the hotel bar drinking herself into a crying jag, where Tony and Anita have disappeared to, and, above all, why Glory's room is empty and her car is gone. How am I supposed to get a show together without any actors?"

For once, Leo was speechless. He clutched the cigar box full of keys as if one of them might give him the answers to Larry's questions. Behind him, Emmy Jackson crept quietly down the stairs. The stage was deserted except for Tina Elliott settled comfortably close to the coffee urn and cookie tin, and Pev Martin, who was stretched out, apparently asleep, on a seat-sprung sofa shoved up against the rear wall. From the open door of the loading dock came the sound of a guitar and young voices singing a country ballad.

Larry Devine paced. "I tried to talk to her. Joe and Elena tried to talk to her. She won't say anything. Just shakes her head and cries. And she won't go to her room. Joe says she had two double shots of Scotch to start out with, and now she's nursing her third. And bawling her head off. Thank God, there's nobody else in the bar this time of day. Joe wants to give her a sedative, but I told him to wait until you try to find out what's wrong. Maybe she'll talk to you."

"I'll go right away," said Leo. "But would you just run the rest of that past me again? You say Tony and Anita are missing and Glory's cleared out completely?"

Devine ran a hand through his shock of graying hair. "I don't say they're missing. They're just not where they're supposed to be. And nobody's seen them since we took a break. They'll probably turn up. It's Hilda I'm worried about. And Glory, too, of course. Although if she has run out on us, it's no great loss. Bud God damn it, Leo, people just don't walk out on rehearsal and not come back. I can't operate that way. It's your job to make sure everybody's here when they're supposed to be here."

"Mercy me!" breathed Emmy Jackson over Leo's shoulder. "You should calm down, Mr. Devine. You're liable to fret yourself into an apoplexy."

Larry opened his mouth to roar at Emmy, but Leo cut him short.

"Emmy's right. Cool heads all around. I'll go up and do what I can for Hilda. Do you want to come along, Unk?"

"No," he said bitterly. "She doesn't want to see me. It seems the mere sight of me is enough to give her the screaming-meemies."

"You're overacting, Unk, and you've no idea what pleasure it gives me to tell you that." Leo handed the box of keys to Emmy. "Here, my love, put these in a safe place. You never know what other doors they won't be able to open." He walked across the stage, picking up his clipboard along the way, and started down the stairs at the side. There he paused and looked back. The bare stage, lit by unshaded work lights, was stripped of all illusion. Tina Elliott, her eyes fastened on her script, reached absently for yet another cookie and stuffed it into her mouth. The old man on the sofa shook himself awake, peered round the stage, and, when he saw that rehearsal had not yet resumed, settled himself down to continue his nap. From the loading dock, a thin mournful voice, accompanied by plaintive guitar plucking, wailed inconsolably about having been loved and deserted by the wagoner's lad.

Leo Lemming hurried away through the darkened auditorium.

CHAPTER XXXI

What a surprising day!

It's so quiet. You would think, wouldn't you, that by now there would be loud outcries and swarms of local yokel policemen trudging about in heavy boots.

Not so. Not a peep. Nothing. But something is cooking. Something is definitely rotten in the state of Denmark, and in the state of Michigan as well.

Well, there's not much I can do about it. I can't very well go rushing off to the sheriff or the marshal, or whatever they police themselves with in this dreary backwater, screaming, "Murder most foul as in the best it is!"

Although it's really not so dreary today. Not with the sun shining and the lake sparkling. It was such a good idea to take a little walk before lunch. It never occurred to me until I saw that pesky little boy out on the breakwater that he could point the finger at me. I hadn't meant to leave the thong around her neck. It's not as though I were a professional at this. Amateurs make mistakes, and I suppose you could say that I am a true amateur of murder. Well, that mistake was easily remedied.

Poor, pretty Glory. She thought she had such a glorious future ahead of her. She thought she'd be rich and famous. Who knows? She might have made it. With that face and that body, she might have been a nine-days wonder. But without the talent to go with it, she wouldn't have lasted long. Just think of the disappointment I've saved her. One day, a sensational new discovery. The next day, wondering what went wrong. I've seen it happen that way. She really ought to be grateful that I've eliminated the possibility of defeat. Can the dead be grateful? Why not? Isn't there a rock group that proclaims it to be so? *The Grateful Dead.* You might say that I've taken their advice to heart. What a lot of gratitude I've earned! It's too bad I'll never receive any thank-you notes from the beyond.

But I do wish they'd get on with it. It would be interesting, for once, to be right on the spot while the investigating is going on, instead of reading garbled reports in the newspapers.

Which reminds me. I must find out if there's any possibility of getting *The New York Times* in this remote outpost. Must catch up on recent developments in the City. Such as the discovery of young victims in grim little rooms. I really ought to start a clipping scrapbook. Apart from my theatrical clippings. A grateful dead scrapbook. I'm sure I could fill it in no time at all. There's bound to be lots of press coverage here once the news breaks. I can just see the headlines: **"Hollywood Starlet Brutally Strangled."** Or: *"Actress Slain in Resort Town."* Or how about: "WHERE WILL THE DUCK CREEK STRANGLER STRIKE NEXT?" It might even make *Variety:* **Hix Nix Pix Chix."**

Although, in the interest of accuracy, "Duck Creek Strangler" is a ghastly misnomer. But you know how newspapers are. So far, we have two by water, one by blade, and only two by strangulation, unevenly divided between Duck Creek and New York City. I might be tempted to set the record straight. I might even be tempted to improve on the record. But not today. Today, I've done enough, and I feel so good. The sun is shining, and I am content to await further developments. With great interest.

CHAPTER XXXII

I couldn't tell him, Leo. I said I would, but when it came right down to it, when he was standing right there where you are, looking at me with those sad, trusting eyes, all I could do was order another drink. I thought the first one would give me courage, but all it did was make me want the second. And the third. I might as well go straight back to the funny farm and turn myself in.''

Hilda Kramer crouched in a booth in the hotel's tiny cocktail lounge, guarding her drink with both hands. Although her face showed unmistakable traces of tears, her eyes were dry and feverish. She spoke in a low, emotionless monotone. Leo, shocked at the change in her appearance, sat beside her and watched helplessly as she drained her glass and crunched a piece of ice between her teeth.

"Be a good boy," she muttered, "and get me another one of these. And get something for yourself. It's hell to drink alone.''

Leo nodded to Joe St. Cloud who was standing impassively behind the minuscule bar. To Hilda, he said, "Let's ask Joe to send the drinks to your room. We'll be more comfortable there.''

Stubbornly, Hilda swung her head from side to side. "The only way you're going to get me back into that room is unconscious. Or dead. Hah! Wouldn't that be a good one? Adjoining rooms for adjoining corpses. But who would carry me away and dump me in the lake? Would you do that for me, Leo? You were always a good relation. When we were related. If I were to die, would you hide me in the cool, cool water? I can't face the man. I can't be the one to tell him what's happened. I'd rather die.''

"Isn't that a bit extreme, Auntie dear?" Leo pried one of her cold hands away from her empty glass and held it palm upward between his own. "Will you tell me what's happened or shall I read it in the crinkles of your palm? What's all this about corpses? Have you poisoned the popsie? Can't say as I

197

blame you. I confess to some murderous feelings myself in that direction. Ow, take it easy!''

Leo's howl of pain resulted from Hilda's convulsive grip on his hand. Her fingernails bit into his flesh as she turned, hollow-eyed, to gape at him.

"Did you do it?''

"Do what?''

"No! No!'' She shook her head wildly. "You couldn't have. Not you. Please help me, Leo.''

"Sure thing. Help is at hand with Leo, the helping hand. Only you're rather destroying my good right one with that death grip you're exercising. Would you mind loosening up a bit?''

Hilda sighed and sank back against the red leather of the banquette. Her hand went limp in Leo's hand and she closed her eyes wearily.

"I shouldn't have come here,'' she whispered. "I wasn't ready. Maybe I'll never be ready. The world is a dangerous place, Leo, and I'm not strong enough to cope with it. When I get out of prison, *if* I get out of prison, I'll go to some little town where no one knows me and live in a little room and try very hard to stay off the booze. I'll get a job selling books or scrubbing floors. Nice clean, easy, safe work. And I'll never be seen within a million miles of Larry Devine or anything resembling of a stage. I'm too old to start all over again. And by the time all this is over, I'll be even older and who's going to pay money to see a decrepit, alcoholic jailbird has-been make a public fool of herself? Leo, what do you think it's like in prison?''

"Well,'' said Leo, "they won't be serving Scotch on the rocks for afternoon tea. Here's your drink.''

Joe St. Cloud stood over the table, tray in hand. He placed Hilda's glass in front of her and removed her empty one. Hilda opened her eyes and gazed sourly at the brimming amber liquid. She sat quietly while he served Leo's Bloody Mary and waited for Leo to scrawl his name on the bar chit. Then, as Joe turned to leave, she spoke.

"Joe, please sit down. I have a confession to make and since it concerns you and the hotel, you might as well hear it.''

She picked up her glass and took a long swallow, shuddering as the whiskey passed down her throat. Joe slid into the semicircular booth, his dark eyes questioning Leo. Leo shrugged his bewilderment. Hilda set her glass down and pushed it a few inches away. She sucked in a deep breath, folded her hands schoolgirl fashion on the table, and fixed her eyes on her crossed thumbs. But there the resemblance to a naughty child owning up to a bit of mischief ended. Her voice came clear and strong.

"Glory Hayes is dead," she said. "She was strangled last night in the bathroom that we shared. I'm not confessing to killing her. I don't know who did. It may have been you, or you." She glanced in turn at Joe and Leo, and after a pause returned her gaze to her folded hands. The ice shifted in her glass. "It might have been anybody. Believe me, this isn't a drunken fantasy. Glory Hayes does not have laryngitis and she hasn't skipped out. That was the fantasy. It didn't work. She's not only dead, but her body is missing. Here's where the confession begins. She came to me last night, before dinner, upset and frightened. She asked me to help her and I refused. I thought it was a lot of nonsense. I thought she was trying to grab attention with her Tarot reading and her insistence that someone was out to get her. I admit I didn't like her. She was a terrible actress, and she knew about my past romance with this stuff." Hilda picked up her glass and raised it halfway to her lips, but she changed her mind and set it down again. "I was afraid she'd tell Larry. I didn't want him to know that I'd been a disgusting drunk and had to be put away for my own protection. So I turned Glory away when she needed a friend."

Leo put an arm around her shoulders and hugged her gently. "He already knows, Hilda. You know what gossip is like in this business. But he promised not to mention it unless you brought it up. He's on your side."

Hilda lifted her glass again, and this time she drank deeply from it, putting it down only when it was half empty.

"He won't be when he finds out what I've done. I didn't kill her, but I might as well have. If I'd paid attention to her, I might have prevented her death. But instead, all I could think of was some way to keep her quiet. Now she's quiet all right, but who's going to believe I didn't kill her?"

Joe St. Cloud, who had been absently filling a corncob pipe while listening to Hilda's story, now lit it with a kitchen match, puffed out a cloud of fragrant smoke, and murmured a question.

"Shouldn't the police be notified?"

Hilda shook her head. "I didn't want to. I thought we could still make it look as if she had left. But Tony and Anita insisted. They went to the police station about an hour ago. I don't know why they're not back yet."

"What have Tony and Anita to do with it?" Joe asked.

Hilda sighed and finished off her drink. "I really shouldn't have another one of these, should I? Not if I'm going to have to tell it all over again to the police. Okay, no more. Tony . . . Tony was with me when we found Glory in the bathroom. He helped me set it up so it would appear that she was ill this morning. But it was my idea. He just did what I asked him to do. Apparently, he didn't do a very good job of it. B-r-r-r. Doesn't that sound callous? I think I don't want to talk about it anymore. I think I want to lie down and close my eyes and sleep and sleep and sleep. And if perchance to dream, it can't be any more horrible than staying awake."

Leo lurched out of the booth, nearly toppling his untouched Bloody Mary as he got to his feet. "Come on. You can lie down in my room" he said, "and we'll move all your gear to another room while you're resting. We can do that, can't we Joe?"

"I'll see what we have vacant," said Joe. "There shouldn't be any problem. I'll send one of the maids up to pack your things."

"I'm sure they'll have a vacant cell for me. Accessory before and after the fact. You'll stay with me, won't you, Leo?" Hilda clung to him as she began to struggle her way out of the booth. "I don't want to be alone."

She swayed slightly but managed to stand erect with only a hand resting on Leo's arm. Joe stood at her other side, ready to lend his support if necessary. Step by step, they moved slowly toward the door. From the lobby came the sound of inquiring voices, followed by the appearance in the entrance to the cocktail lounge of two figures.

"So here you are! Is this some kind of exclusive party? We've been waiting and waiting for the rehearsal to get started again, but everybody's disappeared. What's going on?" Tina Elliott filled the doorway with her bulk. Behind her, Pev Martin hovered like an anxious gray shadow. "We didn't know what to do," he said. "Larry said to check with you, Leo, and then he took off. Will we be needed anymore today?"

"Needed?" said Leo. "Oh, my yes. You'll be needed. We'll all be needed before this day is out. In fact, Tina, I need you right now. Come along and help me get Hilda settled down.

Then you stay with her while I try to round up the rest of the gang.''

Hilda raised her head to protest, but Leo silenced her with a look. "Pev," he continued, "we'll need you, too. And Joe, I think a gallon of black coffee wouldn't hurt. Sorry, Hilda, but I can't let you sleep it off just yet. I'm going to get Larry. And we'll all sit tight together until Tony and Anita get here with the police. Come along, everyone. Up to Leo's room where we will all hear news to our considerable disadvantage.''

"What is it? What's going on?" demanded Tina Elliott, blocking the doorway and scowling mulishly. "What's this about the police?''

"Patience, dear child," said Leo. "All will be revealed in due course. You and Pev take Hilda up to my room and stay with her. Joe, if you'll round up Elena, I'll scamper off and dragoon my favorite uncle. And we'll all be glad of that coffee.''

'Right on,'' said Tina. "And if I've got to be patient, I can do it a lot better with a few doughnuts on the side.'' She pressed an elephantine arm around Hilda Kramer's frail waist. "Come on, honey," she urged. "God, but you're skinny. Drinking's okay, and I've tied on a few lulus in my time, but it rots the liver and addles the brain, and I've got a funny feeling that whatever Leo's cooking up, we're gonna need all the smarts we can muster. Pev, stop standing there like a superannuated scarecrow. Give us a hand.''

Pev Martin, drooping listlessly against the doorjamb, hauled himself erect and offered Hilda a courtly but trembling arm. "Come, dear lady," he murmured close to her ear. "'Away, and mock the time with fairest show; False face must hide what the false heart doth know.'''

But whatever conclusion Hilda might have drawn from the old man's whispered words was lost in the general exodus from the cocktail lounge. Tina Elliott chattered encouragingly. Leo dashed back to the table to retrieve his clipboard and rejoined the group in the lobby. He watched as Pev and Tina guided Hilda toward the stairs. Hilda turned once to gaze pleadingly over her shoulder.

"Hurry!" she called to him, and then allowed herself to be led away.

When the group reached the landing, Leo turned to Joe St. Cloud with a puzzled frown.

"Do you believe it?" he asked. "Do you believe any of it, or

201

all of it, or none of it? Or do you think she dreamed it all up under the influence."

"She believes it," said Joe. "And she holds herself responsible for Glory's death, whether or not she actually had any part in it. If Glory's not dead, where is she? For that matter, if Glory *is* dead, where is she? I took the liberty of searching her room this morning. She wasn't there, dead or alive, and all of her belongings are gone. So is her car. So that much of Hilda's story is true. Anita knows something about it. I met her coming out of Glory's room before I searched it. She told me Glory was sleeping and shouldn't be disturbed. I'll call Sam Welles and find out if she and Tony have turned up there."

"Poor old Sam." Leo shook his head sympathetically. "He's probably never had to deal with anything more criminal than pot parties on the beach. I still can't believe it," he went on, "I keep expecting Glory to come barging through the door in full spate, with a bad word for everyone. Well, let's gather our wits and see what we can provide Sam in the way of alibis, mendacious or otherwise."

CHAPTER XXXIII

Hilda lay on the bed in Leo's room staring up at the ceiling. Her frail body, tensed as if for instant flight, trembled visibly while her fingers plucked at loose threads in the coverlet.

Across the room, Pev Martin stood like a weary gray sentinel beside the door, while Tina Elliott hovered solicitously at the foot of the bed.

"Do you want a blanket?" she asked.

Hilda swung her head listlessly from side to side. "No," she whispered, "no blanket." She was silent for a moment. Then she added, "I think I need my tranquilizers. They're up in my room. Tina, would you mind . . ."

"Sure thing," said Tina. "Anything else while I'm up there?"

"No, I don't think so." Hilda groped in her handbag. "Here's the key. You'll find them in the top dresser drawer."

"Be right back." She waddled to the door. There she turned and playfully waggled her fingers at Hilda. "Don't go away," she warned. Hilda smiled weakly and closed her eyes.

Pev Martin opened the door for her and stood aside as she passed through. He followed her out into the hall and watched as she trundled away and began laboriously to climb the stairs. Then he came back inside the room.

"You shouldn't let it trouble you so," he remarked, walking softly toward the bed. "And you shouldn't take tranquilizers on top of liquor. Don't you know you can kill yourself that way?"

Hilda's eyes opened wide. She pushed herself into a sitting position, her shoulders braced against the brass rods at the head of the bed. "The easy way out?" she asked. "I've been tempted, but somehow I always resist that particular temptation. I guess I still think I have something to live for. Although, sometimes, it's hard to figure out what it is."

Pev lowered himself cautiously onto the foot of the bed. His clasped hands fell between his knees and his head drooped.

"And if you had nothing," he murmured, "what then? What would you do?"

Hilda shrugged and reached again for her handbag. "I don't know. Maybe I'd swallow all the pills in the bottle, and maybe I wouldn't." She rummaged in the bag, keeping an eye on the defeated curve of his back. "Maybe I'd try to find something to stay alive on. Most people get by on very little in the way of purpose. Or if I really felt I'd had enough, that there was nothing left to live for, I'd try to make my death mean something. Oh, damn!" She tossed the handbag aside. "Pev, would you be a darling? I think I left my cigarettes in the bar. Would you run down and get them for me? Please?"

Pev swung around and looked at her, his eyes sunken in misery. "Leo said not to leave you alone."

"Leo's a mother hen. He worries too much. I'll be all right. Really. I'll stay right here and lock the door till you get back. And Joe'll be along any minute with that coffee. I'd like a cigarette to go with it. Please?"

"If you're sure . . ."

"I'm sure."

"Well, all right." The old man hauled himself to his feet and reluctantly trudged to the door. "You shouldn't smoke either. It's bad for the voice."

"I know. I know. Maybe tomorrow I'll stop." Hilda got off the bed and placed one hand on his arm while with the other she opened the door. Beneath her fingers she felt his aged muscles quiver. "Hey!" she said, "you've got the shakes almost as bad as I have. Aren't we a lovely pair? Off with you now. And hurry back. I'll be waiting for you." She pushed him gently out of the room.

"Hilda, wait. I want to tell you . . ."

"We'll talk some more when you get back."

She closed the door and Pev Martin stood alone in the hall. It would have been good to talk things over with Hilda. She alone, out of all of them, would have understood his dilemma and possibly could have helped him decide what to do. Soon it would be too late for that kind of talk. Hadn't Leo said something about the police being on the way? Once they arrived, there would be no time for a sympathetic discussion of his problem. Perhaps he should have insisted that Hilda listen to him. But he'd never been any good at insisting on anything. That's what had been so nice about talking with Glory Hayes. She seemed to want to hear his stories. She hadn't seemed a bit bored by them, as people so often were. And she had made him feel young and full of possibilities. And now she was . . . gone. Behind him, he heard the key turn in the lock. Pev Martin shuffled away and slowly descended the stairs.

Minutes later, when Elena and Joe St. Cloud were able to free themselves from a kitchen crisis—the cook's son had run his motorcycle into the rear end of a boat trailer—and arrived at Leo's room with a huge pot of coffee and tray of cups, the room was empty.

CHAPTER XXXIV

She hasn't moved.

No, poor chick, nor will she move again. But she will very soon be moved from this place. No doubt she will be peered at and probed into by the curious daggers of officialdom, so that she may be declared officially dead of such-and-such causes. Perhaps I should have hidden her away from their slicing knives, a peaceful burial in a lonely country grave with a dignity she never knew in life.

See now, how she lies with quiet dignity. The gown was an inspiration from the wardrobe room next door. White satin, with a modest touch of lace at the throat to hide the angry scar of death. A scrap of veiling over the face. There was nothing I could do to bring tranquility to those distorted features. The veil gives her a bridal look. I'm sorry, dear child, that your flowers are false, mere dusty replicas of sweet lilies of the valley, thrust into your pale cold hands. But they will serve. Rest easy, my lady. I've straightened your limbs and clothed your nakedness. I've combed your hair until it lies like golden bands across your shoulders. I've done everything for you that I can. If I could kiss you back to life, I would. But all an old man's kiss can do is promise a swift reunion on the other side. Perhaps we'll meet and I'll tell you more stories of the grand old days that weren't so grand after all. Adieu, adieu. . . .

"Pev!"

The word was whispered, but no less shocked and shocking. The old man, who had bent to press his lips to the veiled brow of the figure that lay on the long table, whirled round to answer to his name.

"You killed her!" the voice came again. "It was you! But why? What had she done to you?"

"No! Hilda, wait!" The old man lurched forward. "You don't understand."

Hilda Kramer stood frozen in the open doorway of the prop room in the murky upper regions of the Duck Creek Playhouse. To either side the open shelves which once held cannery supplies were cluttered with the disused artifacts of previous summers' entertainments. Chalices and coffee pots, swords and canes and ruffled parasols, toy pistols looking real and real telephones looking oddly false, an entire gardenful of plastic flowers, papier-maché boulders, and painted cardboard trees uprooted and lying flat waiting to be resurrected for some future sylvan setting. In the center of the room, the long work-table, where clever hands fashioned illusion out of scrap, now served as a bier. Hilda could not take her eyes from the white-gowned form that lay there.

The old man moved, stiff-legged and awkward, his mottled hands extended like the grasping talons of a predatory bird. Hilda opened her mouth to scream, but found she could not force a sound past the choking fear lodged in her throat.

"Sssh!" the old man cautioned. "Don't you hear it? There's someone else in the building. We can't let them find us. I'm not ready for them yet. Don't be afraid. I won't hurt you. I didn't hurt her."

"You brought her here," Hilda whispered. "You dressed her like that."

"Yes, yes," the old man agreed. "Come in and close the door. You'll be safe with me. You can help me. There's danger out there. Don't you hear the footsteps on the stairs? There isn't much time."

The old man's fingers touched her wrist. She shuddered and wrenched away, pulling the door closed as she backed out into the deserted corridor. The narrow stairway that led down to the backstage area lay some thirty feet away through the crepuscular gloom of the passageway.

She had fled the hotel, after sending both Pev and Tina off on contrived errands, in order to be alone with her thoughts, to separate what she actually knew about Glory's death from what she felt. The playhouse was a logical choice for solitude; Larry had dismissed everyone and Leo had gone to fetch him from the *Hilda Kay*. But after sitting for a few minutes in the darkened theater mulling things over, Hilda had heard faint noises overhead. She had gone up to investigate and had found out more, much more, than she had bargained for. Who would have thought the old man to be a murderer? Yet there he was behind that door, brooding over his handiwork and muttering crazily about danger. Danger! Of course there was danger! He might come bursting out at any moment and wrap those ancient claws around her throat. Hilda ran for the stairs.

Behind the door, Pev Martin picked up a length of nylon rope, passing it between his fingers in a rosary of grim intentions. His lips moved. His fingers worked. His eyes went to the ceiling where the sprinkler pipes obediently conformed to fire regulations. Aainst the wall, a rickety stepladder waited. Far away, he heard a scream, abruptly terminated, and a series of jarring thuds that briefly shook the floor beneath his feet. He worked swiftly then, and when all was ready, paused only to make certain that the folded sheet of paper was correctly positioned in his breast pocket, the edge of it protruding like a freshly laundered white handkerchief.

There was a quick scuffling sound, a crash as the stepladder fell to the floor, and then silence.

CHAPTER XXXV

She asked me to get her tranquilizers for her. When I got back, they were both gone. You can't expect me to keep track of drunks and lunatics." Tina Elliott glowered truculently around the room. She was seated on the sofa in the hotel lounge where, only a few nights before, Glory Hayes had rested after her encounter with the broken power line.

"What did you do then?" Sam Welles was asking the questions. He paced thoughtfully back and forth before the fireplace, pausing now and then to rock back on his heels and jingle the coins in the pockets of his baggy gray uniform trousers.

"What did I do then?" Tina echoed. "I went down to my room to change my clothes. It's almost dinner time, in case you hadn't noticed."

Leo exploded. He leaped to his feet from the armchair where he had been sprawled, the picture of dejection with his fingertips pressed dramatically to his temples. Before anyone could stop him, he pounced on Tina, gripping her flagrant red hair in both hands and pulling her head back so that her face was held up to his angry words.

"Don't you ever think of anything but food, you fat cow?" he shrieked. "I asked you to take care of Hilda, and what do you do? Run off and leave her alone with someone who may be a killer. While you lick your chops and get your grotty self ready to be stuffed!"

"How was I to know?" Tina whimpered, wriggling helplessly on the couch. "Nobody told me anything. She asked me to get her pills. I couldn't find them. I looked everywhere. Even in the bathroom."

Larry Devine intervened. He lumbered to the center of the room and roared, "People!" It had always worked on dissension in rehearsal, and it worked now. All eyes turned toward him. Leo relaxed his grip on Tina's hair. Tina slumped back into the sofa, mopping up tears on the sleeve of her voluminous turquoise gown. Her tiny feet in golden mesh slippers hung helpless, inches from the floor.

"People," Devine repeated, but softly this time. "Apparently we have a problem. We *all* have a problem." He gazed round at the group assembled. "It appears that some of you have been playing at keeping secrets. Guilty secrets. And it appears that I'm the last to know. I appreciate your attempts at sparing me the news."

Leo retreated to his armchair and subsided into it, crossing his legs fussily and finding his clipboard tucked handily into the space between the cushion and the arm. He improved the moment by doodling fiercely sharp-pointed stars on the top sheet of paper. Tony and Anita stood side by side near the window overlooking the front porch, taking very good care neither to touch nor to look at each other. Elena St. Cloud stood in the doorway, her attention divided between the proceedings in the lounge and the activity in the dining room just across the lobby where guests were beginning to assemble for the evening meal.

Larry Devine frowned and swung round on Tony. "You," he barked, "you were the first to know. Why on earth didn't you tell me right away?"

Tony Brand, still ignoring the woman who stood beside him, shrugged and muttered, "I don't know . . . Hilda. . . . We both . . . thought it would be better if it seemed that Glory had skipped out. Hilda had her reasons, and I guess I had mine. We were both afraid we'd be blamed for it. And besides, I thought maybe . . . I thought . . ." He faltered and fell silent.

"You thought I'd done it!" Anita broke in to finish his sentence. "How could you? Did you think I was *that* desperate for a job? Or did you think I was so jealous of the way she was climbing all over you that I would kill her just to keep you for myself? That's so ridiculous, it doesn't even deserve an answer."

Tony rounded on her angrily. "No more ridiculous than you thinking I'd done it. I thought you trusted me. I thought you knew me well enough to know I couldn't have done such a thing. I admit to behaving stupidly last night. But I didn't kill her. Even if no one else believes, me, I thought you would. So much for love and all its works."

"That's a knife that cuts both ways," Anita fumed, and would have continued had not Larry Devine interrupted.

"All right, you two," he soothed. "Let's not waste time accusing each other. The main point right now is that Hilda and Pev aren't here, and we don't know where they are. If anybody's seen them, or has any idea where they could be, now's the time to speak up. Right, Sam?"

Sam Welles, who had been quietly observing the interplay among the characters scattered about the room, much as if he had been seated in the front row at one of the playhouse's dramatic productions, now stepped forward to take part in the action.

"We'll know whether or not they're still in the hotel as soon as Joe and my boys get back from their search. Meanwhile, let's go over once again the last time each of you saw them. Tony?"

Tony sighed and raised his eyes to the ceiling. "At the theater," he intoned in a bored voice. "Anita wanted to go to the police. Hilda didn't want to, but she finally agreed that Anita and I should go. We left her there to tell Larry what was happening. That's the last time we saw her. I don't remember where Pev was when we left."

Anita nodded her agreement, adding, "Hilda was very upset. But when I looked back before we left the theater, she was heading down the aisle toward the stage. I remember thinking that if she could bring herself to talk it over with Larry, she would feel a lot better. He cares about her, you know." She cast an accusing glance at Tony, who continued to regard the ceiling.

"Fine," said Sam Welles. "And that would be about what time?"

"Three-thirty, four o'clock," said Anita. "Something like that. We'd been waiting about half an hour at the station before you came in."

"All right," said Welles. "Next?"

"I guess that would be me," said Larry Devine. "I called a long break because I was getting pretty annoyed with Glory behaving like a prima donna. I wanted to talk to her myself and find out what she was up to. Laryngitis! At least, that's what they told me. Leo and all the rest of them."

"Don't blame me!" Leo protested. "They had me fooled, too. It was just the kind of dumb trick the silly popsie would play."

"Anyway," Devine continued, "I went up to the hotel to give her warning. I don't mind telling you that if I didn't get a satisfactory answer out of her, I was just about ready to ship her out and let Anita here take over. But she wasn't there. I banged on the door and shouted, but no one answered. When I came back downstairs, Joe told me she'd cut out, bag and baggage. Then I saw Hilda in the bar. I went in to talk to her, but as soon as she saw me, she started crying and carrying on about how she should never have come back into my life and that she was bad luck for everything and everyone she touched. She begged me to go away and leave her alone, and then she ordered another drink. What could I do? I went back to the theater. But I sent Leo up to see if he could straighten her out. She always liked Leo."

"Right," said Leo. "I dashed up to the hotel, and found her in the bar brooding into her ice cubes. She told us the whole story, Joe and me, and she wanted to go sleep it off. Tina and Pev came in and I sent Hilda up to my room with them. I figured that if I could keep people together, watching each other, nothing else could happen until the police got here. The last I saw of Hilda was Tina and Pev helping her up the stairs while I went to fetch Larry." Leo had been addressing himself soberly to Sam Welles, but now he turned venomously to the fat woman huddled on the sofa. "I distinctly remember asking certain people not to leave her alone."

"But you didn't tell me why," wailed Tina. "And I didn't leave her alone. Pev was with her. If I'd known what was going on, I never would have gone looking for those stupid pills. I didn't find them anyway. You know what I think? I think it was a wild goose chase. I think she wanted to get rid of me. Why would she do that unless she wanted to be alone with Pev? How do we know *she's* not the killer? She's probably murdered that poor old man and while we're all sitting here twiddling our thumbs, she could be on her way to . . . to Canada or God knows where."

"How would you like your fat lips made a little fatter?" snarled Leo. "You didn't like Glory any better than anyone else. As long as we're slinging accusations around, how do we know *you* didn't do the popsie in because she called you a pregnant hippo? And not far off the mark, if you ask me."

"Me!" squealed Tina. "Oh, I wish I'd never come here. I could have gone to five or six other places. I had a choice. And I had to choose to come here where I'm insulted every time I turn around and accused of murder on top of it. It's a good thing I'm not vindictive, or I might point out that Glory was

214

pretty outspoken on the subject of gays around us. Maybe you killed her in a fit of pique."

The fat woman flounced self-righteously upon the sofa, causing it to creak and shudder alarmingly. Leo was about to retort, but Sam Welles held up both hands admonishingly.

"Easy on, easy on," he rumbled. "You folks are making this country boy's head spin with all this hullabaloo about who did what and why and when. So far's I know for sure, we don't even have us a body yet, let alone a murder. All we've got is your word on it." He nodded at Tony and Anita. "But I'm willing to listen, providing you all stick to what you know and what you saw."

"I didn't see Hilda," said Elena St. Cloud from the doorway. "But I saw him. The old man."

"Where was that?" asked Welles.

"In the lane. Joe and I had gone up to Leo's room and found it empty. I went back to help out in the kitchen. The cook's son was in the infirmary and she had gone to stand by while he was being stitched up. Nothing serious, and she's back now. But while I was chopping salad greens, I looked out the window and saw the old man going up the lane toward the theater. I thought nothing of it. You people always use the lane."

"The theater!" exclaimed Leo, half rising out of his chair. "Hilda might have gone there. And he might have gone with her. Or followed her. We ought to. . ."

But whatever Leo was about to propose was interrupted by the sound of hurrying footsteps on the front porch and the crash of the door being thrown open. This disturbance was followed by the appearance in the entrance to the lounge of a flushed and agitated Emmy Jackson.

"You've got to come," she panted. "Oh, I'm so glad I found you, Larry. All of you. Call an ambulance! Quick! And come with me. I think she's still alive. I hated to leave her but there was no one else around and I didn't dare move her."

Devine moved swiftly to the trembling woman and gripped her heaving shoulders. "Where is she, Emmy?" he demanded. "It's Hilda, isn't it? Where?"

"At the theater," she gasped. "Backstage. At the foot of the stairs. She must have fallen."

Leo glared at her. "Let's go," he shouted. "If she's dead, somebody is going to be very, very sorry."

215

"I'll call the ambulance," said Elena, running across the lobby to the phone at the registration desk.

"You stay here, Emmy," said Devine. "We'll take care of her." He started for the door, but was held by Sam Welles's hand on his arm.

"Wait," said Sam. "I'd like you to ride over with me."

Leo was already out the door, followed by Tony and Anita. Tina Elliott heaved herself from the sofa and waddled in their wake. Devine tried to lead Emmy Jackson to a chair, but she insisted on returning to the theater.

"Might be I could help," she said. "Oh, the poor thing. Lying there so pale and scarcely breathing. It's a darn good thing I decided to go back and try to get that prop room door open. I found a bunch of old keys at home and I thought maybe one of them might work."

"Was there anyone else in the theater?" asked the police chief.

"I don't think so," said Emmy. "I didn't look. Why, Sam Welles! What on earth are you doing here? I heard about young Jerry, and I'm real sorry. But shouldn't you be with Alberta?" Concern spread itself over Emmy Jackson's round face and she patted the police chief's gnarled hand with her plump one.

"Never mind that right now, Emmy. Suppose you ride back to the theater with us."

"Mercy!" cried Emmy Jackson. "I've never in my life had a ride in a police car! What would Henry have said, rest his soul?"

"He'd have said. 'Go along and stop dithering, woman.'" Sam Welles crossed the lobby in three or four long strides, Emmy Jackson bobbling along beside him. He stopped at the registration desk, where Elena was just putting down the phone.

"The ambulance is on the way," she said. "And they'll have a doctor standing by at the infirmary. If it's serious, they may have to take her into Traverse."

While she was speaking, Joe St. Cloud and two young policemen clattered down the stairs. The two marched smartly up to Chief Welles and gave their report.

"Search completed, sir," said one, standing at attention.

"Subjects do not appear to be on the premises," said the other.

"Okay, fine," said Welles. "Now get your tails over to the playhouse and keep an eye on things. The lady's been found and she's in bad shape. Don't let anybody move her. Could be the old geezer's there, too. If he turns up, latch onto him. I'll be there directly."

"Sir!" chorused the two, wheeling about and marching out the front door.

Sam Welles shook his head. "Make me feel like a Marine Corps drill sergeant," he commented. "But they're good boys. Don't know how they manage to keep a crease in them uniform trousers." He glanced ruefully down at his own baggy gray pants, and then looked up at Joe St. Cloud. His eyes, keenly alert, belied his casual approach. "Joe," he said, "I don't have enough men to cover both the playhouse and the hotel. If the old man turns up here, will you make sure he stays put?"

Joe nodded.

Welles turned to Devine, who had been waiting impatiently near the door. "This kind of puts the skids under your season, doesn't it?" he asked.

"That's not important," said Larry. "Hilda's the only thing that matters now. I should have walked over with the others."

"We're on our way," said Welles, stepping aside to allow Emmy to precede him out the door. "I asked you to ride with me because I want you to tell me everything you know about these people. Start with the old guy. What's his name?"

The blue and white police car was parked right in front of the hotel. Welles helped Emmy into the back seat and motioned Devine around to the front.

"Peverill Martin," said Devine, slamming the door as Welles keyed the ignition to life. "A good, reliable character actor. Been around for years. Started way back in vaudeville, but never made much of a name for himself. Just another one of the thousands of actors who keep body and soul together on a diet of hope, unemployment, and a couple of jobs a year. You'd think they'd give it up and find another way to make a living. Some of them do. But Pev and all the others like him keep on year after year, even when there's nothing left to hope for. I'm always glad when I can give one of them a job."

The car swung around the corner of the hotel and lurched down the lane toward the playhouse.

"Sam," said Emmy from the backseat, "aren't you going to turn on the siren?"

CHAPTER XXXVI

"Don't touch her. Don't anyone touch her. Just keep away."

Leo Lemming knelt beside the still figure crumpled in a heap at the foot of the stairs. Hilda Kramer lay curled on her side, one arm flung away from her body, the other twisted beneath her, and her knees drawn up. Her eyes were closed and her face, paler than usual, gleamed whitely in the dim backstage area. "Can't you find those lights, Tony?"

"Just a minute," came Tony's voice from the opposite side of the stage. "I think I've got it."

The harsh unshaded work lights came on, bathing the scene in a pitiless glare. Leo, his fingers pressed to the wrist of Hilda's outflung arm, bent closer to the pallid face, murmuring, "Come on, Auntie Hilda. You can do it, old girl. Let's have a little flicker of a pulse, just a little thumperoo. That's all it takes. Do it for Leo."

"How is she?" whispered Anita, standing just behind Leo and peering over his shoulder. "Will she be all right?"

Leo straightened up. "I don't know," he muttered. "I'm no doctor. I *think* I can feel a pulse. I *think* she's breathing. But it's so faint I can't be sure. Where the hell is that ambulance?"

"It's on its way, sir."

The two policemen had marched onto the stage and taken up positions on either side of the pale, still woman.

"You mustn't touch her, sir. Please stand back."

Leo got to his feet. "She could be dying and all you can say is 'please stand back.' Can't you *do* something?"

"Orders, sir. Wait for the ambulance."

His companion seemed to relent a trifle. He said, "We can give first aid in an emergency, but it's better to wait when we know an ambulance is coming. They'll be here soon."

Leo scowled and moved reluctantly aside. Tony had rejoined Anita in keeping a silent vigil a few feet away. They still

218

avoided looking at each other, but Anita's hand found its way into Tony's and he gripped it warmly. Leo was about to join them when he heard his name called.

"Leo, come here a minute."

It was Tina Elliott. She stood on the first step of the stairway, peering up into the gloom above.

"What is it?" he asked ungraciously, with no intention of complying with her request.

"I don't know. There's something on the stairs. Maybe you can tell what it is."

Curiosity won, and Leo joined the fat woman on the stairway, mounting a few steps beyond her and gazing upward. Tina clung to his arm.

"Look," she whispered. "I'm sorry about leaving her with Pev. I had no idea she was in danger. I still don't understand what's going on here."

A siren shrieked in the distance. Leo looked back at the two policemen, who nodded encouragingly.

"You see, sir," said one. "Here they come."

"But, Leo," Tina insisted. "There *is* something on the stairs. Look, it's near the top. I'd go up and see what it is, except I'm a little bit afraid. What if Pev is lurking about up there?"

Leo ascended two more steps with Tina following close behind, still clinging to his arm. Dimly, he saw a small dark shape extending out from the edge of the third step from the top. It was impossible to discern exactly what it was. Something left carelessly on the stairs. Something for Hilda to trip over in her less than sober condition. So it may have been an accident. But what was Hilda doing on the stairs in the first place? Was she going up or coming down when she fell? What had drawn her to the theater when she should have been safe in his room, waiting for the police to hear her story? And where was Pev Martin? Could he, as Tina suggested, be hiding in the warren of rooms on the upper floor?

"Let's go see what it is," said Leo. He shook off Tina's clinging hands and bounded up the stairs. The two policemen watched him go, but made no move to stop him. Their orders were to guard the injured woman and to prevent the old man from leaving if he turned up. Nothing about people going upstairs. Tina Elliott breathed heavily as she followed Leo up the narrow staircase.

Near the top of the stairs, Leo paused. "It's a shoe," he

called down to Tina who was by then halfway up and toiling onward. "It looks like hers. We probably shouldn't touch it. Can you see if she's missing a shoe?"

Tina looked back down the stairs. "Can't tell," she said. "Both her feet are underneath her skirt." She continued her climb, coming to a halt a few steps below Leo. She stood still, clutching the rail and panting. "Stairs'll be the death of me yet," she gasped. "Well, now that we're up here, maybe we should take a look around. Find out what she was doing up here."

She peered past Leo into the dimness of the long corridor that ran the entire length of the building, illuminated only by tall unshaded windows at either end. Through one of them, the golden rays of the early evening sun penetrated a few feet before they were lost in the dust-filled, murky air. "Aren't there any lights?" she asked.

Leo reached around the corner of the stairway housing and pressed a switch. At intervals along the ceiling, low-watt light bulbs in wire cages flickered into feeble life making the corridor look longer and more scabrous than it had in its disguising gloom. Dirty cream-colored paint was peeling from the waist-high wainscoting and the plaster above was riven by cracks that ran like mighty rivers from the ceiling. The floor was covered with an ancient brown-patterned linoleum that was worn bare in places and buckled in others. Up and down the corridor, brown painted doors with white porcelain doorknobs were closed and uncommunicative.

"What do you people keep up here?" asked Tina. "Bodies?"

"Not funny," said Leo, keeping his voice low. He glanced back down the stairs to where the creased trousers and polished shoes of Hilda's guardians were visible beneath the slanted overhang of the enclosed stairwell. "I should go back down and stay with her."

"Oh, come on," Tina urged. "Now that we're up here, we should take a look in these rooms. Pev could be hiding up here. Don't you want to find him?"

"Sure I do," said Leo, "but maybe we should wait until Sam Welles gets here."

Outside the building and muffled by the surrounding walls, two siren voices competed for prominence and then whined into silence.

"He's here," said Tina. "If we run into trouble, we can just yell. Is there any other way down besides those stairs?"

"No."

"Then come on." Tina surged past him and waddled importantly down the hallway. Reluctantly, Leo followed.

At the first door she came to, Tina twisted the knob and, with elaborate caution, slowly edged the door open and poked her head into the room. She drew back quickly, colliding with Leo who was hovering apprehensively behind her. Her face was a wrinkled mask of repugnance.

"Phoo!" she exclaimed. "What a smell!"

"Mothballs," said Leo. "Emmy takes very good care of our costumes. Is there anybody in there?"

"I don't know," said Tina. "If there is, they've probably suffocated by now. Shall we look?"

She took a fine lace-edged handkerchief from her pocket and held it over her face as she pushed the door open wider.

"Yoo-hoo," she called into the shrouded racks of costumes that filled the room. "Pev, honey, are you here?"

"Shut up!" Leo hissed behind her, resisting the urge to pinch her fat arm. "If he's here, he's not going to answer you. We'll have to search between the racks."

Despite his antipathy for Tina and his desire to know whether or not Hilda was alive and likely to recover, Leo found himself drawn into the search. If Pev Martin were responsible for Hilda's accident, assuming it was an accident and not a deliberate attempt to kill her, Leo wanted to be the one to face him with it. If he was a killer, and Hilda herself had been terrified that someone among them had strangled Glory and might be inclined to strike again, then Leo was not at all averse to making the capture. But it was hard to believe that the old man, thin, fragile, and weary, had been physically capable of choking off the life of such a strong, healthy young animal as Glory had been.

He followed Tina up and down the racks, lifting the dust covers to be sure that no one was crouched among the ball gowns or frock coats, the limp shreds of marabou boas, or the silver-painted knitted leggings pretending to be chain mail. He found nothing but memories of past seasons' triumphs and disasters: *Joan of Lorraine,* in which he'd played the Dauphin; *Hedda Gabler,* when on opening night the pistol refused to fire and he'd had to improvise with a leftover Fourth of July firecracker fortunately confiscated from a plague of children who had been tossing them under the loading dock. Memories. This season would yield memories of quite a different sort.

"Nobody here," said Tina, waving her handkerchief in front of her face. "What's in all those other rooms?" She led the way back into the corridor.

"Oh, props, odds and ends of furniture, some of them we haven't even cleaned out yet. There's a room full of labels for canned cherries."

He listened to the voices rising up the stairwell from below. Apparently, the ambulance attendants were getting ready to move Hilda. That must mean she was still alive. "Let's go downstairs. Sam Welles can finish the search."

"No. Wait. Pev is an old friend of mine. I think he'd like to see a friend before he has to see Sam Welles. Let's try one more room." Tina rolled away down the hall, knocking on doors as she passed them. "How about this one?" She had stopped at a door about halfway down the corridor on the same side as the costume room.

"I don't think you can get in there," said Leo. "That's the prop room. Somebody locked it and must have gone off with the key. Emmy and I have been trying to get it open for two days."

"Oh?" said Tina. "Well, there's a key in the lock now." She turned the knob and pushed. "And the door isn't even locked."

"Wait!" cried Leo. "Don't go in there!"

He sprinted down the hall, but was too late to stop the fat woman from flinging the door open.

"Why not?" she inquired, and then turned to enter the room.

Leo reached her just as she began to buckle. He caught her, his hands fumbling amidst the folds of her gown, and managed to thrust his arms beneath hers and brace her sagging weight against his thigh. He locked his hands under her enormous breasts, while her head lolled back against his chest. Her eyes sought the ceiling, rolling frantically from side to side. Her fat cheeks wobbled and beads of moisture ran from beneath her frizzled fringe of red hair. Beneath her musky perfume, Leo smelled the rankness of sweat and fear.

"Oh my God!" she muttered over and over again. "Oh my God! Oh my God!"

"Yes," said Leo as he gazed in awe over her limp body at Peverill Martin, who swung gently at the end of a rope, his feet only inches from a table which held a white-clothed form whose face was covered by a lacy veil, but whose golden hair lying in gleaming strands on the table left no doubt as to her identity. "Oh, yes," Leo repeated. "I should have guessed."

CHAPTER XXXVII

The boys in the creased trousers cut him down and laid him on the floor, their composure at last shaken by the sight of ugly self-inflicted death. The old man's face was not pleasant to look upon. Sam Welles covered it with his own red bandanna handkerchief, a jarring note, but less so than the bulging eyes and empurpled cheeks it hid.

Out in the corridor, Tina Elliott sat propped against the wall, her short legs extended and her tiny golden-slippered feet pointed in a dancer's arch beneath the hem of her turquoise gown. Leo knelt beside her, alternately bathing her face with a cold, wet cloth and chafing her plump, twitching hands. The others—Larry Devine, Anita Stratton, Tony Brand—stood uncertainly about the corridor, helpless in the face of the old man's suicide, for suicide it undoubtedly was, not wishing to seem ghoulish but, all the same, eager for news of the contents of the note that had been found on the body. Emmy Jackson, as practical as ever, had gone to fetch the smelling salts, kept handy for fainting members of the audience, from the first-aid kit in the office.

Leo looked up from his ministrations. "How is Hilda? Is she. . . ."

"She'll be all right," said Devine. "Just bruised and shaken up, but they'll X-ray her just to be sure. She came around while they were lifting her onto the stretcher, and she even made a joke about it. She looked up at me and said, 'Don't worry, Larry. I was always good at taking pratfalls.'"

"Thank God!" said Leo fervently. "Did she say anything else? How it happened?"

"No. She just smiled and tried to blow me a kiss while they rolled her away. Poor Glory, I couldn't believe she was really dead until I saw her, in there. She said it was in the cards, and this might just make me a believer. I guess I'm going to have to call Barney Gross before he reads about it in the newspapers."

Tony Brand pulled himself off the wall and slouched forward diffidently, his hands rammed into the pockets of his jeans. "I don't want to seem insensitive," he muttered, "but what about the season? Anita and I ought to see about getting other jobs if you're going to close down."

Devine hunched his shoulders and shook his head. "I don't know. I just don't know. If Hilda's really all right, well, maybe. . . ."

"Anita can take over for Glory," said Brand. "She already knows the part."

"And I can play old men," volunteered Leo. "I've done it before. In fact, I've done it so often, I think I'm having premature prostate problems."

"Ooh," moaned Tina Elliott from the floor. "The show must go on, mustn't it? Oh, 'that it should come to this! But two months dead; nay, not so much, not two,' and not two days, not even two hours dead, and you're all ready to forget him. Well, I can be as cruel as you. I'll play my part. Pev would have wanted the show to go on, so let's get on with it." She struggled to get up from the floor, but slipped and fell back down. Emmy hovered, waving the smelling salts bottle.

"Take it easy, Tina," said Leo, crouching beside her. "We're not as heartless as we seem. It's better to keep doing what we can than to brood about what we can't do. And there's nothing any of us can do about Pev or Glory now."

Emmy pressed the bottle into Tina's hand. "Here, dear. Take a whiff of this if you feel giddy. It'll blow your socks off."

Tina clutched at her and dragged her down, until Emmy was forced to sit beside her on the floor. "He was good to me," Tina moaned. "You don't know, none of you know. He used to buy me ice cream and take me for rides on the merry-go-round. He even took me up in an airplane once, joyriding was all. A dollar a ride. A long time ago. He was good and kind and gentle. And now he's dead and all any of you can think of is who's going to take over his part. That's show biz, all right, and it's rotten. It stinks. But he would have understood. He would have done the same thing." She wept then, with Emmy's grandmotherly arms around her, vast, gulping sobs of a child bewildered by grief.

"Can't we get her out of here?" Emmy asked. "I can take her home with me and put her in the spare bedroom. She shouldn't be left alone."

"In just a few minutes, Emmy." Devine glanced at the closed door of the prop room. "Sam asked us all to wait until he finished in there. And we'll leave the question of whether we go on or not until tomorrow. Tony, is that all right with you? One day won't make that much difference, will it?''

Tony shrugged and leaned indolently against the wall. ''I don't know what all the fuss is about. He's a murderer, isn't he? I should think you'd all be glad he's put himself out of business. I am, because it gets me off the hook. I won't be blamed for something I didn't do. And I can't pretend to feel sorry for the old creep. He must have been pretty perverted to dress a corpse up like a bride and stick a bunch of flowers in her hands. In my honest opinion, he's better off dead.''

The group fell silent after this, except for the continued sound of Tina's weeping. Anita, who had listened shocked and embarrassed to Tony's tirade, moved quietly away from him to offer Tina a fresh handkerchief. Honesty, she thought, was all very well so long as you didn't use it as a club to belabor the helpless. And Tina, at this moment, was the picture of grief-stricken helplessness. Evidently, Pev Martin had some special relationship to her, something going back a long time. Tony's honest opinions were having a devastating effect on her. And Tony, if you wanted to be perfectly honest about it, was not disinterestedly devoted to the truth. So far, he'd said not a word about his previous acquaintance with Glory. As she bent to comfort the weeping fat woman, no longer a ridiculous figure in her sorrow, Anita wondered if Joe St. Cloud would give her a separate room at the hotel. She had a lot of decision-making to do, and it would be easier to do alone, even in one of those monastic rooms up under the eaves. Anything would be preferable to spending another night sharing Tony's bed.

The prop room door opened. Sam Welles, his face grayer, if possible, than before, came into the corridor. He held a folded sheet of paper in his hand.

''You folks,'' he began, and had to stop to clear his throat. He unfolded the note, appeared to read it, shook his head, and began again. ''You folks can go now,'' he said. ''There's nothing more to be done here, except to carry them away.'' He nodded toward the prop room, from which came the slow dragging sounds of official activity. ''My boys'll take care of that.'' He paused and seemed to drift into a reverie.

''The note,'' Devine prompted. ''What does it say?''

''The note?'' Welles stared at the paper in his hand as if it were written in a strange, undecipherable language. ''It says, well, to put it plain, it says he killed them both, your young lady and my Alberta's Jerry.''

"Oh, Sam," breathed Emmy Jackson. "That's awful. You ought to let someone else take over the case."

"There isn't any case, Emmy. It's all over but the burying. Oh, there are one or two things to do before that," he went on earnestly, but a sad weariness permeated his words. "We'll have to make sure this was written in his own hand. I don't think there's any doubt that it was, but we'll have to check it out. And then, we'll have to notify the next of kin. For both of them."

"Pev didn't have any next of kin. I guess I'm the closest thing he had to a relative. And I'm only a friend. A very old friend." Tina Elliott had risen from the floor and now stood like a short rotund monument to grief. Her face, despite its gaudy frame of frizzled orange-red hair, displayed a kind of mournful dignity, while her loose dress, in contrast to its garish color, fell in classic folds about her ample form. She might never be chosen to play Electra or Medea, but for this moment she stood among the great queens of tragedy and held her own. "I'll see to his burial," she said. "He would have done the same for me."

If she had been on stage, she would have received a spontaneous round of applause. In the narrow confines of the shabby corridor, her words were followed by a moment of respectful silence. Then Larry Devine spoke.

"Is that all it said? The note?"

"Ah," Sam Welles pondered. "That's about it. He said it fancy, and I'm a plain man. But I don't think I missed anything. He didn't call Jerry by name. He didn't know his name. 'The boy,' that's what he called him. How can you kill someone without even knowing his name?"

Devine took the note from Sam Welles's hand. Welles let it go without objection.

"Do you mind if I read it?" Devine asked.

Welles shook his head.

Devine looked round the group, and then read the words that marched across the page in a thin precise array of neat copperplate script.

"'I hear the knell that summons me to heaven or to hell.' That's how it starts. There isn't any salutation."

"Pev was always quoting," remarked Tina. "He loved Shakespeare."

Devine continued reading. "'I cannot tell you why I've done the deeds that make my course today imperative. The reasons if there be reasons go with me to be hammered on the anvil of the gods. If there be gods. I need not tell you how they died. By now you know, or soon will. What, then, must I say? That I have taken lives, young lives, brief lives, quenched them as mercilessly as the candle is snuffed when the feast is over. My feast is, indeed, over and I leave the table sickened at myself. She was young, beautiful, eager for all that she could grasp. No shame in that. Don't we all, each in our way, clutch to ourselves the symbols of safety: money, power, a person stronger than we are to shield us from the perils of the world? And he, the boy, younger still, innocent and unaware of his role in the tragedy. To me he remains nameless. His death, now that I look at it, was unnecessary, and I am sorry for it. But now, no more. I've said my piece. It's best I should be brief, before I lose my nerve. An outpouring of remorse would serve no better purpose than my present death. I wish, dear Tiny, for your sake, that I could do this nobly, in Roman fashion, and run upon my sword. But I am gallows meat and take my everlasting farewell suitably dangling from the end of a rope. Forever and forever, farewell.'"

Devine looked up from the page. "That's it," he said.

"Well," said Leo. "That seems to say it all. Come along, kiddies. We might as well toddle." His voice cracked, but he chattered on. "There'll be funeral baked meats and all that sort of thing to take care of. Tina, my love, what's your pleasure? Back to the hotel? Or would you like us to escort you to Emmy's rose-covered cottage on the village green?"

Tina Elliott glanced shyly at Leo and then at Emmy. "All of a sudden," she said, "I'm terribly hungry. If we hurried, do you think we could still get some dinner at the hotel?"

CHAPTER XXXVIII

The Duck Creek Playhouse survived the season. In fact, you might say it had its most successful season on record. Publicity never hurts, and people came from as far away as Chicago, just to see the plays and the place where murder and suicide had happened. The St. Clouds did a roaring business, although, for some reason, they refused to rent out Glory's room. A photographer came and the newspapers ran a lovely picture of me in costume. It makes a nice addition to my new scrapbook.

I read in *Variety* the other day that Tony Brand was off to the West Coast. I wonder what he's up to. Something in the movies, no doubt. Good for him.

I went to see Anita Stratton last week. She's appearing in an Off-Broadway production of *The Lady's Not for Burning*. Got good reviews, too. Well, she deserves them. I like to see people get ahead. For a while, I thought she had something going with that good-looking Indian. But obviously, that didn't work out. She's not the sort to bury herself in a town like Duck Creek.

That same issue of *Variety* had a little item on the back page, just after the obituaries. Hilda Kramer and Larry Devine got married. Second time for both of them. That's all it said. Funny they didn't invite me to the wedding. After all, I visited her in the hospital every day until she got out. She never could remember very much about falling down those stairs. No matter how many times I asked her, she just wouldn't talk about it. I cut the clipping out anyway. It adds a little touch of romance to the scrapbook. I pasted it on the page that follows Pev Martin's final notices.

He made it, old Pev did. Made it big. He made it in the trades and he made it in *The New York Times* and *The Los Angeles Times* and *The Detroit Free Press*. With pictures. Of course, the pictures didn't look anything like him. Not the way he looked there at the end. What a way to go! Suicide by hanging. How could he do that to himself? And what a shock it was

231

to walk into the prop room and find him dangling from a sprinkler pipe. A good thing Leo was with me. I could have had a heart attack. Believe me, I won't forget that face for a long time.

He shouldn't have done it. Nobody asked him to do it. Hanging there like a sack of desiccated old bones with a confession sticking out of his pocket. I could have killed him, I was so angry. But it was too late. He'd already stolen my thunder. Talk about upstaging, he really did a number on me. And not just the confession. The letter. A personal, private letter to me left on top of my bedside box of chocolates where I'd be sure to find it.

Dear Tiny, it said. Dear Tiny. It's there in my scrapbook just in front of his obituaries. I've tried to do it in chronological order. Dear Tiny. Some nerve when he knew exactly what he was doing to me.

"Dear Tiny," he wrote, "it is a far, far better thing that I do, than I have ever done."

Leave it to old Pev always to be quoting somebody. I guess we all do it. There's always a line that springs to mind to cover just about any situation. That's what you get for living your life spouting other people's words. Anyway, on with the drivel in his letter. I've read it so often, I could stand up before an audience and deliver it word for word.

"How I wish I could speak that line to you, instead of merely writing it down. But by the time you read this, I shall be beyond words of any kind. I could have played that role, you know. Oh, Ronnie Colman was handsome. But so was I in those days. It's always been one of my chief regrets that I never even got close to a screen test for that one. I could have made my career with that role, 'Peverill Martin in *A Tale of Two Cities*, and then I would have come for you and told you the truth and you would have had a decent life instead of being hauled around from pillar to post by Tom Elliott.

"The truth. The truth is that Tom Elliott is not your father. I am. You were born in hard times, and my darling Mitzi's life wasn't made any easier when Tom found out she was pregnant with you. He knew, although he'd never bothered to tell her, that he was incapable of fathering children. He was brutal to her. Even before we met, he was in the habit of beating her at the slightest excuse. If his shirts were not properly laundered, if she forgot to polish his shoes. If they failed to get a booking, it was always her fault and liable to gain her a black eye or a swollen lip. Many's the time I helped her cover ugly bruises with a thick layer of greasepaint.

"I begged her to run away with me. We could have left the stage entirely and gone to live in a small town where you would have gone to school and had friends and birthday parties and maybe even a puppy. But she really believed in 'for better or for worse' and wouldn't consider divorce, let alone living with men in what the whole world at that time considered sin. My God! How times have changed!

"So, my dear Tiny, she died, and how many times have I wondered in the years since that dreadful day whether it was truly an accident, or whether in desperation she threw herself in front of that streetcar. All I could do was try to stick close to you and Tom to make sure he didn't mistreat you. Officially, he was your father, and once he found out that you were a good little money-maker, he wasn't about to let you go. Although he didn't mind letting me baby-sit when he had more important things to do. Do you remember all the good times we had together? You used to call me Uncle Wiggly because I wiggled my ears for you.

"I'm afraid I'm boring you with all this ancient history, but some of it is necessary if you are to understand what prompts me to do what I am about to do. My life is over. There have been moments of glitter, but very little pure gold. Your mother was the only gold that ever came my way, and I was careless enough and cowardly enough to lose her. I could have, I should have, taken you away from Tom and given you a father's love. Again, I lacked courage. He told me once that if I ever tried it, he would have me arrested for kidnapping. So instead, I dreamed of the great starring role that would make me rich and famous, so that I could come for you and whisk you away into a life of splendor. It was a dream that never came true. It's only now that I can see it for what it really was—an evasion of my responsibility. While I was dreaming, you were growing, into a young woman and finally into the person you are today.

"I saw you, Tiny. Both times. Did you never sense that someone was watching? I didn't deliberately set out to spy on you, although that's what it amounts to. At first, I was merely looking for a chance to talk with you, to help you, because I could see that you were miserably unhappy with yourself. I followed you from the theater that rainy night. I knew it would be at least a half hour before either of us would be needed on stage. I hoped to have a few minutes alone with you. But when I got to the hotel, you were already going up the stairs with Glory. I waited for a few minutes, wondering what to do—go back to the theater or find out what you were up to. I'd seen you drop that note on her chair the day before, and I knew you bore her malice for the things she'd said about you.

"I followed you up the stairs. I listened outside the door. I couldn't hear anything, except once the sound of breaking glass. After that, I hid on the stairway to the attic. I saw you come out. You looked, forgive me, Tiny, like a vengeful fury, your hair wild, your face pale, your eyes glittering. I thought surely you would see me crouched on the stairs, or at least sense that someone was watching you. But no. You went away. I waited a few minutes and then knocked on Glory's door.

"There wasn't any answer. Of course, there wasn't. I pushed open the door and went in. I saw immediately what you had done, the thing that you had left on the bathroom floor. 'If you have tears, prepare to shed them now.' I told myself that. I should have wept for Glory, and for you. But I had no tears. I am a dry old man, long since cut off from decency and emotion. Maybe that's why I've never been a success. I've been faking it too long.

"I think I knew even then how it would all end. My last grand gesture in an effort to make up to you for all my years of neglect. But first I wanted to see what you would do. I wanted to see for myself what this act meant to you. I have to confess, I'm still not sure. But that doesn't relieve me of my responsibility. I owe you.

"I went back to the playhouse and watched you go through your paces. You're a real pro, Tiny. You carried on as if nothing had happened. And no one seemed to have noticed that we had both been gone for a while. At least, no one said anything about it. Later, after rehearsal was over, I couldn't sleep. I sat out on the porch beneath the overhanging lilac bush, breathing its thick scent, listening to the rain, and pondering how I could save you. From discovery, from yourself, from your terrible legacy of neglect. I wanted to give you a chance to redeem yourself. I saw your light go out and heard your steady breathing through the open window. Perhaps I should have crept in and held a pillow over your sleeping face. But I could never have done that. If I had, that little boy would still be alive. And perhaps I would be, too.

"Later, it seemed like an eternity, I heard scuffling noises and whispering in the hall. I sat very still under the lilac, praying that the wicker chair would keep its peace. I saw Tony Brand and Hilda Kramer carry a shrouded bundle out the side door and away toward the parking lot. Others, it seemed, were determined to keep your secret, too. I watched them disappear into the rainy night. And then I went to bed.

"But not to sleep. I lay there, in the room beside yours, listening for some sound, a nightmare cry, a restless prowling in the guilty hours, that would tell me you suffered for your sins. Then, I think I might have gone to you to offer comfort and to share your agony. They can help people like you, Tiny. There are doctors. But you didn't cry out. Apparently, you slept quite peacefully, while I lay and listened to the rain until it stopped and the gray dawn appeared at my window.

"I got up then and went for a walk in the fog. The beautiful embracing fog. I had no thought in mind except how to convince you to ask for the help you so obviously needed. I realize now that my concern was not entirely on your behalf. I wanted to free myself from my ancient complicity in creating a murdering monster. I had visioned you an innocent Cordelia, myself a foolish and misguided Lear. Instead, you are more bloody that ten thousand vicious Gonerils and Regans. Am I still a fool?

"Perhaps. The fog swirled around me as I wandered, wondering what to do. I found myself high on a dune staring down into a gray abyss. Suddenly, I heard muffled footsteps behind me. I drew back into the shelter of the pines that rimmed the dune, unwilling to share my solitude, and waited. I saw a figure rush through the fog, pause for a moment on the brink, and then plunge over the edge of the dune. I was alarmed lest there be further tragedy, but still I waited and watched.

"The fog was a comfort to me. It obscured the vision and dulled the other senses. I can bear eternity if it turns out to be a soft gray infinite fog that wraps the soul and blunts the memory of earthly torment. But soon the fog began to shred and drift away. I looked down on glimpses of the beach: dank sand, sullen water, and a woman sitting on a log taking off her shoes. I recognized her as Anita Stratton. I watched her walk down to the water's edge and bend to examine something there. Then she ran wildly through the shallow water and fell to her knees, retching into the lapping wavelets. I almost leaped down the dune to help her. She seemed to be ill, maybe poisoned. I thought of you. But then she got to her feet and looked back the way she had come. If she had looked up at the dune, she would have seen me and I would have come down. But she didn't. Instead, she ran back and began tugging at something in the water. The fog continued to lift, and by this time I could see what it was that she had found. It was the thing you had left on the bathroom floor.

"Once she had pulled it part way out of the water, she seemed suddenly to droop with despair, as if she had suddenly realized that the arm she was holding was indeed dead, absolutely and irredeemably lifeless. She dropped it and backed away, and then began walking toward the dune. I hid among the pine trees. She hadn't seen me watching her, and it seemed an inopportune moment to reveal myself. I might have frightened her. And again my cowardly nature asserted itself. I knew that her friend, Tony, had taken the body from the hotel, and yet I didn't feel that it was my place to tell her so. Perhaps she knew it, too. Undoubtedly she would go for help, raise the alarm, bring the police. Soon the whole world would know what you had done.

"I needed time to think about that. I needed to examine why I felt responsible for the death of the poor, silly, pretty creature. I had given you nothing in your life to make it agreeable or easy or even secure in the knowledge of who you were. I had left you in the hands of that brute, Tom Elliott, who used you to shore up his meager talents. Even at that moment, I had the notion that somehow I could do something that would save you, change you, and make up to you for all my neglect. For those reasons, and because I couldn't bear to think of poor Glory lying on the beach like a stray piece of flotsam washed ashore to be gawked at by an insensitive mob, I decided to take her away.

"As soon as I was sure that Anita had left, I climbed down the dune. It wasn't easy for me to carry Glory. She was heavier than I expected, and no matter how I held her she kept slipping out of my arms. I had to drag her up the side of the dune and along the sandy track to the playhouse. And I was so afraid that I would bruise her beautiful tender skin. Ridiculous fear. I should have been afraid that someone might see me, but it never entered my mind, and no one did. It was still very early in the morning.

"The playhouse was unlocked. A stroke of luck, I suppose. But this is still a part of the world where people don't lock their doors. I guess they will now. I don't know why I chose the playhouse for Glory's hiding place. It was nearby, but I think it was also a bit of the homing instinct on my part. The theater, any theater, has always been a place of safety for me, where I could lose myself behind the mask of the characters I played.

"It was exhausting work, carrying her through the deserted theater and struggling with her up the stairs. I found a room that could be locked, laid her on the worktable there, and played the part of wardrobe mistress to the dead. I left her looking like a sweet Juliet, asleep and waiting for a lover's kiss.

"When I got back to the hotel, you were eating breakfast with a good appetite.

"I should have spoken to you then and told you all I knew. Instead, I chose to wait and watch, hoping on the one hand that you would speak, and on the other that you would keep silent and escape discovery through the intervention of the others. And for a while it looked as if you might. When it was announced at rehearsal that Glory was ill, I realized that Tony and Hilda, for reasons of their own, were covering up the fact of her death. I didn't know if they were concealing, as I was, the identity of her killer. I decided to keep an eye on you, and only step forward if you needed my help.

"But you didn't need my help, did you, in killing the boy. It happened so quickly, so smoothly, I couldn't believe my eyes. I'd never seen a murder committed before. How many of us ever do? It was stunning in its simplicity and its inevitability. I was watching from the doorway of the last shanty near the pier. I saw you walk out onto the breakwater and I thought, well, she wants to be alone to think things over. I didn't notice the boy until you stopped to talk to him. And then, before I could shout a warning, the thing was done. One moment the boy was there with his fishing rod, as idyllic a picture of boyhood as could be seen outside of Norman Rockwell, and the next moment he was gone, and you were trudging back along the rocks of the breakwater. I slunk away among the shanties, wondering why, and what I could have done to stop you.

"I'll never know why. Just as he never knew, and no doubt Glory never knew. I wonder if you know. I'm not sure you do. And that is why, dear Tiny, I want to give you this gift. The only one I've ever given you. It's a gift of time and freedom to find your way. It's all the things I never gave you when you should have had them. Take it and use it well. It's all I have left to give.

With love from
Your father"

Well.

Long-winded old coot, wasn't he? As soon as I got back to New York, I went up to the old actors' home to see Pa. He's really gone downhill since the last time I saw him. I said to him, "How about this, Pa? Pev Martin says you're not my father."

But all he could do was babble his Mitzi-talk. "You're losing your looks, Mitzi," he said, looking right at me with that crazy mean glint in his eyes that always meant a slap in the face or a pinch on the arm in the good old days. "You can't afford to lose your looks, Mitzi. Audiences don't like fat, ugly, old broads."

"Is it true, Pa? You're not my father? Is that why you used to hit me so much? You always said it was because I did something wrong in the act."

"Sing, Mitzi! Dance, Mitzi! It's all you're good for Mitzi-baby."

He sat there in his wheelchair, a skinny, shrunken old man with a half-century of meanness and deceit oozing out of his eyes and running down his withered cheeks. He wheezed and gasped, and I wished he would choke to death while I stood by not lifting a finger to help him. He didn't. He was laughing.

"Sing, Mitzi! Let's have your version of 'My Heart Belongs to Daddy.' It does, doesn't it?" Again he wheezed and gasped at his own joke. "Nobody else would have it. Sing, Mitzi!"

I sang.

Mary Martin I wasn't. But I sang, and sang it as well as I could under the circumstances. I always gave my best performances for Pa. It was habit. If I didn't please him, it meant going to bed without any dinner, or worse. While I sang, I was remembering all those times I didn't please him. Some of the times, I knew what I had done wrong the instant I did it. That always made it hard to finish the act because I knew what would happen to me afterward. But other times, I would think that I had done everything right and we would get a nice round of applause, but as soon as we got offstage I would see that look in his eyes and know that when we got back to our hotel room there'd be hell to pay. Once, when I was twelve, I got blood all over the back of my costume. Well, nobody told me what *that* was all about. I thought I'd hurt myself and I was scared, but I couldn't tell him about it because of where the blood was coming from. He really gave it to me that time, for ruining the costume. And then he had the hotel maid come in and tell me what I'd done wrong and how to take care of myself. I felt really stupid after she told me. And ugly and disgusting. After that, he didn't beat me so much when I made mistakes. He did other things. I wish Pev hadn't made me remember the old days.

My heart belongs to Daddy. I finished singing and waited for him to say something. He sat there in his wheelchair, his gnarled and stiffened fingers tapping impatiently on the armrests, his head wagging implacably back and forth, back and forth, like the pendulum of a clock that would never run down.

"No good, Mitzi," he crowed. "No damn' good. You'll never make it in the big time. Don't know why you keep on trying."

I walked away and left him sitting there. I'll never go back to see him again. I walked to the train station, shoved all my loose change into the candy machine, and got on the train. By the time we got to Grand Central, I was feeling a little better, although I did have a headache. Since then, I've been making the rounds, answering casting calls, and I got some new photographs taken. Nobody seems to need fat comic character actresses right now.

I'd like to believe what Pev Martin said, that things could have been different. But what good would it do me? I can't go back and be a kid with a puppy in a little town. I can only go on doing what I'm doing, being who I am.

Anita Stratton's show is still running. Maybe I'll go and see it again. Maybe this time I'll go backstage and say hello just for old times' sake. Maybe we'll go out and have coffee afterward. She must be lonely now that she and Tony have split up. Maybe she needs a friend to talk to. We'll go up to her apartment; I'll bring along some pastries or a rum baba. She'll tell me all her troubles and we'll talk about the future, how we're both going to be famous someday if we get the right roles. The big break is coming. It's just around the corner. I can feel it in my bones.

If only I didn't have this terrible headache.

Delightfully baffling mysteries from

James Anderson